Renegade Nuns
Sisterhood is Powerful

A novel by

LISA JONES

Published by Verbal Construction, LLC
Denver, Colorado, USA
www.VerbalConstruction.com

First edition: March 6, 2017

Front cover photo: Clemence Plane Memorial at Cimetière Marin in Sète, France © 2016 Lisa Jones. Back cover photo: Château de Puivert © 2015 Lisa Jones.

ISBN: 0-9826544-5-6
ISBN-13: 978-0-9826544-5-3

For Dana

"Courons à l'onde en rejaillir vivant."
Paul Valéry

ACKNOWLEDGMENTS

Thanks to my whole family, all of my friends, and everyone who read and commented on portions of this book as a work in progress. Thanks for making publication possible.

Thanks to all the paramedics, firefighters, dispatchers, doctors, nurses, social workers, police officers, investigators, neighbors, friends, colleagues, and affected bystanders in Long Beach and beyond who did their best in a weird situation. Thanks to everyone who cared, wondered, or asked questions. Thanks to all who prayed, and to all who still pray.

Thanks to Lisa Brown and everyone I met through LEVA and NCMF for their professional commitment to advancing the field of digital media forensics.

Thanks to Emmanuelle Auzias for French inspiration. Thanks to Deb Kennedy, Annie Morrissey, and many friends for journeying and lightwork.

Thanks to John and Natalie Bates for insight and story sense. Thanks to Paula Kurtz for proofing. Thanks to Vanessa Johnston for tireless editorial enthusiasm.

Thanks to my sister, who read my worst drafts and urged me to not give up on the story of Eternals.

"The very fact of your being alive is the first of your fruits."

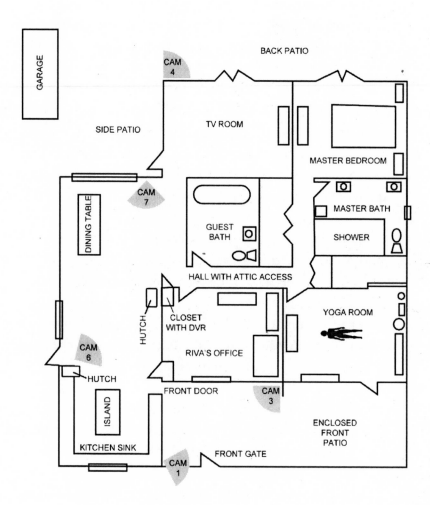

1

MACK LIKE THE TRUCK

My sister's skull was cracked. Her scalp was split with a gaping laceration. By the time she arrived in the hospital's emergency room, she had sustained severe, irreversible brain damage. Her heart was still beating, tenuously, but she was brain dead already. Her husband claimed that she had fallen to the floor while doing yoga at home.

What had happened to her, really? My questions to the Long Beach Police Department were answered with denial, evasion, and disdain. To find out what had happened, I needed the Sisters of the Tower, the so-called renegade nuns. Answers are always in plain sight, according to the nuns, if only we are able to see.

LBFD Dispatcher: Long Beach Fire Department and Paramedics. What's the address of your emergency?
Mack: 7053 Starboard Street.
LBFD: Is this a house or an apartment?
Mack: It's my home. It's my home.
LBFD: Is this for you or someone else?
Mack: It's for my wife. She was doing yoga, doing a headstand, fell, and she's bleeding from behind.
LBFD: Bleeding from the back of her head?

Mack: Yes.

LBFD: Did she lose consciousness?

Mack: Yes.

LBFD: Is she alert and aware of what's going on right now?

Mack: You can tell she's concussed, for sure.

LBFD: Any difficulty breathing?

Mack: She's calm and steady. She's sitting. I'm holding her upright.

LBFD: Can you lay her down?

Mack: I tried but she's a little combative.

LBFD: How old is she?

Mack: Fifty.

LBFD: She was doing a handstand when she fell?

Mack: Correct.

LBFD: Did you see her when it happened?

Mack: No. I heard a loud crash and came running into the room.

LBFD: Is there a possibility of her having a neck injury or a back injury? Did she twist her neck when she fell?

Mack: At this point, I'm going to say no.

LBFD: How heavily is her head bleeding?

Mack: Massive.

LBFD: Do you have a clean, dry cloth you can grab?

Mack: I'm applying pressure with a yoga towel. At some point, I have to go unlock the gate.

LBFD: I need you to keep an eye on her breathing and alertness. Help is on the way.

I had just backed my sporty-but-aging car out of my garage when Mack sent me a text message. It was a chilly, bright, Monday morning in early March in Denver, Colorado. I didn't know that I was about to be thrust into family tragedy, ancient mystery, and contemporary conspiracy. All I wanted was to arrive on time for once at my workplace.

With a cup of hot coffee in my hand, I felt ambitious— righteous, even. I was ahead of schedule rather than my usual fifteen-minutes late. I worked as a financial-donor profiler at Holy Cross Health, Denver's oldest nonprofit hospital. I had a new philanthropic donor to investigate: the Ashton Foundation of New York. I was eager to get to my office.

Urgent, Mack's text message said. *Call me.*

Mack and I rarely exchanged messages. *If something is truly urgent, Mack will call me*, I thought.

I watched my garage door slowly close. My phone rang. It was him, my brother-in-law Mack. I answered the call. "What's the emergency?" I said, impatient, as my car idled in the alley behind my house.

"Becky," he huffed as if he had just run up a flight of stairs. "Riva was doing yoga." He was referring to my sister Riva, his wife. His voice broke. "She fell down. She hurt herself."

"Is she okay?"

He whimpered. "She went to the hospital."

"Hospital?" I asked, perplexed, wondering what injury from a yoga fall would require a visit to a hospital. "Why? What happened?"

"I found her on the floor," he said. "She tried to fight me. She's strong like that. She was fighting me, saying that she needed to finish her yoga routine, but I could tell there was something wrong. I'm scared. So scared."

From Mack's description, I could not imagine what sort of injury Riva had sustained. If she was arguing with him about whether to continue doing yoga, how bad could it be? "She'll be fine," I said in a tone that did not conceal my annoyance. I was irritated by Mack's histrionic moaning and gasping. Why was he calling me about this?

Mack had a tendency to be melodramatic about minor mishaps involving Riva. One such instance came immediately to mind. A few years earlier, the three of us were visiting a geothermal pond while we were on vacation in Hawaii. When Riva got out of the pond, she slipped on wet lava-rocks as she was walking to her towel. Thanks to the physical coordination she had developed through her yoga habit, she was able to land on her butt and avoid serious injury.

I was in the pond, and I watched Riva as she fell. From my vantage point, I could see that she was uninjured. If she had tried to break her fall with her hand, or had hit her head on the rocks, it could have been a vacation-ending accident. Fortunately, all she suffered was a bruise on her butt, which we jokingly referred to as her "ass tattoo from Madame Pele."

Regardless, Mack came unglued. He shouted frantically to get the lifeguard's attention, as if we were in a war-zone and Riva had just been shot. "My love!" he shouted. "She's hurt!"

I swam to the edge of the pond and got out. "Mack, she's fine!" I yelled. "Calm down." Mack appeared to be crying, but he wasn't shedding any actual tears. He was trembling and sobbing like a talentless actor in a bad film. His response was completely out of proportion to what had happened.

"I don't know what I would do without her," he sobbed hoarsely, as if in defense of his overreaction. Riva and I exchanged a look of baffled concern. We wondered why he was being so melodramatic about nothing.

As my car idled in the alley behind my house on that chilly morning in early March, while I listened on the phone to Mack's blubbering, I assumed that *again* he was overreacting ridiculously to whatever might have happened in the course of Riva's morning yoga routine. He was pointedly demanding my attention and sympathy. *But why?* He and Riva lived in Long Beach, California—a thousand miles west of Denver. What did he expect me to do for him in this so-called emergency?

"Are you at the hospital with her?" I asked. "Can you put her on the phone?"

"I'm s-s-still at home," he stammered. "I need to take a shower. I n-n-need your support."

My support? For what? In a serious situation, he would be at the hospital already, wouldn't he? If Riva had been healthy enough to drive herself to the hospital, the injury couldn't be too serious. Mack was putting on an act, pretending that things were worse than they actually were.

"Mack, how can I help?" I asked, facetious.

"Get on a plane. Get out here right now."

Mack and I had never been close. We'd barely managed to tolerate each other—and only for Riva's sake. In the past, we had traveled together, and had enjoyed ourselves, but it was never effortless. Mack grudgingly permitted my many visits and phone calls with my sister. Why was he now begging for my company?

"Mack, does Riva have her phone with her?" I asked.

"Becky, get here as fast as you can." Mack's deep, demanding voice changed to a thin, helpless whine. "Don't abandon me." He repeated it half a dozen times. "Don't abandon me."

Suddenly, I was alarmed. I wondered whether Mack was having a psychotic break. He sounded unhinged. Regardless of what had happened to Riva, I knew that she would welcome my help in dealing with Mack's inexplicable anxiety. She would want my moral support, if nothing else. She would want me to be there with her. She needed an ally. During the incident at the thermal pond in Hawaii, I was glad that Riva and I were both there, as if protecting each other, as if serving as each other's corroborating witness to Mack's bizarre behavior.

Now, Riva was going through something similar, and she was dealing with Mack on her own. I felt that I needed to be there for her, to be a witness for her at the very least. My research report regarding the potentially-deep coffers of New York's Ashton Foundation would have to wait.

"I'm going to the airport now," I told Mack, gritting my teeth at the thought of dropping several hundred dollars on a last-minute plane ticket. Mack wasn't worth it, but Riva definitely was. "Tell Riva I'm on my way. Tell her to keep me updated."

"Thank you, Sis," Mack sniffled.

I hated it when Mack called me Sis. He was the only person who ever called me Sis. I always heard a mocking tone in his voice, and this time was no different.

"Stay strong, Bro," I said. It was the most insipid, insincere thing I could say to a grown man who had been rendered hysterical by—what? His wife's yoga sprain? I ended the call.

I waited for my garage door to roll back open. I parked my car and sprinted into my house. "Family emergency," I explained to Lola, my boss, on the phone. "Some sort of yoga accident," I added, aware of how outlandish it sounded. Lola was always gracious and understanding toward me. She knew that I would never take advantage of her laissez-faire management style. When I told her I needed to be away from the office for a day or two, she trusted that it was for a good reason. She kindly told me not to worry, to stay calm, and to focus on my sister.

I stuffed a change of clothes into my backpack. I grabbed my passport. I had become accustomed to using it as my primary form of identification when traveling, even though my passport photo was not flattering. It showed a middle-aged woman with shoulder-length brownish-to-gray hair, tired-looking gray-green eyes, and a resigned, closed-mouth smile. Not flattering, but accurate. I scrolled through a list of available departing flights. I booked one. I drove to the airport.

I sent a message to Mack: "The plane leaves around noon. Plan on an hour to get a car, plus another hour to drive to Long Beach. What hospital?"

I waited but received no reply from him. I boarded the plane. I asked again in another message: "Which hospital is she at, Mack?" I heard nothing from him. Was he toying with me? Was this all a test to see whether I would come running when he called?

I wouldn't put it past him. Mack was manipulative, in my opinion. His tactics worked on Riva, but not on me. Mack knew that I shook my head in disgust at his frequent, bullying appeals for pity and indulgence. He blamed my lack of sympathy on the fact that I'm a lesbian. "Becky doesn't like me because she hates men," Mack would sulk to Riva. In truth, I was unsympathetic toward him for many, many reasons. No matter what I said or did though, Mack could always depend on Riva's soft heart.

I sent her a message: "Where are you, Riva? I will be there this afternoon. I'm turning my phone off for the flight."

Over the previous 14 years, the only substantial disagreements between Riva and me had centered on Mack. She thought he was a genuinely kind person who sometimes protected himself by wearing a mask of callousness and cruelty. I saw him in the opposite way. I thought he was a cruel, callous person who was wily enough to disguise himself with a mask of kindness and sensitivity.

From the very start of their relationship, I had a gut feeling that Mack was up to something, working an angle, trying to con people. But I never had any solid evidence. All of my "proof" was anecdotal and ambiguous. I had never caught him in a lie that he couldn't wriggle out of. Believe me, I had tried. He was slippery. It was hard to tell whether he was cunning, or just obtuse and socially awkward. Each time I thought I had caught him in a lie, in his defense he would plead confusion, misunderstanding, or ignorance. He played stupid. He played stupid very convincingly. Still, I felt that a fiendish, unfathomable intelligence was at work. But what was he up to? Why? I couldn't imagine a motive for his deceptiveness other than he simply found it amusing.

Often, when I expressed to Riva my skepticism about Mack's truthfulness, Riva would defend him by saying that perhaps he was unpolished and naïve, but he didn't have the personality of a conniver. Of course, to me, he was a conniver who pretended to be a clueless rube. When he abruptly changed his name, for example, I knew he was up to *something*, but I didn't know what.

Mack was born into the name Carlos Velasquez. When Mack was very young, his mother fled in fear from his father. His father had raped Mack's aunt—his mother's sister—or so Mack claimed. Mack's aunts on his mother's side avenged the crime in a way that Mack never specified when he spoke ominously of the episode. Mack told Riva that he was related to Depression-era cop-killer and populist gangster Pretty Boy Floyd. "We don't tolerate disrespect," Mack would say, summarizing his family motto.

After Mack's mother fled from his father, she married a country-club golf pro named Rick "Whitey" Johnson. Riva told me that Whitey Johnson never formally adopted Mack, a fact which Mack bitterly and perpetually resented. Even so, Mack became known as Carl Johnson. When he was in high school, he acquired the nickname "Mack" because of his physique.

With his powerful build and broad, square shoulders, he resembled a Mack truck.

In middle age, after ten years of marriage to Riva under the name Carl Johnson, Mack suddenly changed his first name to King and took Riva's last name—and my last name: Pine. When Riva told me about his name change, I sneered, "King Pine? Does he want people to think he's a lumber baron?"

"Don't tease him," Riva chided me.

Mack explained that he had always been troubled by the fact that he and Riva had different last names. Therefore, he took Riva's last name. He told me that I should regard it as a compliment to the Pine family. Mack said he wanted to honor my whole family by legally becoming a Pine.

Oddly, around this time, Riva told me that Mack had searched for and succeeded in locating his father, the alleged-rapist named Velasquez. The man was living somewhere in the Inland Empire of California. Mack discovered also that he had a half-brother—or maybe two half-brothers—living near Riverside. I couldn't recall the details. Riva told me that Mack had never introduced her to these men, and she didn't know their names.

Riva said it was ultimately a disappointment for Mack to have found his father's side of his family. She told me that, after visiting his father a few times, Mack felt that he had nothing in common with him, and dropped the relationship. It was a shame, Riva thought, because Mack had always longed for brothers and a strong father-figure in his life. "He's like a puppy who wants to run with big dogs," she remarked.

At the time, Mack's mother had been dead for five years, and Whitey Johnson had recently died. Riva told me that Mack had panicked at the thought of having no family. "Family means everything to him," she insisted. "That's why it makes him so sad that you and he don't get along."

Mack's appropriation of our family name grated on me. My parents would've hated it if they had lived to see it. They had never been fond of Mack. Still, they always had smiled and behaved agreeably toward him for Riva's sake.

Even after changing his name, he continued to introduce himself to people by his nickname. "Call me Mack," he would say. "Mack like the truck." It was the most fitting name for him, considering how he barreled through life without concern for other people, without tapping the brakes.

"Why doesn't he just legally change his name to Mack Truck?" I asked Riva.

She shrugged. She and I agreed that "King Pine" was a grandiose-sounding name. By that time though, we had learned that our opinions had no influence over Mack's convoluted processes of decision-making and self-rationalization. For instance, he decided that he needed to spend thousands of dollars getting elaborate tattoos all over his body. He traveled to Hawaii, Vancouver, and San Francisco to be inked by artists he admired. He had become fanatical about tattoos.

Why? Riva and I both wondered.

Mack insisted that getting tattoos was crucial to his mental health and continued existence. He explained that when he was a teenager in high school, he felt insecure and suicidal as the brown-skinned, presumed-stepson of a Caucasian country-club golf-pro named Whitey Johnson. Also, Mack pointed out that he'd had severe acne as a teenager. Therefore, acquiring tattoos as an adult would heal the skin-related psychological wounds of his adolescence. Tattoos would fix whatever was wrong with him. Riva gave him the benefit of the doubt.

I had no way of knowing it at the time, but one day I would see Mack's tattoos in photographs taken by the Long Beach Police Department. On his abdomen, a figure of a Buddha was tattooed alongside an image of a rooster. On his chest, two tattoos of Japanese Oni masks faced each other, one mask above each of Mack's pectoral muscles. Between the two Oni-mask tattoos, Riva's diamond engagement ring hung from a chain around Mack's neck.

Later, seeing the Oni images tattooed on Mack's skin had eerie resonance for me. In Japanese folklore, Oni are demons or ogres armed with iron rods or wooden clubs. These demons supposedly bludgeon people and drag them into hellish death-realms. The Oni drawings on Mack's chest depicted horn-headed demons leering at each other with gape-mouthed grins, showing off their fangs and blood-gorged mouths.

Mack thought these Oni faces were cool. He had gone so far as to acquire a collection of actual demon masks. He put them on display in the yoga room. Riva thought they were creepy. Mack had told her that they were antique Noh masks carved from sacred wood by enlightened masters. They had been used in an ancient form of Japanese stage performance, and had great spiritual significance, he claimed. Regardless, they were a disturbing addition to the décor of Riva's house, which she did not appreciate. She insisted that Mack install a curtain rod and curtain in the yoga room, allowing her to cover up the wall of masks when she wished.

Strangely, for all the money Mack spent on his tattoos, he kept them scrupulously concealed, at least in my presence. I had seen his arms, but not much else. After Riva's death, I found pictures that he had shared online showing off some of his ink. Mack's arms and legs were tattooed with an assortment of Hawaiian turtles, Japanese koi fish, Chinese pictograms, and lotus blossoms. In the police photos, I saw that his back, surprisingly, was free of ink—no tatts on his back. This surprised me because Mack had told Riva that the primary purpose of his tattoos was to cover up teenage-acne scars on his back and shoulders.

This was Mack: he lied effortlessly and seemingly pointlessly. He was skilled at salting lies with small truths, making it extremely difficult for me—and for Riva—to delineate fact from fiction in all things pertaining to Mack.

Once upon a time, Riva told Mack that she would gladly pay for him to consult a licensed psychotherapist. He told her that the last time he had sought therapy, years before meeting Riva, the consultations only made him feel more troubled and suicidal. I called this Mack's Get-Out-of-Therapy-Free Card: *If you make me seek professional help, I'll kill myself.* It worked like a charm on Riva. She redoubled her efforts to placate and understand him. "All he really needs is love," she said, and she meant it with her whole heart and soul.

As I saw it, Riva was a selfless, industrious giver—a perfect match for Mack, a self-absorbed, all-consuming taker. She was endlessly empathetic toward him, projecting her own guilelessness and kindheartedness onto him, always finding excuses for his bad temper and crass manner. I couldn't understand why she put up with him.

At the same time, I knew she would never be rid of him. When he changed his last name to ours, I was certain that Mack would never leave Riva alone, regardless of the formalities or legalities of their relationship, regardless of divorce.

"If you're going to divorce him, you'd better do it now," I said to her at the time.

To my surprise, she told me that she had already talked to a divorce attorney. "If I divorce him, I'll have to pay a fortune in alimony," she said, resigned. "If I'm going to support him, I might as well stay married to him," she reasoned. "At least he knows how to do household repairs."

"Mack can fix a toilet," I said, mocking. "Not that he ever does, but he can. So he's worth keeping."

"I consciously chose to marry him, Becky," she said with sharp rebuke in her voice. "I choose to stay married to him."

She was hell-bent on proving that Mack, if given enough love, would blossom into a joyful, caring, thoughtful, creative person—a person like her. She had failed to accomplish this with Brad, her first husband. She refused to fail with Mack. She was determined to succeed. This was pure Riva: her heart could never be hardened, and her will could never be softened.

Many years earlier, Riva had tried to ditch first-husband Brad, who was her boyfriend at the time. Brad was a soft-spoken, slightly-built aerobics instructor with a delicate constitution and a Carolina drawl. To get away from Brad, Riva had moved from Raleigh, North Carolina, to Savannah, Georgia. She enrolled in a master's degree program at Savannah College of Art and Design. She took a job selling kitchen appliances. As soon as she was gainfully employed, Brad followed her to Savannah. He pleaded with her. He elicited from her just the right blend of sympathy and romantic hope, I suppose, because Riva let Brad move into her new apartment in Savannah.

A few years later, after she had earned her master's degree, she tried to ditch Brad again. She moved to Long Beach, where I was living at the time. She got a job with a kitchen-design company. As soon as she was earning money, Brad followed her to Long Beach. He insisted that he truly loved her. Exhausted from trying to get away from him, she married him.

Riva and Brad looked good together in photographs. They were both wholesome-looking blondes with large eyes, prominent cheekbones, and dazzling smiles. After years of Brad's financial irresponsibility and skillful lies, however, Riva finally faced the hard truth that she was dragging an anchor. Brad was nothing but a burden. The fact that Brad had been arrested for trading sex acts for cocaine in an alley behind a gay bar had helped her reach this conclusion.

Even after their divorce, Brad continued to contact Riva, pleading with her for money and sympathy. A dissolution of marriage is just words, after all, not an emotional shield. A restraining order is just a piece of paper, not a physical barrier.

Riva started dating Mack soon after she divorced Brad. Mack was a gruff, semi-literate construction contractor. Riva met him while he was installing a kitchen that she had designed. To Riva, Mack seemed to be the opposite of Brad. Mack had jet-black hair, deep brown eyes, and a powerful build. He looked as if he could strangle a person with one hand. Mack knew how to swing a hammer and re-wire a house. Mack was licensed, bonded, and occasionally employed. He made her feel safe.

This was the irony. Riva wanted a man to protect her from other men. The presence of Mack would repel Brad and all other would-be Brads, Riva thought. But who would protect her from her so-called protector?

From their first meeting, Riva insisted on seeing only the best in Mack. Riva wanted to give Mack every opportunity to "find himself," whether as a builder, an artist, or an electrician. Early in their marriage, however, Mack revealed himself to be the same as Brad. He announced that he was too sensitive to be weighed down with the responsibilities of earning a living. He told Riva that financial obligations and workplace commitments were too stressful for him to handle. He stopped accepting jobs. He allowed his contractor's insurance bond to lapse.

Riva worked feverishly and expertly. She paid all of their bills. She built a booming business as a kitchen designer. Mack could've been equally busy installing the kitchens that Riva had designed—and, at one time, Riva wished for them to have a working partnership. She saw that he had talent and potential. However, as time went by, she came to see that his workmanship and customer service were not up to the professional standards that she had set for herself. She did not want to admit this to Mack because she believed it would crush his fragile self-esteem. Instead, it was easier for her to work hard enough for both of them.

Mack spent his days surfing, skateboarding, and smoking pot like a surly teenager trapped in the body of a now-middle-aged man. Riva told me, and told herself, that this was just a phase—a phase that had lasted a decade.

Who was I to criticize Riva's devotion to him? While I could see the problems in Riva's marriages so clearly, I didn't have the same clarity about my own relationships. In retrospect I could see that I had chosen romantic partners who, like Brad and Mack, had great potential but zero desire to take the concerns of other people—me, for example—into honest consideration.

In my relationships, everything was always about *her*, whoever she happened to be at the time. At first, I thought that my girlfriend-of-the-moment was kidding. I thought that no one could be so self-involved, not *really*. I thought she'd snap out of it as soon as she relaxed into the relationship, if only I could be patient, pliant, and agreeable enough for long enough. But no. It always ended with my feeling taken advantage of, and her complaining that there was something fundamentally wrong with me.

Maybe there *was* something wrong with me. Why did I always involve myself with the same type of person? I always chose women who were fantastically entertaining and delightfully captivating. Over time, however, I came to see that she, whoever she was, expected my role in the relationship to be that of an adoring audience. The awful thing was that I sincerely tried to meet this expectation by suppressing my own thoughts, feelings, and critical analyses. So it's not as if I was being authentic in these relationships. I behaved more like a willingly brainwashed fangirl. It was bitterly disappointing all the way around when I suddenly stopped applauding.

Through all my relationships, Riva was my ally. She wanted me to be happy on my own terms. She would never tell me that she disliked my girlfriend, even when I asked Riva for her frank opinion. Riva wanted me to reach my own conclusions without her interference. I, on the other hand, vocalized my dislike of Riva's men often and in withering detail, for all the good it did.

Riva and I had similar relationship patterns. The difference was that Riva had more patience. I would get fed up, whereas Riva would patiently wait, watching for microscopic signs of improved mutual regard in her relationships.

I finally escaped the pattern, I told myself, when I made the decision to relocate to Denver. I had been living in Los Angeles and had been out of work for several months. I told potential employers that I was open to relocating. A health-care charity in L.A. offered me a job. My girlfriend at the time informed me that if I took the job, she would break up with me because she had her heart set on living somewhere else with me. I turned down the L.A. job and accepted a better one in Denver. My girlfriend told me, on second thought, she would never relocate.

I had gone along countless times prior to that particular moment, always putting my girlfriend's opinions and concerns ahead of my own. I had tacitly consented to being undermined. *To hell with that*, I told myself. I accepted the job in Denver— my current job at Holy Cross Health. I broke up with my girlfriend, moved away, and didn't look back.

When I left California, however, I also left Riva. Secretly, I hoped that she would join me in Denver. Years earlier, in her attempt to escape from first-husband Brad, Riva had moved to Long Beach because I was living there. I was quietly—and sometimes loudly—rooting for Riva to escape from Mack in a similar fashion. I would be ready and waiting for her in Denver. I hoped that, one day, both of us could leave our disappointing relationships in the California dust, a thousand miles away. Since relocating, I had not had any more failed relationships. Then again, I hadn't had *any* romantic relationships at all in Denver. I couldn't exactly claim success.

Now I was on a plane, heading back to California, awash in ghosts of girlfriends past. Riva would tell me not to dwell on them. She would tell me to stay optimistic and dream big because some day, somehow, the perfect one for me would find me at last. "Follow your heart," she would say. "It will never steer you wrong." And yet, it always seemed to do precisely that.

When the plane landed, I turned on my phone. I had a message seemingly from Riva: "This is Mack on Riva's phone," the message read. "Saint Mary the Tower Medical Center. Intensive-care module 5 bed 3."

Intensive care?!

I could not imagine what might've happened in the course of her morning yoga routine to put my sister in intensive care. Did she have a stroke? Or a heart attack? My heart pounded in my chest. My hands trembled as I sent a reply: "Just landed. On my way."

Mack responded immediately: "She is out of surgery. Resting comfortably."

Surgery?! My head swam. *Why?*

I hesitated to send another message to Mack. I didn't like the fact that he was sending and receiving messages from Riva's phone. I didn't like that he was volunteering only the bare-minimum information. He acted helpless, but he was controlling the situation in his ever-controlling way. Something serious had happened, obviously. I didn't trust Mack to be an intermediary between my sister and me. I hurried to get off the plane.

The atmosphere in Los Angeles felt heavy and damp. The sky was overcast with what locals called the marine layer, light fog rolling in from the Pacific, mixed with air pollution. As I waited outside on the curb for the car-rental shuttle, I could smell car-exhaust fumes and the rotting scent of the ocean. With these smells came a deluge of memories, jumbled and ambivalent, from the time when I called the city my home—a mix of fond feelings and lost hopes, but I couldn't remember specifics. I had been young here, once, a very long time ago.

I rented a car and drove as fast as possible in slow traffic on the freeway down to Long Beach. Afternoon sunshine had dispersed the marine layer by the time I reached downtown.

I had never been to St. Mary the Tower Medical Center. I had never even heard of it. It was an old institution located a mile inland from the harbor. At one time, the hospital's neighborhood had been a wealthy suburb. Over the past century, the area had been overtaken by poverty and crime. I drove past fast-food restaurants and discount stores, past men pushing carts full of trash, and others drinking from bottles wrapped in brown-paper bags. Palm trees swayed above it all like sardonic reminders of California's reputation for balmy elegance.

The medical campus looked like a movie set comprised of 1920s Art Deco palaces and 1930s Craftsman bungalows. The campus of St. Mary the Tower reminded me of Holy Cross, the hospital in Denver where I worked. It was a mélange of architectural styles built over many decades. I followed signs to the main entrance. I parked near a modern-looking tower of steel and glass.

Mack waited outside the building. He was wearing camouflage commando fatigues and an olive-drab jacket. I had seen him wearing the same clothes at Christmas. Quasi-military attire made him look hip, he believed. I had heard him describe his fashion sense as "cool warrior," and "grown-up surf punk." To me, it meant, "middle-aged man trying to look like a teenager."

He looked terrible. His graying black hair was wild, as if he had been in a wind storm. He looked as if he hadn't shaved his face or trimmed his usually neat Van Dyke beard and mustache in days. His facial hair was grayer than I remembered. His brown skin looked unusually ashen.

I walked toward him.

He glanced up from his phone and saw me. A beat passed as he remembered that he was distraught. He started to cry. He outstretched his arms. He hugged me.

"Thank you for existing, Becky," he blubbered into my shoulder.

I got the distinct impression that Mack was acting— overacting, really, like a honey-glazed ham. He was being fake— more fake than usual. I suspected that I was being hoaxed. "What happened to her?" I demanded, breaking his embrace.

"I don't know," he sobbed. "Ask the doctors."

"I want to see Riva," I said.

"I can't go back in there," he retorted, as if I'd told him to drink poison. "People think I'm a tough guy because I look tough. But I'm a teddy bear on the inside. I can't take it anymore. All this stress." He wiped his eyes. "I've been here all day waiting for you." He said it in a way that sounded accusatory. "I need to go home and feed Caldo."

Caldo was Riva's beloved dog, a devoted, reddish-brown Vizsla, a Hungarian pointer.

"Fine," I said. "Go feed Caldo."

"Will you sleep with me tonight?" Mack blurted. When he registered my appalled expression, he clarified: "Will you stay at our house tonight? You can use the air mattress in the yoga room. I don't want to be alone."

When I visited Riva, I usually slept on the air mattress in their guest room, which Mack had recently converted to the "yoga room," the room with the Japanese masks. I didn't want to make any arrangements before talking to Riva, so I lied. "I checked into a hotel already." I took a step toward the door.

"I don't want to be abandoned," he said.

Why was he so worried about being abandoned? It struck me as odd—but everything about Mack struck me as odd. "I hear you, Bro," I said.

We parted.

I went into the hospital. A receptionist wrote down my name and gave me a visitor-badge to wear. She directed me toward the nursing staff station for the intensive-care unit.

Intensive care. I repeated the phrase as I walked. *Intensive care. Why?*

When I arrived in intensive care, I explained that I was Becky Pine, sister of Riva Pine in module five, bed three.

The nurse was a young-looking man, Filipino I guessed from his name badge, which said *Aquino.* "Someone will be here to talk with you." He gestured for me to sit in a waiting area filled with empty chairs.

I sat. I fumbled with my phone. I hoped to see a message from Riva. No message.

After several minutes, a woman hugging a clipboard to her chest came into the waiting area. I think her hair was blonde. She was my age, I assumed. Fortyish. I doubted that I would recognize her if I were to see her again. I suddenly felt as if my eyes weren't working properly.

The woman said, "Are you Becky?"

I nodded.

She told me her name and job title. For some reason, I wasn't able to remember it, but I understood that she was a social worker. She sat next to me. "How are you related to Riva?" she asked.

"She's my sister."

"Not your sister-in-law?"

I thought for a moment. Why would she question me on this point? Then I remembered: *King Pine*. "No, I'm Riva's actual, blood sister. Her husband changed his last name to our last name a few years ago."

"I'm very sorry," she said. She wrote a note on her clipboard. "Your sister Riva sustained a severe blow to the back of her head. Her brain swelled rapidly. Doctors performed emergency surgery to reduce pressure on her brain. They will run a test to find out whether brain-stem herniation has occurred."

The woman's face was a blur. She was speaking in a way that made no sense.

"What does that mean?" I asked. "Is Riva unconscious?"

"No, her reflexes are not responding."

"What does that mean?" I asked, confused. "Is she in a coma?"

"No, she is not in a coma. The test will confirm whether her brain function has stopped."

I tried to decipher the woman's hyper-cautious medical-speak. "Meaning, she's brain dead?"

"Doctors won't be able to make an official declaration until after the tests."

"But you're telling me my sister is dead?"

"State laws govern the declaration of brain death. It's not decided by one person."

"She's dead?" I asked, softly. "Is that what you mean?"

"It's not something I'm allowed to say," she said, pursing her lips as if trying to hold back words.

"What *are* you allowed to say?"

The woman looked at her clipboard. I could tell that she wasn't reading anything. "We were told that your sister fell and hit her head on a bare concrete floor while doing yoga at home this morning. Her husband was in another room. He heard a loud thump. He found her on the floor and called paramedics."

"And she's dead now?" I spoke calmly, quietly, and intensely. "That's insane. You know that's insane, right?"

I did not know it at the time, but many months in the future I would remember this moment as pivotal. Many months in the future, I would hear this social worker's voice again. I would hear a recording of her call to the police: "The doctors are saying that it could be foul play. She's going to be declared brain dead. Her injuries are suspicious." In the recording, the social worker sounded hesitant; she didn't want to cause trouble for anyone, but she had a duty to her conscience to notify the police.

Ultimately, I would be grateful to this woman forever for making this phone call, but I had no way of knowing it on that terrible day. She stood up wordlessly and led me out of the waiting area and down a hallway. We walked through a doorway. We walked past several occupied hospital beds. She pointed at a door, and she left me to walk through it on my own.

Inside the room, machines beeped and clicked. On a white bedsheet, I saw Riva's hand. An intravenous tube had been taped to it. "Riva?" I said. I stepped closer to her. The Filipino nurse was on the other side of her bed, adjusting one of the racks of machines that flanked my sister.

Riva's blonde head was half shaved. An incision had been stitched across her scalp by doctors trying to save her life. A blood-filled plastic pump protruded from her skull. Riva's swollen tongue lolled from her mouth, pressing against her respiration tube, straining against a strip of white adhesive tape. Dried blood was caked in the corners of her mouth. The nurse explained that the lower back of Riva's scalp was split with a deep laceration that had been surgically repaired in the emergency room.

I stood at the foot of her bed, shocked at how distorted her face looked, and wondering why her left eye was purple and swollen, as if she had been punched.

"Riva, it's me." I rubbed the soles of her feet. I gently squeezed her toes. I watched her face. Despite obvious signs of extreme medical intervention, she appeared to be asleep. I expected her eyelids to flutter open. "Riva," I said, louder. I shook her foot, trying to wake her up. I knew that when she woke up and saw me standing there, she would smile.

"Is she knocked out on painkillers?" I asked.

"She's not on any painkillers," the nurse said gravely. He explained brain-stem herniation to me. When the brain is injured inside the skull, the brain swells. To reduce pressure from the swelling, doctors perform a craniectomy. Meaning, they cut open the skull to give the brain more room. If they can't relieve the pressure soon enough, the brain swells downward toward the brain stem, crushing brain tissue as it expands through the hole in the base of the skull. This is catastrophic and irreversible because it destroys neural function and blood flow.

"I'm going to check her reflexes," the nurse said. He pressed his fingers into Riva's eyebrows and around her jaw. "I'm not seeing any reaction," he said. "Earlier, we did a cough test and a gag-reflex test with no response."

With his thumb, he lifted Riva's eyelid. I expected her to wake up and blink her eyes. She didn't move. Her eye was dilated and motionless. The nurse flashed a light into her gray-green iris. "No response," he said. He checked her other eye, the one with the swollen eyelid. I expected Riva to wince with pain. "Nothing," the nurse said.

"How did this happen?" I asked softly.

The nurse moved nearer to where I was standing. "Earlier, we thought we were getting a reflexive response in her feet." He ran a metal point across the arch of her left foot. "I'm not getting anything now." He ran the point over her right foot. "No, nothing."

"She's dead?" I whispered, not comprehending.

"She'll have a cerebral perfusion scan, and an apnea test. There are more tests to run. But her condition is not going to improve," he said gently but firmly.

"So she won't wake up?" I asked, dazed.

"Brain death means irreversible damage to the brain caused by trauma," he said. "Your sister cannot breathe on her own. We are giving her oxygen and glucose, which is why her heart is still beating. Brain death does not mean *sort-of* death. The key word is *death*." As he talked, he moved toward the door. "You'll have a chance to talk to the neurosurgeon in the morning." He seemed hesitant to leave. "You're welcome to stay here with her as long as you want," he offered. He nodded at a nearby chair. He sounded both sympathetic and resigned.

"Thanks," I said, letting him know that it was okay for him to leave. There was nothing he could say that would help me grasp the enormity of the situation. Riva was dead. What more could be said?

I stood at my sister's side, looking at the needles and tubes taped to the backs of her hands. Her heart continued to beat because of medical intervention. A ventilator breathed for her. A plastic blanket filled with cool air regulated her body temperature. Riva could no longer think, feel, or even twitch. She was completely helpless and humiliated.

"Riva, what happened to you?" I asked. I touched the backs of my fingers to her cheek. Her skin felt hot and feverish. "Riva?" I said, trying to wake her. Delicately, I put my thumb on her right eyelid just below her brow. I looked into her clear, wide, silently-staring lens. I tried to smile. "Riva, it's me. I'm here." I watched for a contraction in her iris, or any sign at all that she could see me. There was nothing.

I pulled up a chair next to her bed. I sat. I rested my hand on her forearm. I was still sitting there hours later when Mack called.

"Get here now, Becky," he commanded. "The cops won't let me in my house."

2

NIGHT OF THE HUNTER

"Get me a lawyer," Mack said over the phone.

"Are you under arrest?" I asked.

"No," he huffed, indignant. "They think I hurt Riva."

"If you're not under arrest, you don't need a lawyer," I said, vaguely disappointed. "I'm on my way."

As I drove, I tried to recall my most recent conversations with Riva. We had talked about her kitchen-design clients and my job. We had endless things to discuss. For instance, she told me about a huge kitchen that she had been hired to design in Newport Beach. "They want an entire cabinet dedicated to storing special trays that they use for serving breakfast in bed," she had told me. We marveled at the peculiar luxury of needing such a cabinet.

At the time, I figured that Mack was within earshot while Riva and I were talking. He hated it when Riva talked to me about him. She did anyway, though, especially if something about him was troubling her. Or at least she *had*, until she stopped many weeks ago. Right after Christmas—that was when something had changed. All of a sudden, Riva stopped talking to me about Mack. I hadn't wondered why until I was driving to her house that night.

As I drove, my suspicions grew. I imagined Mack pushing Riva during an argument. What if she had fallen backward onto a kitchen countertop, or a bathroom sink? I could see him panicking and making up the flimsy story that she had fallen while doing yoga.

On second thought, I knew that Mack wasn't the type to lash out in a fit of rage. Rather, Mack was more likely to express his anger by toying with Riva over the course of days and weeks, by confusing and annoying her. For example, a few weeks before Christmas, Riva told me that Mack had changed her clocks—on her computer, in her car, on her phone, all over their house—so that each clock told a different time, well behind the actual time. As a result, she was late to an important client meeting. Later, she confronted him. Mack claimed to have no idea what she was talking about.

"He did it to sabotage you," I told her.

She disagreed: "He would never deliberately harm me, Becky. Never."

I turned onto Riva's street. She lived in a residential area that usually was dark and sleepy after sunset. On this night, however, red-and-blue lights lit up Riva's block. Her street was filled with police cruisers. I lost count at ten cars with flashing lights and squawking radios. Police officers canvassed the neighborhood, knocking on doors and talking to people who lived in modest, middle-class houses located on the edge of a public golf course.

Because there were so many police cars, I had to park my rental car several houses away from Riva's. Small groups of neighbors, some holding dogs on leashes, stood on the sidewalk. I heard what they were saying as I walked past.

"It's just routine questioning," I heard one woman say to another. "One of the officers told me that there's no foul play. Police have to investigate anyway because Riva died."

The woman looked familiar to me. I realized that she was Carleen Biggars, a neighbor of Riva's. Carleen was relatively short in stature, just over five feet tall. She had brown, curly hair. Her natural hair-color was gray, I guessed, because she appeared to be in her late fifties. The thing I recognized about her was her New Age hippie vibe. She wore granny-style, wire-framed eyeglasses. She wore a flowing, multicolored cotton dress, a shawl around her shoulders, and Birkenstock sandals on her feet. I recalled that she worked as an emergency-room nurse as well as an acupuncturist and herbalist.

I had met Carleen several years earlier. Riva had designed a remodel of Carleen's master bath, and Mack was doing construction work on the project. I had stayed overnight at Riva's house during this time. Riva told me that it was exhausting to have Mack working on a project in the neighborhood because he would come home a lot during the day and interrupt her. She said that it was hard for her to get any work done because Mack and Carleen both kept interrupting her with project-related questions and constant crises that, according to Riva, were baseless. "It's almost as if they enjoy bothering me for no reason," she said.

Carleen and Mack had become close friends, and had been spending a lot of time together. "They're doobie buddies," Riva said.

I laughed. "What does that mean?"

Riva confessed that Mack was in the habit of smoking marijuana in their garage. Riva was uncomfortable with this because, at the time, it was illegal to smoke pot in California. The garage was directly behind their house, abutting a public golf course. Riva worried that someone on the golf course would smell pot smoke and report it to the police. Riva didn't care that Mack smoked, although she felt that it made his personality even more self-centered, if such a thing was possible. Mostly, Riva didn't want illegal activity happening on her property. "I was worried about my liability as a homeowner and business owner," Riva told me. "So when Mack started going over to Carleen's to smoke with her, I was relieved."

"Are they *just* doobie buddies?" I asked. "Or do you think there's more to their relationship?"

Riva smiled. "After you meet Carleen, let me know if you're still suspicious."

When I met Carleen, I wasn't suspicious of her in any way. I found it hard to imagine that Mack would be attracted romantically to her. Carleen's vibe was indulgently maternal toward Mack. She seemed to dote on him in a way that I found patronizing, almost as if he was her prized pet poodle. She referred to Mack as "Macky" in a cloying, sing-song way.

That night on the street, in the hubbub of police activity, Carleen Biggars' voice held the same babying tone that I had heard years earlier: "Macky would never hurt Riva. He is such a gentle soul. Riva is Macky's whole world. Honestly, I have never seen such love and devotion." I smelled Carleen's strong patchouli perfume as I walked past her.

Her voice and scent faded as I walked closer to Riva's house. As I approached the driveway, I saw Mack sitting on a low wall. Two police officers in blue uniforms stood in front of him with their backs to me. Two men wearing business suits and neckties had just arrived. I assumed that they were detectives. One detective was small and wiry. The other was tall and broad-shouldered like a football player. The tall one reminded me of actor Martin Milner, who had played a policeman on TV. Later, I would learn that this was Detective Anderson.

I expected Mack to be angry and belligerent toward the police, as he had sounded to me on the phone. Instead, I heard him laughing his unmistakable laugh, which sounded like growling and barking. I heard the police laugh, too.

I paused on the sidewalk and observed. Mack appeared to be swapping chummy stories with the cops. I heard Mack talking about the video-camera surveillance system that he had installed around the house. "The whole place is wired with motion-activated cameras," he said, bragging. "It's all automated. I can run it from my phone." He loved to boast about the elaborate electronics he had installed in the house. He had spent countless hours and dollars puttering with home electronics.

The police seemed very interested in what Mack was saying about his automated "smart home."

"The whole house is on camera?" the larger detective asked.

"You can watch the recordings from this morning," Mack said. "You'll see it all. She fell down. She had an accident."

Involuntarily, I quietly gasped. The tone of Mack's voice startled me. He sounded supremely confident, almost daring the police to prove him wrong. He sounded as if Riva's "yoga fall" had been captured on camera, but I knew this could not be true. Despite all of Mack's surveillance cameras, no camera was in the room where Riva customarily did her morning yoga routine. I knew, therefore, that Mack was lying. Police were canvassing his block. Crime lab technicians were about to scour his home. Detectives stood in his driveway. Yet Mack seemed untroubled.

I took several steps toward Mack before an officer stopped me. "Stay on the sidewalk, ma'am," he said.

"I'm family," I said.

Mack heard my voice. "Becky," he cried, suddenly dropping his braggadocio and trying to sound frantic and vulnerable. "Sis, thank you for coming. Please explain to these officers. Tell them how much I loved Riva."

I opened my mouth but didn't know what to say. "I'm Riva's sister," I muttered after an awkward pause.

One of the officers gestured for me to follow him to the other side of the street. "Over here, ma'am," he said. He led me toward a patrol car. He asked me to stand near a bright light. The officer was a lanky man in his early thirties with a dark mustache. He stood just outside the glare of the light. He asked to see my driver license. He wanted to know when I had arrived in Long Beach.

A group of neighbors stood several yards away, looking at us, speculating about my identity in hushed voices. I saw that Carleen Biggars was among this group. I got the distinct impression that she said something disparaging about me to the others.

As the officer copied my name and address onto his notepad, I looked at his name tag. It said, "Smith Gordon." The officer had been relaxed and jocular toward Mack, but his manner toward me was brusque and unsmiling. He handed my ID back to me. "My condolences about your sister," he said as if required to say it. "Anything you want to tell me about King?"

It was strange to hear someone use the name "King" in a serious tone in reference to Mack. "Everyone calls him Mack," I said.

"Anything I should know about Mack?" The officer sounded accusatory, but not toward Mack. He sounded as if he suspected me of something.

"Look," I said, feeling awkward, not sure whether I should share my suspicions, but unable to keep them to myself now that a violent scenario had occurred to me. "I think Mack might've done something stupid. I think he might've hurt her."

I tried to explain the dynamics of their relationship. "She supported him. He just lazed around all the time. It created tension in their relationship. He always did whatever he wanted to do, and sometimes she wasn't happy about it." I knew it sounded implausible as a motive for murder.

"Did they argue?" the officer asked.

"Sometimes."

The officer smiled wryly, as if I had said something obvious. "All couples argue, ma'am. Did he hit her?"

"Not that I know of," I admitted. "I'd like to think that if he ever hit her or threatened to physically hurt her, she would have left him immediately. It was far more effective for him to threaten self-harm. *Do what I want, or I'll kill myself.* That's how it was. He used threats of violence."

The cop blinked as if trying to make sense of what I had said. "How is threatening to hurt himself a threat of violence against her?"

"It's emotional extortion," I said. "Like threatening to hurt the dog."

"Did he threaten to hurt the dog?" His tone suggested that *this* was a serious allegation.

"Not to my knowledge," I said.

The officer nodded slowly. Across the street, I saw the detectives usher Mack through the front gate of Riva's house and into the enclosed courtyard near the front door. I knew that Mack couldn't see or hear me from there. I felt as if the whole neighborhood had fallen silent. The neighbors had seen Mack go through the gate. Next, they turned their attention to me. I felt as if everyone was watching me with suspicion. I crossed my arms defensively.

"Let's put it this way," Officer Smith Gordon tacked, as if interviewing an unhelpful witness. "As far as you are aware, did he ever physically threaten your sister or their dog?"

"There weren't *physical* threats, no, but there was coercion in their relationship," I said. I didn't speak loudly, but I tried to speak confidently. "Mack belittled her constantly. Nothing was ever *his* fault. His feelings were always more important than hers. Arguments with him lasted for weeks, or however long it took for Riva to concede that Mack had been right all along. He holds grudges about petty things for years. He sees himself as a victim, always, which justifies everything he says or does."

"Being a jerk doesn't make him a murderer," the officer interrupted, as if correcting me. "Besides, he says he was the housewife. She was the boss of everything. He cooked, cleaned, and took care of her. He was a loving, supportive servant."

I hated how simplistic this sounded, and how tempting it might be for people to believe it. "It doesn't work that way," I said. "The power dynamic doesn't change just because you think the stereotypical domestic roles have been flipped. He dominated her. He made a point of telling people how he treated Riva like a queen. He claimed that he waited on her hand and foot—as if she would ever want such a thing. It was all for show. In reality, he acted like a defiant teenager. He acted like she was his mom—a mom he resented. Mack was a parasite, not a partner. In a very slow, bloodsucking way, he had been killing her for years."

"Did he ever fool around with other women?" the officer asked as if it was a routine question.

I sighed, embarrassed to be talking about Mack's sex life with Officer Smith Gordon. "Mack told Riva that he was a recovered sex addict," I confessed quickly. "Riva told me that infidelity was her deal-breaker, though, and Mack knew it. If she ever found out that Mack was cheating, she would divorce him in a heartbeat. She tolerated a lot of nonsense from him, but infidelity was a big, bold line that he knew not to cross.

But—but." My voice trailed off. For the first time, I wondered seriously: *Was Mack cheating on Riva?*

Many women swooned over Mack. They found him handsome and sexy. He flattered women like Carleen, convincing them that, despite his "bad boy" persona, he was deeply sensitive.

I sometimes wondered if Mack might be gay. He was an avid viewer of mixed-martial-arts fights, which featured nearly-naked men. He watched these fights on TV as if mesmerized by the homoerotic spectacle of men grappling with each other's bodies. He had started taking classes to learn a martial art, too. I wasn't sure *which* martial art. It was one in which he wore a "gi," a loose-fitting canvas uniform tied at the waist by a belt.

There were men in Mack's life whom Riva had never met, and for whom Mack expressed admiration. Mack shared few details about these men with Riva, except to say that they were "mentors" to him. One was a tattoo artist in Venice named Samadhi Masterson. Another was a surfer in Huntington Beach named Roy Dumond. *Who were these men?*

Officer Smith Gordon cleared his throat. "So was Mack fooling around, or not?" the officer pressed.

"If he was, I didn't know about it. Riva probably didn't know, either."

"Can you think of any real reason why Mack might have intentionally hurt your sister?" The officer sounded genuinely perplexed. "What would his motive be?"

"Financial freedom," I said. "Riva wasn't rich, but she had assets. I'm guessing that she had at least six figures in investments and savings accounts. Plus, she had equity in the house. Now, all of it belongs to Mack. He can do whatever he wants with it."

Several years earlier, Riva told me that she and Mack had drawn up a living trust in case either of them became incapacitated or died. The trust would allow the survivor to control the other's assets and avoid probate. Mack had no significant assets to put into the trust. It was all Riva's—her business, her investments. Living trusts were commonplace, I knew, and did not arouse suspicion. I was bothered, though, that Mack had cajoled her into it, just as he had pressured her to add his name to the deed for the house.

At the time, Mack was angry because my parents had structured their estate to prevent Mack from ever having access to Riva's inheritance from them. My parents must've had an intuition about Mack. After they died, their assets went into a trust shared by Riva and me. Even in the event of Riva's death, Mack would never have access to money from my parents. It was a brilliant plan on their part, and Mack was quietly furious about it. To placate him, Riva set up their marital trust in such a way that he was guaranteed to get everything of hers with as little fuss as possible.

"Mack inherited money from his mother when she died a few years ago," I added. "After his stepfather died, Mack sold his mom's house in Menifee. He has probably pissed away the proceeds by now."

I paused, sensing that I needed to say more about Mack's family. "Whitey—Mack's stepfather—ultimately died of cancer, but he had fallen and hit his head at some point," I said. I tried to recall more details as I spoke. "Whitey used to tell Riva that Mack was mistreating him. Mack was always quick to remind everyone that Whitey's allegations could not be trusted on account of his head injury."

I wished I had asked Riva more questions about Whitey's head injury. In light of what had just happened to Riva, this suddenly seemed relevant, and I knew too few facts.

"Mack's only income over the past five or six years has been through inheriting assets from dead family members," I said bitterly. "It wouldn't surprise me if he killed Riva just so he could raid her bank accounts."

Officer Smith Gordon looked at me as if I had completely undermined my credibility.

"Sounds like he had every reason *not* to hurt her," Smith Gordon reasoned. "She was the breadwinner. Why would he kill the goose that's laying golden eggs for him?"

A car drove slowly past us. The driver gawked at the scene. Riva would have been deeply embarrassed by the spectacle surrounding her home, and by public attention regarding the circumstances of her death. I felt my face flush. I was simultaneously disgusted by Mack and sad for Riva. I was heartsick that she had defended and protected him for so long and so passionately that no one could see what a creep he really was. Also, I was frustrated that the cop seemed hostile toward everything I had to say. Why was he defending Mack?

I wanted to shout: *The goose who is laying golden eggs! Exactly! That's my point!* I wanted to explain that this attitude, this idea that Riva was like livestock, like poultry, to be farmed, to be "productive," to provide goods and services—producing golden eggs, like magic—all for the benefit of Mack—*this is exactly what I'm talking about.* According to this mentality Riva was an exploitable resource. According to this mentality she wasn't a person, she was plunder. I wanted to shout all of this, but the words stuck in my throat.

"If he killed her, he killed her because he could," I said, at last, feebly. "His motives were entitlement and disrespect."

Skeptical, almost sarcastic, the officer asked: "If he was so bad, why didn't she divorce him?"

"She *did* consult a lawyer about divorce," I said, seeing a flicker of hope.

"Who did she talk to? When?" he demanded.

"Years ago—I don't know," I admitted, deflated. "When Mack changed his last name to Pine."

The officer spoke in a soothing way. "So you have no real reason to believe he hurt her. It's just your hunch." He put his notepad in his pocket. He seemed to think that our interview had ended.

"Riva loved him," I said, flustered, scrambling for a way to justify my opinions about Mack. "It doesn't mean he was worthy of her love. It doesn't mean he loved her."

"Thanks," Officer Smith Gordon said. "That's all."

"How is that *all*? My sister is dead."

Officer Smith Gordon sounded as if he was suddenly confiding in me. "I'll be honest with you," he said. "We have to assume that Mack is totally innocent. He's cooperating with us. We don't see anything here that suggests foul play. You might as well go home and get some sleep."

I bit my lip, angry that I had not successfully explained Mack's potential for violence. What proof did I have? What physical evidence existed? I brightened. "Will there be an autopsy?"

"Yes, ma'am, there will be an autopsy."

"Thanks," I said.

The officer walked to the house across the street from Riva's, presumably to interview the occupants. I decided not to stay and wait to talk with Mack. I didn't have the energy to humor him.

Carleen Biggars watched me as I walked back to my car. I thought it was odd that she didn't say something to me, since she obviously remembered having met me. She knew that I was Riva's sister. Then again, I had said nothing to her. What could I have said?

Regardless of what the police presumed, I was confident that the coroner would see the truth. This was no yoga accident.

Rather, Riva's death was Mack's doing, somehow. I felt sick and bewildered by the events of the day, but the promise of an autopsy meant that the investigation into Riva's death would continue. Eventually, the truth would be known.

I drove downtown. I checked into a hotel near the ocean. Riva's life had ended, but her story was far from finished.

I turned on the TV in my hotel room and saw *Night of the Hunter*. Riva and I had watched this movie together many years earlier, when she was still married to Brad. The 1955 movie directed by Charles Laughton featured Robert Mitchum in the role of a scheming ex-convict disguised as a pastor. He married a woman, murdered her, and terrorized her young children. Famed actress Lillian Gish played the role of the children's protector and righteous angel.

I recalled that Riva found the movie preposterous. She rolled her eyes at the premise of Mitchum walking around with letters tattooed on the backs of his fingers, with L-O-V-E on the right and H-A-T-E on the left, representing the duality of good and evil, or the idea that good and evil battled each other in the actions of one man. "It's so cartoonish and unrealistic," Riva scoffed. "Besides, no woman would ever willingly marry such an obviously menacing man."

That night in Long Beach, I vacantly re-watched the movie. I found Mitchum's character to be exaggeratedly chilling, but not preposterous.

The next morning, after a night of restless semi-sleep, I arrived at the hospital to find ten or twelve of Riva's friends and colleagues gathered in the intensive-care waiting room. Mack wasn't among the crowd. I recognized some of the women from Riva's book group. They had been friends of Riva's for many years. They expressed their worry and dismay to me. They explained that, using Riva's phone, Mack had sent out a message-blast early that morning. Mack had informed all of Riva's contacts that she had been in a terrible accident. She was in a medically-induced coma, fighting for her life at St. Mary the Tower, he'd said. He had invited her friends to come to the hospital to rally in support of her recovery. Her friends asked me for an update on Riva's condition.

"She's dead," I said bluntly, knowing no other way to say it. "She sustained irreversible, total brain damage due to a blow to her head. She's gone. Mack knows this. I don't know why he told you otherwise."

My voice trailed off when I saw the effect my words had on them. I wished I had found a more tactful way to tell them. They looked stricken, shocked. Some covered their mouths with their hands. Their eyes filled with tears. Profound stillness fell over the room. I was moved, truly, to see how much they cared about Riva.

"Is there anything we can do?" one woman asked, breaking the silence.

"Maybe plan a memorial service for her," I said abruptly, not knowing what else to say. "I don't think Mack is capable of doing it."

"It would be our honor," the woman said with grace and composure. "How can we support *you*?"

I couldn't imagine how I might be helped. The situation was beyond all help. Riva's friends were already heartbroken, and I didn't want them to be troubled further on my account. "There's nothing you can do," I said, sounding pricklier than I had intended.

At that moment, Mack entered the room. He saw the group of people who had gathered there. He started sobbing loudly. Receiving the condolences of others made me extremely uncomfortable, but it brought out a kind of celebrity charisma in Mack. He drew the crowd around him in a circle of support and affirmation. He wailed and moaned. People seemed to find his lamentations touching and cathartic. He welcomed their hugs and their tears. He basked in their attention.

Such a phony, I thought. He had arrived before anyone had a chance to ask me, "What happened, exactly? How did Riva die?" The possibility of Mack's culpability in Riva's death occurred to no one, probably. Why would they suspect him? They were addled at losing Riva, and now Mack was artfully pulling every heartstring. Besides, even if people had wanted to ask questions, they probably felt that this particular moment was an inappropriate time. I left the waiting room and walked down the corridor to Riva's room.

The same Filipino nurse was on duty. I glanced at his badge to remind myself of his name: *Aquino*. Riva had been examined by a second doctor who ran tests and confirmed brain death, Aquino told me. I would have to wait outside Riva's door as the third doctor, a neurosurgeon, completed his examination.

Aquino explained that Riva had elected to be an organ donor. "Her next of kin—her husband King will be asked to sign a series of agreements and authorizations," he said. "According to applicable laws, you as her sister have no say regarding anything." Aquino said this as if breaking bad news.

"I know," I said, resigned. I had already researched my legal standing on a legal-advice website. I whispered, "Police went to Mack's house last night."

Aquino nodded as if he already knew about the police. He handed me a copy of the papers that Mack would be asked to sign. He told me I could stand near Riva's door as I waited for the neurosurgeon to complete the examination. I assumed that Mack was still in the waiting room, playing to his grief-stricken audience.

A half-hour after I had stationed myself outside Riva's door, the neurosurgeon signed the third and final declaration of brain death. I sat with Riva in her room and waited for Mack to show up.

Soon, Mack appeared with Father Murphy, the hospital's priest. Mack seemed giddy. He had asked Father Murphy to perform a Last Rites ritual for Riva, even though she wasn't Catholic, and wasn't fond of religion.

"The police cleared me," Mack crowed, loud enough for the entire intensive care unit to hear. "I've been cleared."

In a more subdued voice, Mack told Father Murphy and me that during the previous night, detectives had talked to him for hours. They had ordered him to take off his shirt, and had photographed him. They had searched his house. He recounted these indignities as if we should feel outraged on his behalf. He spoke at length about how fat and dimwitted the detectives were.

I presumed that Father Murphy was thinking what I was thinking: *Your wife has lost her life, yet here you are, reciting your petty complaints in her presence.* The priest cleared his throat and said something in Latin. "Let us begin," he added. He moved closer to Riva.

Mack growled at me: "Why didn't you stay and support me last night? Why did you abandon me?"

I consciously kept my eyes on Father Murphy. "A cop told me to go get some rest." I shrugged. "They told me you were totally innocent, so I left."

I didn't have to look at Mack to know that he smirked with satisfaction to hear that the cops thought him innocent.

The priest anointed Riva's head with holy oil. He spoke in Latin.

"I'm glad they investigated me. Now everyone knows I didn't do anything wrong," Mack said. He laughed a low, throaty laugh.

I made the mistake of glancing at him. He gleamed with triumph. "Sorry, Sis," he said, as if I had lost a hand of poker. "Sorry about Riva."

He had done *something* to cause Riva's death. I knew it. Aquino and other hospital staffers seemed to know it, too, judging by how they watched Mack out of the corners of their eyes. Father Murphy, too, probably knew that Mack was guilty of something horrible. The priest muttered low, whispering to Riva.

"I'll be back in a minute," I said. I hoped that in my absence, Father Murphy would smite Mack with a crucifix. In the meantime, I wanted to ask the nurse a question.

I saw Aquino in the corridor. "I was told that there would be an autopsy," I said. "Who can I contact about that?"

Aquino looked at Riva's chart. He pointed to the information I was seeking. "This is your sister's case number."

I typed the information into my phone. I followed Aquino back to Riva's room.

The moment we walked through the door, Mack bellowed: "Why, *Padre*, why?" He fell to his knees as if overcome by grief. "Why did God take her from me?"

The nurse, Father Murphy, and I looked at one another with surprise. Mack's thunderous sobs summoned other nurses. Alarmed and curious, they looked into Riva's room.

The priest put his hand on Mack's head. "No words can comfort you, my son," he said. "I will pray for you."

Mack shuddered and gasped. The priest spoke in Latin.

"Pull yourself together, Mack," I said. "They need you to sign the papers." I was referring to the organ-donation paperwork in the nurse's hands.

Mack stood. He rubbed his eyes. As far as I could see, he had cried no tears. "Okay," he said. "I'm ready." His paroxysm of emotion seemed to disappear as suddenly as it had appeared.

The nurse and Father Murphy exchanged a look. "Everyone grieves differently," the priest said, as if he knew that Mack's behavior was odd, but he needed to say something comforting and priest-like anyway. The priest hastily left the room.

"I brought this," Mack said as he reached into the camouflage-motif ballistic-nylon messenger bag that he often carried. He pulled out a folder from an insurance company. Printed on the cover were the words, "Long-Term Disability Care." Mack showed it to the nurse. "Does this help?"

"Long-term disability?" I said, louder than I had intended. I remembered that Mack had pushed Riva to buy the policy years earlier. He claimed to be worried because Riva drew all of her designs by hand rather than with a computer program. Mack worried that she might break her arm and become unable to draw. She signed up for the policy to put his mind at ease. "She's not disabled, Mack," I snapped. "She's *dead.*"

Aquino shifted his weight from one foot to the other, uneasy with the situation. "If you could just read these and sign off," he said to Mack.

Mack skimmed through and initialed the organ-donation papers as the nurse handed them to him one by one. At last, he signed the final authorization form and gave it to the nurse.

"I guess you'll pull the plug on her now," Mack said.

"It's more complicated than that," Aquino replied, casting a thoughtful gaze at my sister. "Riva will be with us for a few more days as doctors test the condition of her organs. Medical teams will work to identify appropriate recipients who are awaiting transplants. In a few days, Riva will be giving others a gift of life."

"Thanks," I said.

Aquino left the room.

"A few more days?" Mack repeated the nurse's words incredulously. "I can't do *days* of this."

I assumed he meant days of enacting over-the-top, exhausting displays of fake mournfulness. I couldn't handle days of that, either. "Everyone will understand if you can't bear to be here, Mack," I said.

"I guess you're going back to Denver now," he sniffled.

"I think I'll go up to Pasadena to visit a friend." It was a lie, but it was plausible. In truth, I planned to be with Riva until her organ-donation surgery. I wondered whether Mack had thought about planning Riva's funeral. "You should ask Riva's friends to help you plan a memorial service," I said.

"It's under control," he said, dismissive.

"You'll need to choose a mortuary," I added. I assumed that he had not read the death-of-a-loved-one information packet provided by the hospital. "The coroner will need to release the body to the mortuary of your choice."

"How do I choose?"

"It's in the information packet the nurse gave you yesterday," I said, irritated at his sudden and presumably feigned helplessness. "There's a list of mortuaries."

"It's too much for me. You do it, Sis."

"Mack, you have to authorize everything. Legally, you're the only person who can sign the papers."

This puffed him up a bit, reminding him of his omnipotence regarding the final disposition of Riva. "I want her cremated," he said.

"I think she would've wanted that, too." I kept my eyes on Riva. I couldn't stand to look at Mack and his smugness. The priest's words rang in my ears: *Everyone grieves differently.* But Mack wasn't grieving. There was nothing sad about him.

"It would be cool to mix her ashes with ink and get a tattoo," he said, sounding a bit like a child dreaming of gifts on Christmas morning. "Lots of guys do it when their wives pass. They get a tattoo made of her ashes."

It occurred to me that I hated the word *pass* as a euphemism for *die*. Riva had died. She hadn't *passed* like an uncomfortable episode of flatulence. She had been killed.

"Remember when we were in Hawaii last year?" Mack continued. "Remember when she slipped and fell and hit her head? Maybe I should have seen this coming back then."

My eyes widened but I did not turn them toward Mack. Yes, I remembered the incident very well. "She landed on her ass, Mack," I said. "She was fine. Besides, that was four or five years ago."

"No," he insisted. "She hit her head really hard on the lava rocks. Maybe she had a stroke, and that's why she fell doing yoga. She has been acting spacey lately. She was having a hard time getting out of bed."

I knew that none of this was true. In fact, when I had seen Riva a few months earlier at Christmas, I had remarked on her healthy, clear-eyed appearance. She said it was because she had stopped drinking coffee, was sleeping better, and had been waking up with lots of energy.

"Mack, you're misremembering things," I said.

"Sis, you're misremembering," he said in a patronizing tone. "You're still in shock from Riva's accident. You're not thinking clearly."

"Mack, you and Riva have not been to Hawaii in *years*," I said, forcefully. On their first visit, they had come to see me in Hilo while I was housesitting. They had returned to the Big Island twice after that. Both trips were for the express purpose of Mack getting tattoos from a tattoo artist named Mahalo, whom Mack admired. Mack wanted to visit Mahalo by himself, but Riva thought it was weird for him to go alone, so she accompanied him on the trip. "Three years ago, Mack," I said. "That's the last time you and Riva were in Hawaii."

"She never saw me naked," he said with a wistful air, changing the subject in an unsettling way, as was his custom.

"I know," I said without missing a beat. "She told me."

Actually, she had told me that Mack was keenly self-conscious about his body. He always insisted on wearing a shirt in her presence, even at the beach. She had told me this while we were in Hawaii at a beach, and Mack refused to go swimming with us. For all of Mack's quirks, this particular quirk struck me as uninteresting. The fact that he brought it up suddenly, as we stood on opposite sides of Riva's deathbed, made me wonder whether this was a crucial piece of information regarding Mack's personality.

"Maybe I'll put the tattoo with Riva's ashes on my back to honor her," he said, dreamily. "I never let anyone see my back."

I distinctly recalled a conversation in which Mack told me that Carleen Biggars had applied acupuncture treatments to his back to help cure a non-existent back injury that, according to Mack, made it impossible for him to be gainfully employed. Why, moments after signing the papers acknowledging Riva's death—*why* was he talking about his back and his avoidance of nakedness? I didn't want Riva's ashes to be embedded anywhere on Mack's body. I wanted to give Riva's ashes a proper honoring—a ceremony, a scattering at sea, something beautiful. I waited another moment before I spoke.

"Do you think we might split her ashes?" I asked. "I want half."

Mack wiped a non-existent tear from his cheek. "It will be hard for me to part with her, Sis," he said.

He wanted me to bargain with him. Riva once told me that to get him to do anything for her, she had to make a deal with him. "I'll pay the mortuary expenses in exchange for half of her ashes," I offered.

Mack and I didn't look at each other as we negotiated. We kept our eyes on Riva.

"You pick the mortuary. You make the arrangements. You pay for it all," Mack said, flatly. "I'll sign the papers and give you half."

"I want a mortuary viewing, too," I added. "I want to see her one last time after the autopsy."

"I don't want to see her again." He checked his phone for messages. A moment later, as if remembering his role as a grieving husband, he added, "It's too emotional for me to see her again."

I tried to sound nonchalant. "Do it as a favor to me."

"As a favor," he repeated, seemingly satisfied with the knowledge that I would "owe" him. In Mack's calculus, my being indebted to him meant that I was under his control. This would give him leverage to manipulate me somehow, he seemed to believe.

He slipped his phone into his pocket. "I'm out, Sis."

"Later, Bro," I said.

He left.

I smiled at Riva ruefully. "Now that you're dead, he's not your husband anymore, which means that I'm no longer related to him. So that's the bright side of all this."

It's not over yet, Becky. I imagined Riva saying. *There's more to come, so brace yourself.*

3

SISTERS OF THE TOWER

What is consciousness? Where does it reside? For several difficult days, I had been at the bedside of my brain-dead sister, my lifelong best friend. I lifted her eyelids and looked into her cool, gray-green eyes. Her pupils were blown black and hollow, staring lifeless, seeing nothing. With her brain destroyed, and her body kept alive by machinery, there was no place for her consciousness to be. I understood all of this. She wasn't *there* or *here* or anywhere at all. She no longer existed. Even so, I felt her presence. She was with me, somehow, talking to me.

Yes, it was true: Riva was talking to me. It wasn't as if I heard her voice with my ears. I heard her in my mind. Sometimes I laughed or whispered a response. Sometimes I remained silent. At times I would concentrate on a thought, feeling, or memory. I felt that Riva remembered, too, simultaneous with my thoughts and feelings.

"Death isn't what you think, Becky," I heard her say. "It's not much different than being alive."

Being alive isn't so easy, Riva, I thought. *Now that you're gone.*

Being dead isn't exactly a breeze, Becky, I heard her reply tartly, in a joking tone.

Was I imagining it? The things she said sounded spontaneous. Did I invent them in my subconscious? If I had invented them, why did her comments often surprise me?

Three days went by as doctors and nurses prepared Riva's body for organ procurement. At the request of the Los Angeles County Coroner, Riva's corneas and other tissues would remain intact for the autopsy. During these three days, Mack had not returned to the hospital. He had sent me several text messages informing me of his deep grief. I did not reply. The Long Beach Police seemed to have dropped their investigation of Riva's death.

"The best is yet to come, Becky, I promise," Riva said. She was an optimist, a stubborn optimist, even in the worst circumstances, even now. She was in perfect health, after all, other than being suddenly, hopelessly dead. She was fifty years old, in the prime of her life in every sense. Her successful design career was rocketing to new heights. She was happy and kind. She had everything going for her, except that she no longer had any physical reflexes, and could no longer regulate her own body temperature. "Look on the bright side," she said.

On the bright side, Riva was a bonanza organ-donor. Her heart, lungs, liver, kidneys, and pancreas would be harvested and transplanted into people she would never meet. She would extend their lives. She was proud of this fact, proud to be of assistance to others, and delighted to be prized for her deep-down vital excellence which her death did not extinguish.

"Mack stole everything from you, Riva," I said in a low voice. "All your dreams and plans. He's unredeemable."

"What if we'll never be free from Mack?" Riva asked as if posing an uncomfortable question. "What if he will be with us always, in lifetime after lifetime? Think long-term, Becky. You can't just discard people. You'll see them again. They'll keep coming back into your life forever. The only way to deal with

Mack is with compassion. If the roles were reversed, you would want him to treat you with compassion. You'd want him to give you the benefit of the doubt."

I didn't want to get into one of our arguments about Mack, especially since Riva was dead, which seemed to give one of us an unfair advantage, although I wasn't sure which one.

"No one can ever say that you gave up on him, Riva. You were forgiving and optimistic and unreasonably cheerful well past the bitter end. But consider. *Consider.* Maybe there comes a point when forgiving and turning the other cheek actually desensitizes and emboldens a person like Mack. It feeds his delusions. He has treated you like crap for so long that it seems normal to him. He takes advantage of your kindness. He routinely disappoints you and hurts you, but you forgive him. He starts to think it's okay to hurt you. He starts to think that hurting you doesn't really hurt you anymore. Next thing you know, he bludgeons you with a 20-pound dumbbell in your exercise room and pretends it's a yoga accident."

She was silent, as if thinking. "I made a promise to him, Becky," she said at last. "I made a promise to myself. I pledged to love him no matter what. I'm not happy about the way everything turned out. No one's more disappointed than I am. Do we have to re-hash it right now? I'm going into surgery soon."

Riva had always regarded promises and rules very seriously and literally. On principle, she would never cheat, cut corners, or go back on her word. It was a wonderful quality of hers. People could count on her integrity and fair play. At times, though, it could be maddening.

I reminded Riva of the time when we were supposed to meet at the L.A. airport for a flight to Toronto. Our tickets had been issued by one airline, while our actual flight was operated by another airline. I had been confused and had gone to the wrong terminal at first. I made it to the correct departure gate with only minutes to spare. But Riva wasn't there. I didn't want to board the plane without her, so we missed the flight. This was before the era of ubiquitous phones and messaging devices, of course. I had a hunch that Riva had gone to the other airline's terminal, so I went looking for her there. I found her standing in a long line waiting for customer service.

"What are you doing over here?" I said, bewildered. "Our flight just left from the other terminal."

"The ticket is for *this* airline," she said, showing me her ticket.

"But the plane is from *that* airline," I said.

"Yes, it says so on the monitor," she pointed. "But it does *not* say that on the ticket." She was right. The information on our tickets was misleading. Instead of going to the other terminal as I had done, Riva politely waited her turn in line to speak to a customer service representative. According to Riva, this is what one does when one respects rules and courtesies. One waits patiently for accurate information rather than running through an airport like a homicidal Heisman Trophy winner. Eventually, after following rules and instructions, we arrived in Toronto a few hours later than we had planned.

"Remember the blisters, Riva?" We had been walking around Toronto having a lovely time when I noticed that she was limping. She took off her shoes and showed me horrific blisters on her heels. She hadn't said anything to me as we walked. She hadn't stopped to buy moleskin or bandages because she didn't want to interrupt our fun, she said.

"Riva, you walked around in agony, suffering in silence, as if stopping to buy a blister-blocker would have been an extravagant inconvenience. I wish you had said something. It was a pointless martyrdom."

"What about now?" Riva asked wryly. "Is this a pointless martyrdom, too?"

I touched her hair. It was golden and soft. I couldn't remember ever having stroked her hair. When we were kids, Riva would style my hair in an effort to make me look more girly, but I remained an incurable proto-lesbian, which in those days was sometimes called a tomboy. I never cared about hair and girly grooming, but Riva wanted me to look my best.

"Maybe it is a martyrdom, Riva," I said. "You loved the unlovable, the way saints supposedly do. Was Mack worth dying for?"

"I didn't *die for him*, Becky," Riva scoffed. "He killed me. I believed in his basic goodness. If I died for anything, I died for that."

Whenever I pressed for details about what exactly had happened to her, Riva would go silent. *How did Mack hurt you? Why?* She would not answer. She would not explain her silence. I assumed that he had hit her in the head with a dumbbell because I remembered that there were dumbbells in the yoga room, and it seemed a likely weapon for an impulsive attack. It occurred to me that perhaps Riva did not know exactly what had happened. She had been pushed, or attacked savagely from behind, after all, possibly without warning.

I thought about what she said: she didn't die for him; he had killed her. Yes, this was an important distinction. She had faith in his potential. That's why she was with him, and why she had stayed with him for 14 years. She believed in his goodness, despite strong evidence that his goodness was nonexistent. And he killed her.

I looked at Riva's mouth. It was swollen with trauma and breathing tubes. I wished more than anything that I could see her smile one last time. "You're a martyr of charity, Reeve."

I heard her say, "Little Boz."

No one but Riva had ever called me Boz. It was her affectionate nickname for me since childhood. Neither of us knew why she called me Boz. When she said it, she said it warmly and protectively. It summed up a lifetime of Riva being my older sister.

I looked for strands of gray on Riva's head but couldn't find a single one. I had streaks of silver in my hair already, and I was two years younger than she. The previous nurse on duty had asked me, "Are you Riva's mom?" I confessed that I was Riva's little sister. I understood why the nurse had asked. Even in death, Riva glowed with youthful radiance.

"No gray and no wrinkles, Reeve. Your skin looks clear and fresh."

I reached out, tentative at first, and smoothed her eyebrow with my thumb. I could have scooped her into my arms right then, bloody tubes and all, but I knew she couldn't feel it. I sensed that what she needed from me—or what I needed to give to her—was an expression of love that wasn't dependent on anything physical or material, because she was beyond that now.

I recounted funny stories about the time we traveled to Cambodia together. One day, an orange-robed monk who, apparently captivated by Riva's blonde hair, aggressively pursued her and tried to grope her while we were touring shrines at Angkor Wat. *Remember that?* The episode disturbed and amused us. The monk was relatively small in stature compared to us, so we did not feel that he posed a physical threat. How hilariously bizarre, we thought, to be accosted by a monk at a holy site.

Afterward, I teased Riva for being outrageously polite to the monk by saying, "Thank you, sir, I'm not interested, sir," and "Please leave us alone, sir."

I said: "Riva, next time, just tell the creep to back off."

Later that day, a barefoot child on a street in Siem Reap said to me, "Please, nice lady, give me one dollar." Riva gave me a sharp look and shook her head. I shrugged and handed the kid a buck. In an instant, six children surrounded us shouting, "One dollar! Nice lady! Give me one dollar!"

Riva and I made a run for a taxi.

"Next time, tell the little punk to back off," Riva teased.

Riva and I had the same vulnerability: we pitied people whom we perceived to be less fortunate than we were. We felt guilty about our good fortune. We felt that "being nice" and complying with the requests of people we pitied would atone for our guilt.

Engaging our pity was the surest way to bypass our common sense and short-circuit our self-preservation instincts. I sneered at Mack for being an oaf much of the time, but he was smart enough to discern this baseless guilt of ours, and to exploit it expertly with Riva.

I reminded Riva about the time we drove all the way around the Big Island of Hawaii in a rental car during a single day, one of our most memorable sister days. We started in the rainy verdure of Hilo near a macadamia nut farm. We drove past rolling pastures and windy hills near the town of Hawi, and down the dry, sunbaked coast past coffee plantations near Kona and beyond. We rounded the seemingly deserted southern tip of the island, stopping to touch black-and-green-sand beaches. We wended our way past lava flows and volcanic plumes on the road back to Hilo. The whole island felt like a living entity. Even the rocks seemed alive. We felt as if we were circumnavigating the leathery shell of a huge turtle floating on the Pacific Ocean.

Remember, Riva? It's like we drove on the back of a giant Honu.

Mack spent that day getting an elaborate tattoo of a *Honu*—a Hawaiian sea turtle—on his arm at a studio in Hilo.

Getting tattoos in Hawaii was more important to Mack than actually seeing Hawaii.

For Riva and me, being together was always the best fun. It didn't matter where we were or what we were doing. *Even now*—tears welled in my eyes. I heard the *whoosh* of the ventilator that inflated Riva's lungs. "Even now, Riva. Being with you. This is the best and worst sister day ever."

Another memory from our trip to Cambodia suddenly became vivid. It was as if Riva had interrupted my thoughts with a shared memory.

One night, Riva and I stood on a beach in Sihanoukville, also known as Kampong Som. We looked out across the Gulf of Thailand. In the distance, an electrical storm lit up the clouds with wild, erupting flashes. We were too far away to hear the thunder. From where we stood, it looked like a blanket of silent bombs exploding across the night sky.

Riva and I talked about the people who were near the storm and how terrifying it must be for them. For us, it was an immense, dazzling display wrapped in eerie silence.

Was this what Riva wanted me to think about, and to understand? Was I standing on the shore while she was in the storm? Was it the other way around? Or were we together now as we had been in Cambodia, marveling at something far beyond us?

Jolting me out of this memory, the nurse named Aquino came into the room with two bags of intravenous fluid. He swapped the old fluid bags with the new ones. I could see that he was sad for me, and sad for the whole situation. "You'll need to leave the room for at least twenty minutes," he said apologetically. "The respiratory therapist and anesthesiologist are coming for a final check before we move her to surgery."

"Anesthesiologist?" I asked. "I thought she couldn't feel anything."

"It's just standard procedure for all surgical patients. We wouldn't operate on anyone without an anesthesiologist being present."

I hoisted my backpack onto my shoulder and followed the nurse out of the room. It was an unsettling possibility to ponder as I walked. *What if Riva's in there, somewhere, unreachable, and feeling pain?* The thought that she might be able to feel the sensation of having her organs harvested—just the faintest glimmer of this possibility—disturbed me so much that I couldn't even hold the thought in my mind.

"Hang in there, Riva," I said aloud, as if to dispel all possibility of her pain. "It will be over soon."

I rode the elevator to the lobby. I walked down a long, wide hallway near the cafeteria. The walls were decorated with historical photos of the hospital. It reminded me of the hospital in Denver where I worked. We, too, had our institution's history on display in our hallways.

According to the placards accompanying the photos, St. Mary the Tower had been founded by an order of Catholic nuns who had come to Long Beach in the early 1900s. In the photos, the nuns all looked the same, wearing identical habits to conceal traces of individuality, as if they were interchangeable parts of one larger organism. The nuns' faces were plain and stern. These women had sustained the hospital through epidemics, earthquakes, fires, and financial crises. Eventually, powerful men in the Catholic Church sold the hospital to a medical corporation. The Vatican later dissolved the order of nuns.

I found it strange that nuns were called "sister." I had Riva, a true sister with whom I had shared my whole life. She and I differed in significant ways. She was diligent and patient. I wasn't. She had respect for rules and courtesies, such as sending timely greetings and thank-you notes. I didn't. Even so, we used to joke that we shared a single brain because our patterns of thought and speech were similar. Plus, we had so much life experience in common. I could not imagine having this same sisterly bond with a random group of women, even if we worked together, wore the same clothes, and professed the same faith.

I flashed on a memory of a woman I used to know when I lived in Long Beach in the late 1980s. I was just out of college when I moved to Southern California to live my life as a newly self-proclaimed lesbian. This woman—what was her name? I couldn't remember. She was ten years older than me, and well-established as a responsible citizen. I was interested in dating her. I met her at *Executive Suite*, a popular if seedy lesbian bar on the Pacific Coast Highway. She worked long days in a medical office. She spent her evenings caring for a gay man named Billy who was dying of AIDS. She had known Billy since high school. They went to prom together because they were the only non-heterosexuals they knew. They were each other's "beard." Later, Billy got sick and was abandoned by his family and friends, so this woman took care of him—cleaning his house, bathing him, and feeding him.

The weird thing was that Billy was a complete jerk to her. I went with her to his apartment once to help her change his bedsheets. The whole time we were there, he hurled bitchy insults at us, telling us what ugly dykes we were, reeling off a sustained, anti-lesbian screed. He literally spat on her.

After we had cleaned up his place, she and I went to a bar for beers. I was still shaken by the experience. "He's terrible," I said. "Why do you put up with him?"

She sighed. "If I don't help him, who will?" She took a swig of beer. She added, sadly: "Truth is, he'll be dead soon. All of us will be dead sooner than we think. It's nice to have clean sheets."

I didn't disagree with her, but I recognized at that moment that we were romantically incompatible. I admired her devotion to Billy. At the same time, I thought she was a masochist. *Yes, we all will soon be dead,* I thought. *Which is all the more reason to refuse to take crap from people who have no appreciation for you.* She dodged a bullet, I suppose, because I was young and smug and incapable of understanding her sense of loyalty. As a couple, we never would have worked out happily.

Why did people end up coupled with certain people, and not with others? Why did Riva end up with men like Mack? Why did I end up with women like Mack?

As I looked at the photos on the wall, I saw a Long Beach Police officer in uniform walking toward me. I hoped he was coming to tell me that Mack was under arrest. Instead, the cop nodded at me as he walked to the cafeteria.

I wasn't eager to be parted from Riva forever. Still, I wanted her to be examined by the coroner immediately. I wanted to be able to say out loud what I knew to be true: Riva's death was a homicide, not a yoga accident. Until I had an official statement of her cause and manner of death, though, I'd have to bite my tongue, something I'd never done successfully for long.

Down the hall, I saw an elderly nun standing near the door of the hospital chapel. She was dressed all in white with a starched white veil. She looked exactly like the nuns in the hospital's archival photos. Her face was exposed from her jaw to her forehead. She seemed to be waiting for someone. She seemed to be smiling at me. I looked behind me to see if she was smiling at someone else. The nun and I were the only people in the hall.

As I walked closer to her, she held out her tremor-wracked hands. "I saw you," she said, as if she knew me. "I hurried to greet you."

I reflexively reached out my hands. The nun clasped them between both of hers. I noticed that she smelled like roses. She pressed something into my palm.

"I think you've mistaken me for someone else, sister," I said.

She looked at me with a strange kind of clarity, which puzzled me. Her eyes were clouded with cataracts. I doubted that she could see my face at all.

"I see the most exquisite violet hue around you, my dear," she said. Her pronunciation was precise and dated somehow, similar to the way actors in American movies from the 1950s spoke. In fact, the nun looked like Lillian Gish in *Night of the Hunter*, only older.

I didn't know what to say. I looked around helplessly, hoping to see someone who might be accompanying this frail old woman, but found no one. I gently turned my hand to see what she had given me. It was a string of beads. Tiny spheres of rosewood were looped together on a silken cord. The beads had been worn smooth and shiny from use. A half-dollar-sized circle of carved rosewood hung from the cord. It looked like a circle filled with smaller circles forming a six-petal flower in the center.

"You must accept this rosary," the old nun said.

I did not initially recognize it as a rosary because there was no cross or crucifix on it. The rosary looked antique, as if the nun had prayed with it all her life. Perhaps she had inherited it from a forebear who had prayed with it for many years, too.

"I can't take this from you," I said, holding it gingerly and awkwardly. "It's too personal."

"You must take it," she said, adamant. "It is not for you."

I shook my head, not comprehending. "It's *not* for me," I repeated. The phrase seemed to explain exactly why I couldn't accept the rosary.

"This is for you," she said. From the folds of her habit she produced a small, clothbound book. She closed my hands over both of the objects. Her hands were very warm, almost hot.

"Sister," I said, "I'm not who you think I am."

Her opaque eyes widened. "Look here." With the tips of her fingers, she tapped my forehead just above the spot between my eyebrows. "Close your eyes."

I closed my eyes. I felt her tap my forehead three times.

I saw a small dot of purple in a field of blackness. It exploded. Purple expanded to fill everything.

"Oh," I said, surprised. I opened my eyes. I blinked.

The nun had vanished. I still held the book and rosary she had given me. I glanced up and down the hallway. I assumed that she had gone into the hospital chapel. I opened the door, which was painted with the word "Chapelle," the French spelling of chapel, which struck me as odd.

I discovered that the door led to a small courtyard which led to another building-within-a-building. The medical tower had been built around a humble but beautiful old chapel. The chapel stood in the center of the courtyard. I looked up at the windows of the medical tower. The height of the surrounding building prevented the courtyard from getting much sunlight.

The chapel must've been protected from demolition because it was a historic structure, I assumed. Otherwise, why go through all the trouble of constructing the tower around it?

The chapel's wide, wooden doors were open in front of me. Inside, artificial light shined through stained-glass windows, giving the room a multicolored, psychedelic ambiance. The place was notably peaceful and empty. I saw no sign of the nun. I assumed that she had taken an exit that I couldn't see.

I turned to leave. I noticed a small plaque on the wall of the chapel. As a philanthropic fundraising researcher for a hospital, I habitually studied plaques on walls, especially plaques on walls in hospitals. This plaque read: "Rebuilt with a gift from the Ashton Foundation, 1933."

The Ashton Foundation? I half laughed at the coincidence. I had been on my way to the office to do research about the Ashton Foundation on the morning days earlier when Mack called me to say that Riva had fallen while doing yoga.

As I walked back to the hospital lobby and the elevators, I thought about my research assignment regarding the Ashton Foundation. I still hadn't done the report. My boss Lola had been very kind about letting me miss work to be with Riva. Getting the Ashton report done as soon as possible was the least I could do in exchange.

In the lobby, I asked the receptionist at the front desk to page the nun for me.

"What nun?" she asked as if surprised by the question.

"The nun who works here," I said, clarifying.

"The nuns are long gone," the receptionist said in a nostalgic tone. "I can page Father Murphy if you need spiritual counseling."

"No, thanks," I said. I figured that the nun was visiting someone at the hospital, or maybe she was a patient.

I took the elevator to the intensive care unit. I saw Riva's nurse writing notes on a chart outside her door. "We're going to take her to surgery in about 15 minutes," he said.

Riva had been slightly re-positioned. Her chin was tilted upward. The foul smell of stale breath lingered in the air, as it did when the respiratory therapist made adjustments to Riva's breathing tube. The first time I smelled it, I offered Riva a stick of gum—*ha, ha, Reeve, let's do something about your breath.* Now, as she was about to leave for organ-donation surgery, the odor reminded me that she was dead. She was in decay.

I told Riva about meeting the nun near the chapel. "She wasn't creepy like the monk at Angkor Wat, but she was weirdly intense. She tapped my forehead, and—well—maybe I had a spiritual experience." I forced a laugh at the absurdity of it. "Why do religious clergy-people find us interesting? Why do they bother with us?"

Riva was agnostic, with no fondness for organized religion. I had dabbled in Buddhism but was turned off by the ingrained hierarchy and authoritarianism that I found even in that ostensibly anti-authoritarian tradition. We weren't religious people, which was one of the reasons why it was so ridiculous that Mack had asked a priest to give Riva Last Rites. We weren't even spiritual.

"The nun gave me a book and these beads, Reeve." I held up the rosary to show her. "I feel bad about it. I wanted to give them back to her. But she left and I couldn't find her. She wanted someone else to have this rosary, not me. Weird, huh?"

Riva said nothing. The ventilator clicked. A stream of air mechanically inflated her lungs.

I tucked the rosary and the book into the front pouch of my backpack and forgot about them. I walked to the other side of Riva's bed. I wanted to be away from the door because I didn't want Aquino to hear my sobbing.

"Riva." I took her hand.

I felt a slight tremor in her muscles as if she wanted to grab my fingers. I had felt this tremor once before. A doctor had assured me earlier that it wasn't an actual reflex; rather, it was just my wishful thinking. I gazed at Riva's face. She looked eager to get out of her broken head. She looked constrained and confined by a body that no longer fit her.

"Maybe someday this will be funny, Riva. I'll say, *remember the time your husband murdered you?* We'll roll our eyes and laugh."

I could feel blood pulsing in Riva's ring finger. With each beat of her heart, it felt as if Riva was squeezing my hand. Her last effort to touch me, to let me know everything would be okay, came from her heart. *Little Boz*, she said.

Three staffers entered the room—Aquino the nurse, the respiratory therapist, and the nurse in charge of organ harvesting.

The respiratory therapist asked in a polite, almost formal way: "Could we ask you to step into the hallway?"

"She's beautiful," the organ-harvesting nurse said to me, kindly.

I wiped my eyes. Yes, Riva looked beautiful—radiant and ready for whatever would happen next. I stood in the hallway while they loaded up Riva's bed with an oxygen tank and the other equipment that she would need for the final part of her journey.

They wheeled Riva's IV-stand alongside her bed as they rolled it down the hallway. They let me walk with them. They invited me to join them in the staff elevator. I knew they felt terrible for me. They even let me enter the surgery area. I was not allowed to cross a red line on the floor, however.

Aquino said sadly: "You'll have to leave her now."

I turned to go. I took a few steps. I turned back. "Bye, Riva." I waved feebly. "Good job." I gave her a perky thumbs-up as if she was going into an important client meeting. I blurted: "Knock 'em dead!"

The instant I said it, I knew it was tactless and thoughtless, considering her recent fatal blow to the head. The respiratory therapist raised his eyebrows slightly and said: "Everyone grieves differently," oddly echoing Father Murphy.

I knew that Riva would laugh and have fun teasing me about saying the most appallingly inappropriate thing ever.

4

ASHTON FOUNDATION

According to the provisional certificate issued by the Los Angeles County Coroner, Riva's cause and manner of death were "deferred." The funeral coordinator at the mortuary explained to me over the phone: "The *cause* of death is the thing that killed the person, such as a disease, or an injury, or lots of other things. *Manner* of death can be only one of five things—natural, accident, suicide, homicide, or undetermined."

The funeral coordinator was named Chutney. She had a high-pitched, rapid, chirpy voice that seemed to suit her unusual name. At times, however, she spoke very slowly, as if making a conscious effort to sound serious and solemn.

"*Deferred* means that the coroner isn't finished investigating," she said, slowly and solemnly. "Sometimes it means they're waiting for the results of toxicology tests. It can take as long as three months for the coroner to specify the manner of death in a case like this. You might have to wait even longer to see the autopsy report. For your sister's manner of death, you can probably rule out suicide."

Unless you consider suicide by marriage, I thought.

The coroner had deferred ruling on the specifics of Riva's death because, I assumed, he or she suspected homicide. Making a final determination would require more information from the police. They would have to investigate further, I hoped, despite their initial lack of suspicion. Meanwhile, Mack remained at large.

After conducting the autopsy, the coroner had released Riva's body to the mortuary. Chutney explained: "Mr. King Pine has authorized a viewing for mourners to pay their last respects to your sister tomorrow morning at 10 a.m." At the viewing, I would be able to see Riva's embalmed body. After this, Riva would be cremated. Her ashes would be divided into two separate containers, one for Mack and one for me. The ashes would be ready for pick-up by the end of the week.

I was looking forward to picking up Riva's ashes and going home to Denver. I felt that returning her ashes to Denver, where we both had been born, would provide a symbolic bookend to her life.

I took a walk on the beach hoping to hear Riva's voice. Every place I went in Long Beach reminded me of her. It seemed wrong to me that the city hadn't stopped, hadn't been paralyzed with grief at the cruel death of the wonderful woman who had walked on these sidewalks, and shopped in these shops, smiling at the world. I wondered, truly perplexed: *How can anything continue to exist without her?*

More to the point, how was I going to get through the rest of my life without her? I couldn't watch movies or television or even read newspapers because everything felt inconsequential to me. Everything seemed irritatingly useless and false, especially scenes of death and grieving. I wanted to issue a memo to every actor in Hollywood to let them know that their grief scenes were laughably inauthentic. Real people don't howl and moan like that. Real people don't scream "No!" and gesticulate wildly as they weep. Rather, they're stunned. They're in shock at the death of a loved one. They haven't even started to grieve.

Everyone grieves differently—Father Murphy's phrase echoed in my mind yet again.

The people who were inclined to put on a big show alongside a deathbed were people like Mack, people who were untouched by reverence and awe. Perhaps it was too harsh and too sweeping an assessment, but I concluded that people who displayed instantaneous frenzied sadness had yet to mourn. They didn't feel, or had yet to feel, the breathtaking power of death. Rather, they were just mimicking what they'd seen on television.

I remembered from my years of living in Southern California: immediately after a major earthquake there's an intense silence, as if everyone collectively recalls that we're all walking a tightrope over an abyss. A long moment passes. Gradually, the noise of day-to-day life resumes, along with screaming and crying, too, depending on what the quake left in its wake. Maybe one day soon, I would wail and flail in response to Riva's death, but during those days in Long Beach, I felt suspended in palpable silence.

My boss Lola had been generous about giving me time away from work. I still owed her a report on the Ashton Foundation, and I was certainly curious to investigate the foundation's link to St. Mary the Tower Hospital in Long Beach.

A woman named Marydale from the Ashton Foundation had called Lola to discuss making a significant financial gift to the hospital. I wondered whether Marydale was a first name or last name. Was it Mrs. Marydale, or Dr. Marydale? Regardless, Marydale was Ashton's manager of charitable projects. She would meet in Denver with Lola soon. In preparation, Lola needed to know more about the Ashton Foundation's philanthropic priorities and financial resources.

During my time with Riva at St. Mary the Tower, I had gained an important investigative lead. I knew that the Ashton Foundation had made a financial gift in 1933 to reconstruct the peculiar chapel-in-a-courtyard at the hospital. I had seen the plaque on the wall of the chapel to commemorate this gift.

As part of my job as a background researcher, I routinely gathered information about foundations as well as individual financial donors and potential donors. I amassed data about their income sources, expenditures, family relationships, social activities, political sympathies, and favorite charities.

Much of this work was necessary to protect the hospital from scandal. It was not unheard of for wealthy individuals to make impressively large pledges to gain publicity, yet be financially unable to make good on their promises. It was not unheard of for philanthropic donors to have buildings and endowments named after them, only to end up tarnishing the reputation of the charity after being indicted for fraud, for instance.

Always, we need to know who is giving us money, and why, Lola would often say. *How did they acquire their wealth? What conflicts of interests might arise?* My job was to answer these questions to Lola's satisfaction.

I walked to the downtown branch of the Long Beach Public Library, which was near the Long Beach Police Department Headquarters, several blocks from the beach, and near my hotel. I sat down at a computer terminal. An online search showed me next to nothing about Ashton. The Ashton Foundation was a private foundation rather than a nonprofit and, therefore, it was not required by law to file public disclosures. I found related references to someone named Anna Bartlet. Bartlet was the executive director of the foundation.

I discovered that Marydale was Diane Marydale, CNM— she was a certified nurse midwife. Marydale and Anna Bartlet supposedly had an office in New York, but I couldn't find a street address. The Ashton Foundation didn't even have a website or social-media presence. All it had was a post-office box.

I found obscure, online rants suggesting that the Ashton Foundation was somehow trafficking in fetal stem cells and providing funding for a network of secret abortion providers. A few online commentaries accused Ashton of promoting witchcraft. This reminded me of ridiculous rumors I had heard about Holy Cross—something having to do with witches and secret anti-Catholic practitioners of Kabbalah in Denver in the late 1800s. I couldn't remember the specifics because I had dismissed the allegations as silly and irrelevant the moment I'd heard them.

The plaque I had seen in the chapel at St. Mary the Tower was my only substantial lead regarding Ashton. The plaque said: "Rebuilt with a gift from the Ashton Foundation, 1933." I wondered whether the local newspaper had published an article about the chapel's reconstruction.

A librarian patiently showed me how to view microfilm. Microfilm was a thing of the past, I thought, like newspapers. The librarian assured me that microfilm was the best, most reliable repository of irreplaceable cultural treasures such as Long Beach newspapers from 1933.

"That was the year of the big earthquake," the librarian said. She was a youngish woman with shockingly purple hair, black lipstick, and chunky eyeglasses with translucent frames.

On March 10, 1933, an earthquake had devastated Long Beach, destroying many buildings, the librarian said. The chapel at St. Mary the Tower had to be rebuilt after the devastation.

I scrolled and skimmed through hundreds of newspaper items. The nuns of St. Mary the Tower appeared in the news frequently in 1933 and 1934. The nuns offered a variety of public health and education programs in addition to hospital care. From what I could tell, the nuns were much-beloved members of the community.

I took a break for coffee. I checked my phone. I had a message from Mack: "Viewing of the wife tomorrow at 10. Much love."

He was always classy like that, referring to Riva as "the wife," as an abstract thing like "the weather," or as an accessory like "the Porsche." Mack once bought a Porsche 911 sports car that Riva had begged him not to buy. It was ultimately, and predictably, a regrettable, money-losing blunder. Mack bought it just so he could impress people by referring to it off-handedly as *the Porsche.*

One of Riva's friends later asked her why she had allowed Mack to buy the car in the first place. Instead of admitting that it was not in her power to prevent Mack from doing stupid things against her advice, Riva said that she hoped it would be a learning experience for Mack. "He believes that acquiring toys will make him happy," she'd said. "Happiness doesn't come from having or not having cool stuff. Mack knows this, deep down, but it hasn't hit home for him. Maybe *the Porsche* will prove it to him once and for all." Sadly, I think the only thing Mack learned was that if he overextended himself financially, Riva would bail him out.

I assumed that the viewing at the mortuary would be another opportunity for Mack to revel in sympathy from Riva's friends and colleagues. He probably would invite his whole neighborhood to it, too, including Carleen Biggars. I wondered whether he might invite the men whom he had referred to as his mentors—Samadhi Masterson and Roy Dumond.

Some of the women from Riva's book group had sent me messages inviting me to have dinner with them. I politely declined. I wanted to be alone. More than that, I was afraid of what I might say. It would be unwise for me to broadcast my suspicions about Mack being a murderer. Whatever I said might get back to Mack.

As far as I was concerned, Mack was a man who believed himself to have gotten away with the perfect crime. What could be more hazardous to my health than a brazen murderer who had always hated me? As long as I had to interact with Mack about Riva's remains, and as long as I was within a thousand miles of him, I wanted to play the role of a clueless, disengaged sister-in-law.

I went back to the microfilm reader. I had seen entries referencing structural damage to buildings at St. Mary the Tower. I skipped forward to newspapers that had been published in the later months of 1934. At last, I found a brief announcement of a re-dedication ceremony at the hospital chapel. I looked at the edition published after the ceremony.

I found an article entitled, "Chapel Rises from Rubble." A photograph accompanied the brief report. The photo caption read: "Mrs. Simon Ashton, chairwoman of New York City's Ashton Foundation, congratulates Sisters of St. Mary the Tower." The grainy black-and-white photo showed a woman in her thirties flanked by six nuns clad in white.

There was something strangely familiar about the woman identified as Mrs. Simon Ashton. She had a proud, almost defiant look about her. Her dark abundance of hair was pulled up on top of her head in a way reminiscent of ancient Roman statuary. *That's it*, I thought, *she looks like a famous statue I've seen somewhere.* But no, this didn't seem quite right. She was more familiar to me than that. I had seen her before in a more personal context, I was certain.

I found it both quaint and appalling that she was identified as "Mrs. Simon Ashton" rather than referred to by her own first name. It was if she had become an appendage of Mr.

Simon Ashton upon marrying him—and by laws and customs of the era, she had indeed become his property.

I searched through New York newspaper archives and found that her name was Anna Ashton, born Anna Seton in 1880. She married wealthy Manhattan financier Simon Ashton in 1904. Together, they had created the Ashton Foundation, which was dedicated to "furthering on Earth the work of Angels in Heaven." The Ashton Foundation had made significant financial gifts to charities run by or serving women.

It was impressive to me that the Ashton Foundation had existed for more than a hundred years and was still operating. Their money managers were obviously doing a great job, I thought.

I looked again with new admiration at the photo of Anna Ashton and the nuns. Facts echoed in my mind: *Born in 1880. Married Simon Ashton in 1904. Photographed in Long Beach in 1934....* I blinked. This made no sense. The woman in the photograph from 1934 looked much younger than 54—by at least 20 years.

I toggled back to New York newspapers. I hunted for Anna Ashton's obituary. According to her four-line death notice, she died of natural causes in her Greenwich Village home on September 14, 1975, after a long convalescence. She lived to be 95 years old, and had not been a topic of public interest for many decades. Honoring her last will and testament, her body was buried somewhere near Puivert, France.

Strange. The woman had founded a well-funded, still-vital philanthropic organization, yet she did not merit a full obituary. The New York paper didn't even print a photo of her along with the death notice. Again, this struck me as unusual. I searched the paper's archives for photos of Anna Ashton and Simon Ashton. I found nothing. As far as I could tell, the only surviving, published image of Anna had appeared in a Long

Beach newspaper in 1934, accompanying an article about the re-built chapel. How could this be?

"Can I save an electronic copy of this photo?" I asked the librarian. I right-clicked repeatedly on the photo of Anna Ashton at St. Mary the Tower.

"Theoretically, yes," the librarian replied. "Technically, no. We've been having trouble copying electronic files from microfilm. Would it be okay if I printed out a paper copy for you?"

"Of course," I said. "That would be great."

I jotted a text message to Lola, my boss: "Ashton Foundation has a history of supporting nuns and women's charities. Not sure how this fits with funding priorities at Holy Cross. More info soon."

A few minutes later, the librarian handed me a sheet of paper that had just come off the printer near her desk. The photo was grainy to begin with, and the printed copy was more blurred, but Anna Ashton's facial expression lost little in translation. She was a powerful, self-assured woman.

"Can I help you with anything else?" The librarian seemed pleased by the novelty of someone attempting to do research. She seemed to welcome my company.

"This is obscure, and I'm sure it happened long before your time," I said, unthinkingly prefacing my question in a way that made me sound condescending. "Do you know anything about the nuns who founded St. Mary the Tower? Are there any nuns still around?"

The librarian eagerly pulled up a chair across from me as if thrilled to talk to someone. "It's quite a story," she said. "They were called Sisters of the Tower. They didn't survive Vatican II."

"What's Vatican two?" I shrugged.

"It was a big reformation of the Catholic Church to modernize it and bring it into the Twentieth Century. Basically, the church became more liberal than it had been. Supposedly, the Sisters of the Tower became too liberal even for the liberalized church. I've heard that the nuns were always radical, but they became more open about their radicalism after Vatican II. At the hospital, they provided free birth control and women's reproductive health-care services, for instance. I've heard that they even provided abortion procedures for women in need. As you can imagine, when the church bureaucracy got wind of this rumor, they shut down the nuns. The sisters were stripped of all their assets, which included the hospital buildings and all the land. The church disbanded the whole order of nuns known as Sisters of the Tower. The sisters were excommunicated from the church."

"Can you help me find newspaper articles about this?" I asked, excited to read more about these scandalous sisters.

The librarian slowly shook her head as she spoke. "There aren't any. There are no documents, no published accounts of this story, nothing whatsoever in print."

I wondered for a moment if she might be joking, but her expression told me that she knew how seriously incredible it sounded. "How did you hear about it?" I asked.

"I grew up around here," she said cagily. "I've heard things. Women's history—the true story of women—is almost never documented. If it is documented, the documents are almost always purged or suppressed. Women have had to find alternative ways of preserving their history." She glanced around the relatively empty library. She asked: "Do you know how to use a hex-reader?"

I frequently used a hex-reader for my job. Studying the hexadecimal coding of a digital photo helped me to determine whether it was original, or whether it had been altered in some way. I remembered one case in which a potential Holy Cross donor had added himself to photographs with politicians and celebrities to make himself appear well-connected. The fake photos *looked* flawless, but the hex code didn't lie. "Yes, I know how to use a hex-reader," I said.

The librarian's face brightened. "Sit at that terminal," she said, pointing to a desk across the room. "Open the folder called *Long Beach Historical Society Trip to Rome*. Look for a picture of a woman in front of the Vatican." Her tone changed slightly, as if she was issuing a dare: "Check the hex on just this one photo." She glanced at a clock on the wall. "I'm going on a break." She stood. "If you can't figure it out, I'll be back in an hour to help you." There was a distinct challenge in the way she said this.

"I think I can handle it," I said, rising to defend my general competence, although I wasn't sure why I suddenly felt defensive.

I sat down at the terminal as instructed. I assumed that, with the help of a hex-reader, I would find a file hidden within another file. This was known as *steganography*, the practice of hiding information within other information. Criminal organizations were known to hide messages to their operatives within the code of innocuous-looking photos, for example.

I saw a folder labeled *LB Historical Society Trip to Rome*. Inside the folder were hundreds of digital photographs of Rome. I scrolled through the images. Dozens upon dozens of these photos were taken in St. Peter's Square in front of the Vatican. Almost all of these photos featured women. I sighed. I understood why the librarian thought the task was beyond me.

Which picture of a woman in front of the Vatican?

I clicked to enlarge the photos. I skimmed over dozens of snapshots of smiling women. I knew that it was possible to hide lengthy text documents and secret videos, even, within the code of an ordinary-looking digital photo. But *which* photo? And why? For what meaningful purpose? It would take hours for me to comb through the code looking for anomalies and hidden messages.

I assumed that a photo containing hidden information would have a larger overall file size than other photos. I was about to compare the file sizes of all the photos when one particular image caught my attention. I paused and studied it.

The woman in the photo looked vaguely familiar to me. Her head was turned toward her right shoulder, and her face was blurred, as if she had suddenly moved just as the picture was being taken. If I hadn't known better, I would have said that it was a color photo of long-dead actress Lillian Gish taken when she was in her forties. Instantly, I recalled the old nun at the hospital, the one who had given me the rosary and the small book. I had thought that she, too, looked like Lillian Gish—an eighty-something Gish.

I opened this Gish-like image to scan the code. I found a text document embedded in it. I opened it. The document read as follows:

During the First Century A.D., the woman who was later called St. Mary the Tower fled from the city of Alexandria fearing for her life. She and her accomplices were forced into a wooden boat and launched onto the Mediterranean Sea with little chance of survival. Mary's crime was that she had succeeded where others had failed in learning her Master's metaphysical arts. She knew how to raise the Treasure Tower from the ground, which is why her Master had called her Mary the Tower. This did not endear her those who had more mundane plans for the legacy of her Master --

plans of conquest and kingdom. The rift between Mary and the others had always been obvious, and it widened after the death of their teacher. Fleeing to a friendlier shore was her only hope of staying alive and teaching others what she had learned.

Without oars, without a sail, and without a rudder, Mary's boat traveled more than 1,800 nautical miles in approximately twenty days. She and her party of seven faithful souls saw the stark, steep, limestone walls and narrow inlets along the coast of what we now know as southern France. The party drifted past the port that we now know as Marseille. They ultimately landed on a sandy coast of the Camargue marshland.

According to popular legend, Mary and her friends set out to liberate all humanity. It is said that Mary taught metaphysical arts throughout the region of Provence. She then retired to live in a cave at the base of the Sainte-Baume mountains. She spent the final thirty years of her life in suspended animation, never eating or drinking, until entering nirvana.

The unwritten part of the story is that, in truth, in the south of France, Mary discovered descendants from her own tribe. She discovered that southern France was populated by her distant cousins, by people who had come to the Rhone Valley in their flight from war and cataclysm in ancient Crete. People had been coming to this valley since Paleolithic times, since the times when saber-toothed cats roamed Europe. These people had lived and meditated in caves. They had left their mysterious paintings on the walls. They carved their histories in the stones of France.

All of these seemingly diverse peoples of the region revered femaleness. Femaleness was the fundamental operating concept of their cultures. They did not denigrate maleness. Rather, they celebrated and revered the female form in all its power and complexity.

A thousand years after Mary had arrived in her rudderless boat, the region of southern France had grown and flourished in a way that the rest of Europe had not. The region was known as Occitania. Its wealth and progress stood in contrast to the relative poverty, ignorance, sickness, and belligerence of the lands influenced and controlled by the Catholic Church.

The faithful people of Occitania practiced the spiritual arts of the Master as taught by Mary the Tower, which coincided with the ancient teachings of the land. They called themselves "the good people."

These good people had no use for the church of Rome with its violent repression of femaleness and its absurd elevation of maleness. In Occitania, both sexes were regarded as equally human. Neither sex was confined to prescribed social roles. Both women and men could be poets, farmers, weavers, traders, and warriors.

What's more, marriage was unheard of in Occitania. Adults conducted their lives in a spirit of mutual responsibility and integrity, not needing contracts, forces of obligation, or threats of punishment to coax people to behave in a civil manner.

To the Roman Catholic Church, the so-called good people of Occitania were an abomination. Their rejection of marriage made them free-love degenerates in the eyes of the church. Their women were unforgivably self-assured, and their men allowed them to be this way. Their greatest affront, however, was their refusal to pay taxes to Pope Innocent III.

In the year 1209, the Catholic Church joined forces with northern warlords to exterminate the good people and to plunder the wealth of their lands. For three decades, the church organized, financed, and blessed mass murder throughout Occitania.

In a desperate attempt to ensure that the teachings of the good people would survive, some men and women of Occitania infiltrated the Catholic Church. They surrendered to the invading armies. They renounced their "errant" faith. They pledged allegiance to the Pope. In exchange, they were allowed to live.

In the most famous instance of strategic conversion, seven Occitan women surrendered themselves to Saint Dominic, founder of the Dominican Order. They gave to Dominic their sacred practice of rosary meditation, a practice that had been taught by Mary the Tower herself, and by many teachers before her. Saint Dominic adopted the practice of the rosary as his own, claiming that another Mary -- Mary, Mother of Christ -- had revealed the practice to him in a miraculous visitation. Eventually, the entire Catholic Church embraced the practice of the rosary, with a few modifications to make the practice more consonant with church dogma.

These seven Occitan women were the foundation of Saint Dominic's order of nuns. He built a convent for them at Fanjeaux, France, which still exists. These renegade nuns were the fore-sisters of the women who founded St. Mary the Tower Hospital in Long Beach.

For centuries, renegade sisters and brothers have existed, hidden within the cloisters and cells of monastic communities. These people are referred to as renegades because they appear to be devout adherents of religion while their true allegiance is to *the all in the all*. They are involved in the ancient, intergalactic struggle against the Captivity. Powerful people within the Catholic Church, including popes and saints, have been among the renegades and their allies, providing cover and support, maintaining an appearance of humble loyalty to the Church. Renegades hide from the Church by hiding within the Church. The alternative is total annihilation at the hands of the Captivity.

I scoffed as I read it, certain that I had found a creative-writing student's attempt to conjure up a fictional conspiracy reminiscent of *The DaVinci Code*. It was exactly the kind of narrative that a bored librarian might dream up. Obviously, she wanted me to find this, and to take it seriously. I felt that the librarian was playing a practical joke on me. But why would she?

All of my questions remained unanswered. What had happened to the nuns in Long Beach? Were they really punished for providing reproductive health-care to women? Was *this* the mission that the Ashton Foundation intended to support with their financial gift to St. Mary the Tower Hospital? If so, why would Ashton be interested in making a gift to Holy Cross in Denver? None of our research involved reproductive health-care.

I felt that I had hit a brick wall regarding the Ashton Foundation. *I need to focus on what's important right now*, I told myself. My mind kept returning to one question: *What had happened to Riva?*

After her organ-donation surgery, Riva's body had been transported to the coroner's office. The medical examiner had conducted an autopsy. I knew nothing about autopsies. I searched the library's resources on the topic.

I studied illustrations and descriptions of standard autopsy procedures. I found it very upsetting that Riva had to go through an autopsy all by herself without my being there to support her. Presumably, homicide detectives had been present. Riva had dutifully endured the examination as the final task she had to complete, I imagined. Her last job in this world was to tell the story of what had happened to her. She had to speak with her skin, skull, eyes, and ruined brain. Her body told a story of homicide, no doubt. I hoped the police were attuned to hear it.

I left the library and went for a walk along the bluff overlooking Alamitos Bay. Riva and I had walked there many times together.

Each Fourth of July, we would stand on the bluff and watch the fireworks that were launched from the *Queen Mary*, the elegant ocean-liner now permanently at anchor in Long Beach Harbor. Riva and I would say "Ooh" and "Aah" along with the appreciative crowds as shells burst over the bay, reflecting blooms of fiery color.

That day in March, the sun was bright and hot. A sea breeze kept Long Beach cool. On the horizon, oil tankers and cargo ships at sea waited to enter the port. People bicycled and jogged along a concrete path that stretched the entire length of the beach. The mighty horn of the *Queen Mary* sounded one low blast, signaling one o'clock p.m. It was a fine day in Long Beach, glittering with perfection, and Riva was not there.

"Where are you, Riva?" I said aloud, softly.

While Riva was in the hospital, I had felt that she and I could communicate perfectly. Now, I felt as if a door had closed between us. I sensed that Riva still existed somewhere, but we could not connect with each other.

I started having dreams about Riva the night she went into organ-donation surgery. I looked forward to these dreams because I wanted to see Riva. I dreaded them, too, because of the way they ended.

I dreamed that I ran into her at the Denver airport. We greeted each other with surprise. "You made it," I exclaimed. "Last time I saw you, you were going into surgery."

"Surgery?" She raised her hand to touch the back of her head, as if remembering she had been injured. Her eyes glazed. She faded into nothingness.

In another dream, I saw Riva in a busy train station. I had become trapped in an online map. I needed to borrow her phone to call for help. "I clicked on *street view*," I explained to her. "Now I'm stuck here."

"You're just in another dimension," Riva said. "Don't worry." She handed me her phone.

"How did it go?" I asked as I fiddled with the device. "Last I heard, they were going to remove your heart and kidneys."

"You're right." Riva looked as if she suddenly remembered that her vital organs had been removed. "Becky, I have no lungs." With that, she was gone.

"Riva," I shouted, frantic. "Riva!"

I had several dreams like this, all with the same story. I would run into Riva in transit. We were happy to see each other. We would remember that she was dead, and she would disappear.

I sensed, however, that she had not become permanently extinct. Rather, she had gone somewhere else. But where? And how could I contact her? Despite all evidence to the contrary, I knew there must be a way.

5

DETECTIVE COLUMBO

On the morning of the mortuary viewing, I woke up later than I had planned. The handy thing about having packed only one change of clothes was that I didn't have to think about what to wear. I put on the lavender shirt that I had worn every other day since arriving in Long Beach, paired with black trousers. Riva had told me once that she liked my blue shirt, the other shirt I had brought with me. I had rinsed it the night before, though, and it was still damp that morning. I had never been fashionable, and certainly Riva would understand my lack of stylish attire on this grim occasion. Besides, what's the right thing to wear when contemplating the dead body of one's sister?

I rushed across town to the mortuary. I didn't want to be late, fearing that Mack would find a way to bar the door and prevent me from seeing Riva. The mortuary parking lot was packed with cars. At last, I found a place to park. I grabbed my backpack and walked briskly into the crowded lobby. I recognized no one. I went to the reception desk. "I'm Becky Pine," I said. "I'm here for the Riva Pine viewing."

The receptionist asked me to wait while she called Riva's funeral planner. A few minutes later, a woman in her twenties with a plump, jolly appearance introduced herself to me as

Chutney. I recognized her chirpy, happy voice from the phone. "I need to prepare you," she said. "Because of the chemicals used by the coroner, your sister is covered in protective sheeting. All you can see is her face. Is that okay?"

I nodded.

Chutney led me down a hallway.

"Are there lots of people here already?" I asked.

Chutney stopped. Her eyes registered mild panic. "More people? You're the only one we're expecting for Pine."

"Mack—I mean, my brother-in-law King. Do you know if he's coming?"

A look of relief crossed her face. "No, Mr. Pine told me that you would be the only mourner." Chutney continued walking. She opened a door. "You have this room for 15 minutes. We're really busy today," she said, apologetic. She left me there.

Chutney was right—I could see only Riva's face from chin to forehead. The rest of her body was draped in white sheets.

Riva's eyelids and cheeks were sunken. During the autopsy, the coroner had removed her eyes, tongue, and brain. The coroner had literally peeled Riva's face off of her skull as if it had been a mask. The mortuary had done a good job of putting her back together in recognizable form. Riva's lips looked pursed, as if she wanted to say something to me and was thinking of how to phrase it.

I looked at her and tried to see the Riva I had known all my life. It was her—but it *wasn't* her.

I touched the backs of my fingers to her cheek. Her skin was cold. She was not the same Riva I had left in the hospital. *That* Riva had a heartbeat. This Riva had no heartbeat. This Riva no longer had a heart, even. Someone else had her heart now. Someone else was alive at that very moment because of my sister's heart.

I suddenly realized: Riva looked like a nun! She looked as if she wore a starched, white habit, just like the Sisters of Mary the Tower. Covered in sheets, Riva looked as if she had joined a religious order. I almost laughed, but I didn't because she looked so earnest.

I remembered the rosary that the nun in the hospital had given me. I had forgotten all about it, until now. I took it from my backpack.

The well-worn beads felt smooth. They still smelled of roses. The scent immediately recalled to my memory the face of the nun, as if she had materialized in front of me. *The rosary is not for you*, I heard the nun say. *It is for your sister.*

I gently placed the beads on the white sheet just above Riva's hands. The rosary's tarnished wooden fob—which looked like a circle with several smaller circles creating a flower-petal design—rested on Riva's fingers.

"Take this with you on your travels, Riva," I said. "*Bon voyage.*" I wiped my eyes with my hands. I wished I had brought a handkerchief. I put my pack over my shoulder. I left the room.

Chutney seemed surprised by the expression on my face. "Is everything okay?" she asked with a slight grimace.

Nothing was okay, but I didn't want to explain it to Chutney. "I left a rosary with my sister's body," I said. "I would like for it to be cremated with her."

"I'll make a note of that in the paperwork," Chutney said. She led me to the reception desk. "One rosary from sister to accompany body," she said as she wrote. "Just sign here." She handed me a piece of paper.

Riva's ashes would be available by the end of the week, she said. Chutney informed me that Mack had already scheduled an appointment to pick up the ashes at 10 a.m. on Friday. "King asked me to tell you that he will take all of your sister's ashes if you are not present at the appointment to collect your half," Chutney said, apologetic. "Legally, he has the right to do that."

I nodded, glumly acknowledging Mack's right to do whatever he wished with everything of Riva's that remained in this world.

"He said that he needs the ashes promptly at 10 a.m.," Chutney added, in a lowered voice. "Because he has a tattoo appointment at 11. What does getting a tattoo have to do with picking up his wife's ashes?" She sounded intrigued.

I shrugged.

I left the mortuary and drove aimlessly. I stopped at a French café that Riva and I had visited several times. I sat at a table and ordered espresso. I reached into my backpack and pulled out the book that the nun at the hospital had given me.

The book was small, perhaps five inches by eight inches. It was bound with worn, blue cloth. I fanned the thick, yellowed pages. It was not a book that had been printed by a publisher. Rather, it looked like a personal diary. It was filled with handwriting and diagrams drawn in black ink. It might be a hundred years old, I thought. The spine of the book had been broken in several places. Upper and lower corners of many pages had been creased, as if the book had been consulted frequently.

The first page was blank except for one word written in block letters: "VICTORINE." I assumed that this was the name of the book's owner—most likely, the elderly nun. This was followed by several pages of sketches of a human figure in various poses. The sketches seemed to suggest repetitive movements, such as raising and lowering of the arms. The order in which the poses were drawn suggested a progression, as if the poses were to be done one after the other in a routine. To me, it looked like a Kundalini yoga workout.

As a devotee of yoga, Riva would've gotten a kick out of the book. She probably would've tried to replicate the routine, just to see how it felt.

I wondered: when did people in the West start doing yoga? Was it possible that nuns in Long Beach were doing Kundalini routines in the 1930s? Maybe the book was from the 1960s or 70s, but it seemed *much* older than that to me.

After the yoga drawings, a page proclaimed in fancy penmanship: "Subtle Techniques." This was followed by more drawings. These sketches illustrated various hand gestures accompanied by a notation or two, such as "to send" and "to receive." One drawing was accompanied by arrows, suggesting direction or movement, but the markings made no sense to me. The illustrated figure held her right hand at shoulder level with the palm facing forward, as if taking an oath. Her left hand was in front of her heart, also with the palm facing forward. I tried to mimic the gesture.

On following pages, the writing changed from elegant script to a hasty scrawl, as if the writer had been trying to take notes in longhand as someone spoke. I was surprised to see that this hasty handwriting looked a lot like my own attempts at writing longhand in cursive script. The notes described an immense tower rising from the Earth and unfolding into unimaginably enormous proportions. This tower floated in space above planet Earth. It was made of wondrous jewels, glittering in all colors. Billions upon billions of living beings "in myriad form, some of light, some of sound" traveled from all over the universe to bear witness to this spectacle.

This didn't sound like Catholicism or Christianity to me. It sounded more like science fiction. What was a nun doing with a book like this, and why had she given it to me?

The French café smelled of delicious, fresh-baked bread and simmering sauces kissed with herbs, but I didn't feel like eating. I downed the espresso quickly. I felt the urge to go back to the library to do more research. I planned to show the mysterious "nun book" to the purple-haired, conspiratorial librarian to see if she could help me make sense of it. Maybe it, too, was part of an elaborate hoax being played on me. But *why* would anyone be hoaxing me? Mack was capable of lying and murder, of course. But book forgery and hiding excerpts of historical fiction in the code of digital photographs were well outside his wheelhouse.

The book fell open to a page that was blank except for one notation: "42.9 N 2.05 E." I typed this into the map on my phone. If these were meant to be geographic coordinates, they landed near a town called Puivert in southern France. The pages of the book had a musty smell of age. Certainly, the notes had been written long before global-positioning satellites and GPS coordinates had been devised.

I recalled that Anna Ashton's brief obituary said that she had been buried in France near the town of Puivert. I did not know what to make of this seeming coincidence.

My phone buzzed in my hand. I saw that I had received dozens of new messages. I immediately understood why. The mortuary had published an online obituary about Riva. A link to the obituary had circulated on social media. Friends and distant family members offered me their condolences.

Chutney had asked me to write the obituary two days earlier. She secured Mack's approval. He had suggested no changes or additions—because, really, he knew nothing about Riva's life. The obituary said that Riva had died suddenly, but it didn't specify *how* she had died. I refused to include Mack's claim that Riva's death was a yoga accident. As far as I knew, the coroner had not yet ruled on Riva's cause or manner of death, so it would be inappropriate to say anything at all about it in the obituary.

Seeing so many messages on my phone made me feel tired and overwhelmed. While in Long Beach, I had been neglecting my communications. My inbox was bursting with messages in need of my thoughtful replies. Instead of going to the library to show the mysterious book to the librarian, I went back to my hotel room. I spent the next few hours catching up on correspondence, reading all the messages about Riva and sending short responses.

Some people interpreted the obituary's statement that "Riva died suddenly" to mean that Riva had committed suicide, which I found hugely upsetting. Many people wanted to know how Mack fared. "My heart aches for Riva's poor husband," wrote one of my cousins. Almost everyone asked me to express warm condolences to Mack.

Several times a day, Mack sent me text messages such as, "Why did she leave me?" and "I feel so alone." I regarded these messages as annoying pleas for my attention and sympathy. I refused to give him any.

Almost everyone who contacted me wanted more details about what had happened to Riva. I could not bring myself to say: "Riva fell down, hit her head, and died," as if she had been a ditzy klutz, as if yoga was a potentially lethal pursuit. It was ridiculous. It was a lie. People who knew and loved Riva, people who knew her impeccable balance, strength, and skill—they would read between the lines, wouldn't they? They would understand that there was more to the story of Riva's death.

Returning phone calls and actually speaking to people was harder for me than responding in writing because people tended to ask many follow-up questions. "I know, I know," I would say. "Her death doesn't make sense. I hope the coroner will have answers for us."

On the phone, one of my cousins asked: "What have the police told you?"

I explained that I had talked to a police officer at Riva's house, but I had heard nothing more.

"You need to contact the detectives in the homicide department," my cousin said. "Make sure they know who you are. Tell them how to contact you. Tell them that you want answers. Go to the police station in person if you can." I assured her that I would do this right away.

An instant later, I received a message from Mack: "Are you mad at me, Sis? Why are you ignoring me? Losing a spouse is the hardest grief a person can face. Why are you abandoning me in my time of need?"

I vowed to myself that I would not let the police forget about Riva's case.

In Long Beach, you can't just walk into the police headquarters building and ask to speak to a detective. You have to go through a screening process. Officers stood at a counter behind a thick, glass window. I lined up behind seven or eight other people who waited their turn to speak to an officer. It was like waiting to buy tickets at a movie-theater box office, except with argumentativeness and people walking away with bitter dissatisfaction. Most of the discussions and questions at the window devolved into frustration and dispute. The waiting room smelled greasy and sour, like days-old fried food. I was relieved when my chance to speak to an officer came at last.

"I would like to talk to the detectives in charge of my sister's homicide case," I said.

The officer behind the window asked me to write down the name and address of the victim. I did. I watched the officer type this into his computer. He studied a screen for a few minutes.

"We don't have a record of a homicide," he said.

Surely, he was mistaken. "Just last week, there were ten police cars in front of my sister's house, with officers going door to door."

The officer checked his screen and tapped a few keys on his keyboard. "We have no record of officers being dispatched to that address. Ever."

Disbelieving, and wondering why he would lie, I said: "But I was there. I saw it. Cop cars lit up the street. I spoke to Officer Smith Gordon."

The officer tapped a few more keys and stared at the screen. "No," he said. "No records."

"My sister is dead," I said, trying to maintain a polite demeanor. "She is a coroner's case."

"Do you have the case number?" he asked, skeptical.

I knew it by heart. "Zero-1724," I said.

He typed. He shook his head. "Nope."

I suddenly understood why all of the inquiries at the window seemed to turn into arguments.

"There appears to be some mistake," I said calmly. "Is there someone you can call in the homicide department? Can you pass along my contact information to them?"

The officer typed on his keyboard for several long minutes. "What's your name and phone number?"

I gave it to him.

"Is that all?" he asked, as if tired of me.

"Yes," I said.

I left the lobby and stood on the sidewalk. On my phone I looked up the number for Long Beach Police Homicide. I called and explained that I was at the police station, and I was upset because there was no record of an investigation regarding my sister. The woman put me on hold.

At last, a man identifying himself as Detective Anderson came on the line. I pictured Martin Milner, the blonde, clean-cut actor who had played a Los Angeles policeman in the TV series *Adam-12*. Detective Anderson listened as I recounted what I had been told at the window.

"Mack had something to do with Riva's death," I said, finally. "I think you need to investigate."

Detective Anderson sounded mildly frustrated at having to explain to me: "It's not a homicide unless the coroner rules it a homicide. The coroner hasn't made a ruling yet."

"But there are so many suspicious things," I said. "The way he's acting." I launched into a heated rant, saying all of the things I had been thinking about Mack. I went on at length before the detective interrupted me.

"You just don't like him," he said, matter-of-factly. "King told me that you've been ignoring him since your sister died. He told me that you are the only family he has left, but you abandoned him in his time of grief."

"He told you that?" I was taken aback. Detective Anderson made it sound as if he and Mack had been discussing the situation over beers. "Are you friends with him?"

"He calls me every day since his wife's accident," the detective said. "The poor guy is really upset."

"Doesn't that seem suspicious to you?" I asked, incredulous.

"Why would a guilty guy want to talk to a homicide detective?" he countered. "We've checked the security-camera video from the house. There's no way he had anything to do with his wife's accident. He was out walking his dog when it happened. King is totally innocent." A beat passed and the detective's tone softened slightly. "Look, your sister was online in the house, using her tablet. She was on a shopping site and a video site. We have proof of this. King was outside, walking the dog during this time. You can see on the video that he comes back to the house, goes inside, finds her, and calls 911. He has an alibi. The video is his alibi."

"He set up the video," I retorted. "He installed the whole system himself. He controlled it. Do you actually see my sister on video that morning?"

"Ma'am, there's no evidence of a crime," he said. "I can't make an arrest in this case unless someone comes in and confesses."

I was silent for a few stunned moments. "So you're saying there's no homicide investigation?"

"I'm saying there's no homicide," Detective Anderson replied flatly. "If his plan was to kill her, why did he call 911 *before* she was dead? He's totally innocent. I have your name and number. I'll let you know if there are any developments."

I must've ended the call. I couldn't remember if I had said anything more. I was choked with outrage.

I walked toward the ocean. I walked and walked. Confused thoughts crowded my mind, but I couldn't make sense of anything.

Mack's comments about Detective Anderson echoed in my memory. The morning after the police searched his house, Mack told Father Murphy and me that the homicide detectives were fat and stupid.

They knew nothing about electronics. They knew nothing about video. I had to explain everything. They were idiots, lazy idiots. Mack had expressed nothing but contempt for the detectives.

Now, suddenly, Mack and Detective Anderson were great pals? How did *that* happen?

I walked for almost an hour before I came to the spot on the bluff overlooking the bay, the place where Riva and I had once stood to watch fireworks. The late-afternoon sun blazed as it neared the horizon.

"Riva?" I said aloud, my voice all but silenced by the stiff breeze off the ocean. "Riva, what happened to you?"

"I've been busy, Becky," she said. "I've been at the library."

"What are you talking about, Riva? *I've* been at the library."

"So have I," she said. "I'm studying the archive of light. It goes back forever."

"What archive, Riva?"

"*The* archive," she said, sounding excited. "I'm seeing all of the records of all of my lifetimes with Mack. He has killed me before, Becky. Time after time. He is a student of some very dubious teachers."

Archive? Teachers? What was she talking about? I worried that I was inventing what I was hearing.

"According to the homicide detective, you weren't murdered," I said. "Also, I worry that you're not really talking to me, Riva. I worry that you're just my imagination."

She said one word: "Columbo."

"What does that mean, Riva?" I replied warily.

"Were you thinking of Columbo before I said Columbo?" Her tone was playful.

"No," I sighed, not in the mood for playing games.

"Think of Columbo," she said. "I'm going back to the archive."

Columbo, I said to myself as I started walking toward my hotel. The image that came to my mind was actor Peter Falk in the title role of television police-detective *Columbo*. Detective Columbo was famous for pretending to be clueless when really he was solving a murder case. In each episode, the murderer usually befriended Columbo in order to keep tabs on the detective's investigation. *Is this what Riva is trying to tell me?*

I hoped that Detective Anderson was doing a Columbo routine with Mack, but I couldn't be certain. What if the detective truly believed that Mack was totally innocent? It didn't change the fact that Mack *had* done something horrible to Riva. I *knew* that Mack was guilty. I needed to remain optimistic that evidence of his guilt would come to light.

My phone buzzed with another message. It was Chutney from the mortuary confirming that Riva's body had been cremated. At last, Riva had been released from her broken head and plundered body. She was free.

On the morning that I went to pick up Riva's ashes, I had a sick feeling in my gut. I was afraid to see Mack again, afraid that I would lose my cool and openly accuse him of murder. Obviously, the coroner had examined Riva. Her body had been cremated. And Mack had not been arrested. *He must be feeling very confident,* I thought. *He thinks he got away with it.* I calmed myself with the knowledge that I would be driving directly from the mortuary to the airport. Within a few hours, I would be home at last, with a thousand-mile buffer between me and Mack.

As I drove, I thought: What if Mack is never arrested? What if he really does get away with murder? I could almost hear Riva sigh, and say: "Don't dwell on it, Becky. He'll never win. He'll never be free or happy. You need to live your life, Little Boz. Don't give him another thought."

I said out loud: "Riva, I don't want revenge. I don't need for Mack to be punished or to suffer. All I want is for the truth to be known. I want there to be a public accounting and acknowledgment of what he did to you. He erased you. If I could have stopped him from doing it, I would have. The least I can do now is stop him from erasing the fact that he erased you."

Very clearly, I heard Riva say: "I was going to leave him." She sounded apologetic, as if confessing a terrible mistake.

"Riva, it's not your fault," I said aloud. "You didn't make him do it. You are not responsible for what he did."

In the uneasy silence that followed, I knew that she wasn't convinced. I steered into the mortuary parking lot, which was almost empty. "Riva, the only thing that could make all of this worse is your believing you are to blame for your own murder. Because you're not," I said aloud.

I saw that Mack had already arrived. He had driven Riva's brand-new car, a white Toyota Prius. She had owned it for less than a month. I parked on the opposite side of the building.

"You know, Riva, I'm glad you were going to leave him," I said. "Maybe that's why he kept saying, *Don't abandon me.* He knew you were done with him, and it terrified him. You were no longer under his spell. Hooray for that."

Mack was waiting in the mortuary lobby. His hair was wild, as if it had grown a few inches since I had last seen him. His eyes were bloodshot. "*Namaste,*" he said, greeting me. He insisted on hugging me.

Hugging him was always like hugging a python; I was quick to break away because I feared he might squeeze the life out of me. Mack wore a bright-orange shirt. Around his neck were strings of Buddhist prayer beads.

Over the previous few years, Mack had adopted Buddhist affectations. He bought dozens of Buddha statues and placed them around Riva's house. He bought Oni masks depicting demonic faces and displayed them in the so-called yoga room. Oni demons weren't Buddhist characters, necessarily, but Mack seemed to think that they had religious significance. He burned incense. He spoke often of karma, but I don't think he knew what it meant. He pretended to meditate, too, and told people what a mellow guy he had become since embracing what I considered to be the superficial trappings of Eastern mysticism. Riva and I found Mack's affectations amusingly ironic at first, but they increasingly became annoying as Mack's Buddhist décor supplanted more and more of the household items that Riva liked.

Seeing Mack at the mortuary, it dawned on me that his interest in Buddhist paraphernalia had developed at around the same time as his interest in "mentors" Samadhi Masterson and Roy Dumond.

Mack noticed that I was looking at the beads around his neck. He said: "These are my *malas*. They help me stay centered." He looked pleased with himself.

"Great," I said. "Does Chutney know we're here?"

"She's getting the paperwork ready," Mack said. "What have you been doing the whole time you've been out here?" There was a probing tone to his question that suggested he was suspicious of my activities. He probably wondered whether I had talked to the police.

"I've been around," I said.

"You didn't call me." He sounded wounded rather than accusatory. "You didn't reply to any of my messages."

"I didn't know what to say to you, Mack," I said, which was true, actually. How is a person supposed to respond when the murderer of her sister sends a message saying, "So tired is my heart at the passing of my true love!"

Mack seemed to grow impatient. "Becky, what have you been up to? I'm asking you a simple question." He said it as if I was being maddeningly evasive.

I shrugged. "I sat around at the library and tried to do some work."

"*Which* library?" he pressed.

"The Huntington. In Pasadena," I lied ridiculously.

"I just hope," he said. He paused to stroke his Van Dyke beard and mustache as if the gesture would convey deep thoughtfulness and great wisdom. "I just hope you can find peace."

He was so sanctimonious I could hardly speak. "You want me to find peace?" I said, choking back my anger.

"Nothing you can do will bring Riva back," he said in a soothing way, as if talking to a child. "You need to be at peace with Riva's passing. You can't go looking for reasons and answers. There are none. The first step in healing is to accept your loss." He touched his prayer beads as he put a hand over his heart. "You need to detach, Becky. Only with detachment will you find peace."

I crossed my arms and looked at the floor. "Yes," I said. "Detachment. I'll work on that." I held back a flood of epithets. How dare he lecture me about detachment and peace?

"Hi, Becky," Chutney chirped. "We're ready now." She appeared at just the right moment to save me from saying something I would regret.

Chutney placed two red-velvet bags on the reception counter. She presented Mack with papers to sign. "Each box of ashes has a separate permit," Chutney explained. "This is because you will be keeping them at different addresses." She opened one of the bags to reveal a black, plastic box. Taped to the box was a document from Los Angeles County certifying that I could keep the ashes at my house in Denver.

"Becky, these are yours," she said. "When you go through airport security, they will want to see the permit." She lifted the lid of the box and showed me a bag of fine, gray sand. The bag was sealed with a metal clip. "We divided the cremains evenly between the two bags," Chutney said. "The rosary was included in the cremation."

"What rosary?" Mack asked.

"I left a rosary with Riva at the viewing."

"Why didn't you say something? I would have given you some of my awesome *malas* to throw in with her."

"Riva would have loved that," I said.

"This one's mine." Mack cradled Riva's ashes in one arm like a baby or a trophy. He signed the papers. "Are we done?"

Chutney laughed her bubbly laugh. "We're done."

"We're done," I echoed. "Thanks, Chutney."

"I'm going to Disney World." Mack laughed in his low, growling way. "Just kidding. What about you?"

"I have a plane to catch," I said, as if I was late for it. I walked briskly toward my car.

"Detach," Mack yelled at me across the parking lot. "Peace."

I waved, got in my car, and drove. I wanted to never see Mack again anywhere except in a courtroom.

As I drove, I seethed. *Riva, how could you live with him? How could you stand his self-satisfied smugness? How did you remain sane?* It said a lot about Riva's state of self-possession that she could tolerate him and *not* be driven crazy.

"Riva, I think Mack is far worse than any of my ex-girlfriends," I said aloud. "And not just because he killed you."

Women can be difficult and even murderous, no doubt. But there's something uniquely soul-crushing about the way a man can erode a woman's confidence in her own accurate perceptions. He can talk down to her and it's considered normal. He can extract resources from her, such as time, labor, attention, affection, and creativity, and erase her when he's done, justifying it all with the lie that women exist to serve men or ennoble men or save men from their own dark impulses and sad pasts. If he succumbs to "temptation" or inflicts violence, it's *her* fault, not his. Worst of all, women accept this as the way the world works, as if it's natural and nothing can be done about it.

"Women do crappy things to other women, Riva, but nothing as crappy as everything Mack did to you," I said.

As I drove up the 405 freeway, moving farther and farther away from Mack, my irritation dissipated. I calmed down.

"Maybe," I heard Riva say, at last, in a soft voice. "Maybe you can forgive him."

"Are you kidding?" I snapped. "Maybe I should give him a cookie and pat him on the head, too. Is this your guilt talking? You're not guilty, Riva."

"I'm saying surrender," she said firmly.

"Riva, you cannot be serious," I said, half-laughing. "You can't—I can't. He stole your dreams. Riva, think of the highly specialized knowledge of kitchen design that you cultivated throughout your career. He robbed the world of that. People in Long Beach will have to settle for mediocre kitchens when you could have given them masterpieces. Doesn't that infuriate you?"

"Actually, yes," she admitted. "Not because there aren't other good kitchen designers. It bothers me that my clients were left in the lurch with unfinished kitchens. It bothers me that my work suffered because of my death. This is the point I'm trying to make, Becky. You asked how I could live with Mack. How could I tolerate him? By forgiving him. This doesn't mean I didn't notice or didn't care what he did. Yes, I noticed. Yes, I cared. He's an energy sponge, Becky. He will soak up every ounce he can get from you. Even *thinking* about him gives him energy. I learned to *not* do that. I learned to put my energy where it mattered. I put my energy into my work. I put my energy into what I wanted to accomplish with my life. Mack would go surfing, eat long lunches at pricey restaurants, and laze around, and I would hunker down and work twice as hard as usual. Because that's the life I wanted. I wanted to be an outstanding designer. I didn't give my life to *him*. I gave my life to my work, and my work gave life to me."

I took the exit ramp toward the airport. What Riva said was true. She was prolific and inventive. Her work truly shined. But I didn't understand why she was telling me to surrender. "Forgive and forget," I said aloud. "Is that what you're prescribing? Surrender? What does that mean, Riva? How do I do that?"

"Forgiving him does not absolve him of responsibility, Becky," she said. "Wanting him to be held accountable will only exhaust you. He's already being held accountable in ways you can't know. Forgive him. Meaning, don't resent him. Don't give him your emotional energy. Don't give him any energy at all. Everything you give him feeds his rage and entitlement. Forget him by remembering what's important. Forget him by remembering *your* work, *your* dreams, and by doing what *you* want to accomplish with your life."

I saw airplanes landing and taking off in the near distance. Thousands of people were coming and going. Thousands of partings. Thousands of new beginnings.

"Don't let Mack block your horizons, Little Boz. Stay above him and look far into the distance."

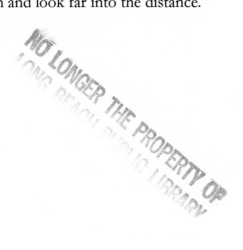

6

BACK AT HOLY CROSS

A moment after I sat down to wait for my flight, my phone buzzed. I glanced at the screen. I had a text message from Riva! My heart skipped. My elation turned to annoyance when I remembered that Mack had commandeered Riva's phone.

Mack wrote: "I want to start a new life, Sis. I am thinking about Denver. If I come to Denver, can I stay with you? I really want to be around family right now. Family is everything. I did not know this until I lost Riva. Becky, I hope it's not too late for us to be like a real brother and sister. This is what I want more than anything."

I felt mildly sick. I took a few deep breaths. Mack was working some sort of plan, I surmised, and his plan involved me. But why? He had never liked me, and I had never liked him. He hated it when I visited Riva. Why did he suddenly want to visit me? What could he possibly want from me?

I remembered a sensational murder case that had unfolded in Denver. A man was found guilty of killing his second wife by pushing her off a cliff during a mountain hike. He claimed that she had fallen accidentally. During his trial, the prosecution presented evidence that he had killed his first wife, too, in a staged "accident" to collect money from a life-insurance policy. It came to light during the trial that he had taken out insurance policies on the lives of other women, too. One of the other women was his first wife's sister-in-law. He stood to reap millions of dollars in the event of this woman's accidental death.

I knew that Riva had been covered by a modest life-insurance policy which would have given Mack just enough to pay off the mortgage on her house in case of her death. Had Mack taken out additional policies? If he had, the police would know about it—wouldn't they? Had the police even thought about investigating Mack's finances?

I realized that my face was flushed. I was uncomfortably warm. I was sweating.

I wondered: Was Mack planning to take out a life-insurance policy on me? If so, he would have to prove an "insurable interest" in me. Meaning, he would have to demonstrate to the insurer that I was a close relative of his.

When he called me "Sis," was he trying to convince himself and others that I was his actual sister? He had changed his last name to Pine—was he planning to pretend to be my actual brother, and take out a huge insurance policy on my life? Would a terrible, implausible accident befall me? Was I next on Mack's kill list?

No—how could I think such a thing? He hadn't *planned* to kill Riva. Maybe he had pushed her, or hit her, or thrown her to the ground. But it wasn't premeditated—no, of course not. It was an impulse.

I typed a reply to Mack: "Thanks for your heartfelt message, Bro. I will be busy catching up with work for the next several weeks. If I was going to start a new life, I'd go to Hawaii, not Denver. We will talk soon." I attached several smiling emoticons to convey lighthearted friendliness. This was the opposite of how I felt. I certainly wasn't going to welcome him into my home, but I didn't want him to feel rejected and angry at me. He was capable of fury and killing, I knew. I didn't want to be within a thousand miles of him. But if he wanted to come to Denver, how could I stop him?

I pulled up the phone number for the homicide division at Long Beach Police. I wanted to alert Detective Anderson about Mack's message to me. But what would be the point? The police would probably roll their eyes at my concerns. They would think I was overreacting.

Maybe I *was* overreacting. Mack probably had no intention of visiting me in Denver. His claim of wanting to be around family was probably just for show. Mack had to keep up his Sincere Grieving Husband act, at least until he cashed the payout check from Riva's modest life-insurance policy.

Back at home, I put Riva's ashes on my fireplace mantel. The last essence of Riva's life had been burned away in the crematorium, hadn't it? Riva had been released completely, converted into flame—*gone, gone, gone beyond*, as the Buddhists say. She had dissolved into brilliant light and now inhabited another dimension. Her earthly, material remains, however, retained a kind of power, a palpable presence that I found unsettling. I wondered whether I had been unwise to include the rosary that the old nun had given me. It, too, had burned to ash and was now intermingled with Riva's remains. I wondered whether some strange alchemy had taken place by mixing the juju of the rosary with my sister's ashes.

I could no longer hear Riva's voice as clearly as I had heard it when she was in the hospital. In fact, I started to believe that I had imagined all of our conversations. All along, I had been projecting my memories and feelings onto an imaginary death-transcending Riva. I had been comforted by her presence— rather, I had been comforted by the *imaginary* presence of a Riva that I had created in my own mind.

As Riva's ashes sat in my living room, and as the hours passed, I became more and more certain that I had imagined it all. It was all in my head. It *must* be, because Riva's ashes kept repeating the same nonsensical message, a message that was clearly an expression of my own fear, paranoia, and general confusion. She kept saying: *He planned it meticulously, Becky. You're underestimating Mack. He has fallen in with bad teachers. You need good teachers, and they're trying to reach you.*

Be realistic, I told myself. Mack was a jerk and then some, but he didn't have the capacity to be a criminal mastermind. I had been dealing with the shock of Riva's death, but facts were facts. Mack wasn't smart enough to plan a murder and fool homicide detectives for long. Dead people don't talk to the living from beyond the grave. Mysterious nuns don't appear in hospital corridors and give people rosaries. I had to pull myself together and recognize that my thoughts and perceptions over the past few weeks were unreliable. I had to chalk it all up to some kind of psychological coping mechanism. I had to get back to reality. I was glad to leave my house on Monday morning and get back to my job.

My boss Lola had asked me to come see her immediately on my first day back at work. When I looked into her office, though, I saw that she was on the phone. She made an apologetic face and mouthed the words, "Five minutes."

I didn't mind waiting for Lola. Being in Lola's presence, even lurking outside her office in anticipation of a meeting, was a highlight of any workday. I could hear the rich, musical tones of her voice as she talked on the phone.

Lola was a tall woman, six-foot-three or thereabouts, with a mane of silver gray hair that added a few more inches of loft to her imposing personage. She had a graceful, regal bearing that commanded respect, combined with a down-to-earth

Midwestern authenticity that made her approachable. She raised millions of dollars in charitable gifts for our hospital each year just by virtue of her personable style. As soon as Lola was off the phone, she would wrap me in her full attention, and my world would sparkle with possibility. In the meantime, I stood in the hallway and studied the haunting photograph that hung on the wall outside Lola's door.

Months earlier, Lola had hired an archivist to find old photographs depicting life at Holy Cross hospital during the institution's founding years, back when it was a tuberculosis sanitarium for poor people. Enlargements of the photos were framed and hung on walls around campus. Financial donors would feel a deeper connection to the hospital's roots if they could see images of the past, Lola said.

My favorite photo was the one next to Lola's office. It was a black-and-white portrait from the early 1900s of the Denver Ladies Mountaineering Society. In the photo, five women stood in a mountain meadow. They looked small and fragile compared to their rugged surroundings. Towering peaks rose behind them. The women wore woolen dresses and leather boots. Some held walking sticks. Some wore hats. One smiled. The others looked stern. Nothing in the photograph foreshadowed the tragedy that would befall them.

The ladies aspired to become the first women to climb Mount of the Holy Cross, a fourteen-thousand-foot peak in the mountains west of Denver. On the eastern side of the peak, the snow each winter would fill two perpendicular ravines that intersected to form a cross. During most of the year, this snowy cross on the mountain was visible for many miles. Reaching the summit of Mount of the Holy Cross became, for many mountaineers, a kind of religious pilgrimage.

Anna Prescott, the leader of the ladies' hiking club, was married to a rich philanthropist. She convinced her wealthy friends to help build Holy Cross Home for Consumptives, a sanitarium for indigent people with tuberculosis. Over the years, the sanitarium evolved into Holy Cross Health, the research institution where Lola and I worked.

Anna and the other mountaineering ladies embarked on an expedition to climb Mount of the Holy Cross in 1903. They all died in a freak, late-summer blizzard in the high country. It's unknown whether they ever reached the summit.

The photo by Lola's door was said to be the only surviving image of Anna Prescott. It reminded me of the photo I had seen in the library in Long Beach. *That* photo showed Anna Ashton at the hospital-chapel ceremony. The two photos were in no way identical. They had been taken thirty years apart. Even so, as I studied the photo on the wall, I clearly recognized that Anna Prescott and Anna Ashton looked startlingly similar—they could have been twins.

The purple-haired librarian had printed out the Long Beach photograph for me. I had folded the piece of paper and tucked it into my notebook. I flipped through my notebook but couldn't find the picture.

"Becky, I am so sorry for your loss." Lola swept me into her office. She closed the door behind us.

I thrilled at the unexpected intimacy of a closed-door meeting. "Thanks, Lola. That means a lot." I took a seat across from her desk.

"In one of your messages, you said that the police were involved. I have to ask, Becky: do you think it was murder?" She said it more as a statement than a question, as if she was already convinced that a crime had been committed.

"Yes," I said, relieved that I could tell *someone* what I truly believed. "I think her husband killed her."

"What do the police say?"

"The detective told me that my brother-in-law is totally innocent," I said skeptically.

"Did the detective actually say the words *totally innocent?*" she asked, coolly appraising the situation.

I nodded.

"Becky, that's a very unusual thing for a police detective to say about *anyone*. Was there an autopsy?"

"The coroner deferred ruling on Riva's cause and manner of death. The funeral planner at the mortuary said I might have to wait months before a final report is issued."

"If the autopsy was inconclusive, there will have to be a thorough police investigation," Lola said, reassuringly. "It's too soon for police to say that he's *totally innocent*. When you told me in your message that it was a fatal yoga accident, I knew right away that foul play was involved. There's no such thing as a yoga helmet, Becky, for a reason. Yoga is not a potentially skull-smashing activity."

I was glad that a reasonable person could accurately assess the whole situation just by knowing the absurd "yoga accident" premise. Still, I knew it was medically possible for a person to fall from a standing height, hit their head on the floor, fracture their skull, and eventually die as a result of brain injury. In Riva's case, however, falling on a smooth, flat surface was unlikely to have split her scalp with a deep, L-shaped laceration.

"It helps me to hear your views, Lola. I was starting to wonder whether I share the same reality as the police."

"You wouldn't want to share their reality," Lola said, not unkindly. "One of my ex-lovers was a detective. His job put him under enormous stress. Be patient while the police do their work."

"I looked into the Ashton Foundation," I said, changing the subject, not wanting to become known as a bore who talked only about her dead sister. "I've found a promising lead. Well, I'm not sure if it's a lead so much as a connection."

Lola looked eager to hear what I had to say. "Every little bit helps."

"It's so off the wall," I demurred, unsure of myself. "Do you know anything about renegade nuns or a group called Sisters of the Tower? Can you think of any way that Anna *Prescott*, founder of Holy Cross, might have had a connection with Anna *Ashton*, founder of the Ashton Foundation—and involving renegade nuns somehow?"

Lola looked surprised. "That makes sense, actually," she said, as if something had suddenly been illuminated. "This was one of the things that critics said about Anna Prescott when she announced that she wanted to establish Holy Cross. Leaders of the church, as well as leaders of Denver, questioned whether Anna was truly a devoted Catholic. She had a reputation for sympathizing with, and financially supporting a group of nuns who provided medical care for impoverished women, including birth control and pregnancy termination." Lola shot a look of caution at me. "Well, pregnancy termination was *rumored* in an attempt to smear Anna," Lola added. "I want people to know the history of Holy Cross, yes, but with a caveat. This chapter of the institution's history has been buried for a long time. Just between us, Becky, it should probably stay buried, considering the current political mood of our country. I don't want Holy Cross to become embroiled in a ginned-up scandal about abortion." She paused. "How is this connected to Anna Ashton and the Ashton Foundation?"

"Ashton has a philanthropic profile similar to Anna Prescott's," I said, my confidence restored by Lola's validating knowledge of Holy Cross history. "Both were notable women—both were named Anna—and both supported these mysterious radical nuns. The weirdest thing is that I saw a photo of Anna Ashton. It was printed in a newspaper in Long Beach in 1934. She looked exactly like Anna Prescott in the photo outside your office, the one taken in 1903. I know it's *impossible* for them to be the same person, but—but."

Lola inhaled sharply as if she'd had a startling insight. "Becky, do not speak of this to anyone. Let me do some digging. Have you ever heard of Eternals?" As soon as the word "Eternals" was out of her mouth, she waved her hand as if to dispel it. "Never mind. We'll talk about it later. In the meantime, we have a more urgent matter." Lola's fingers fluttered over a screen on her desk as she searched for an electronic record. "I have a special assignment for you."

I pursed my lips in anticipation.

"We have a quarantine case," she said. "We need to keep it quiet."

"Quarantine?" I was intrigued.

A couple of years earlier, the U.S. Centers for Disease Control and Prevention put a man under quarantine at Holy Cross to stop him from spreading a nasty case of "extensively drug-resistant tuberculosis." The patient made headlines all over the world. Television news helicopters hovered over the hospital. The incident sparked public worry about a possible TB pandemic in the U.S. and Europe.

"Why are we keeping it quiet?" I asked. "Last time, the media attention was great for fundraising."

"Because *that* patient sued the CDC for violating privacy laws," Lola said. "The doctors are tight-lipped about this case. Use your connections over in the labs, but be discreet. Call your friend."

"My friend?" I asked, wondering whom she meant.

"The doctor in Infectious Diseases."

"You mean Dr. Blanton?" Dr. Blanton and I were both lesbians, so in Lola's mind we were friends. Blanton and I *were* friends, in fact—in a purely non-romantic way—but I didn't know that Lola knew it.

"Yes, call Dr. Blanton. Find out everything you can." Lola's phone rang. She shooed me out of her office.

I loved it when Lola sent me on confidential assignments. Especially now, I welcomed an opportunity to obsess about something other than Riva. I felt a spring in my step as I walked back to my office, which was just down the hall from Lola's.

We worked in a building that everyone called Old Infirmary. It was the oldest building on the Holy Cross medical campus, loaded with architectural charm from the 1880s. The building also had the eerie, mournful mood of a place where generations of patients had lingered through months of respiratory illness. Some recovered their health while many more wasted away, burning with fever and delirium.

The office in which I worked used to be, long ago, a quarantine room at the edge of a larger infirmary. No doubt, countless patients had died on the spot now occupied by my desk. The medical charts of long-dead patients had once hung on the door now marked: *Becky Pine, Director of Philanthropic Intelligence.*

I sat down and rifled through the pockets of my backpack trying to find the photo of Anna Ashton from the Long Beach library. I couldn't find it. I pulled out the book that the nun had given me, thinking that maybe I had tucked the photo between the pages. It wasn't there. *What could I have done with it?*

I jotted the name "Anna Bartlet" on the notepad near my computer. Bartlet was the current executive director of the Ashton Foundation. I couldn't help but notice that I was trying to find out more information about three women—Anna Prescott, Anna Ashton, and Anna Bartlet—three women, all named Anna. I sensed that the name wasn't the only thing they had in common.

I picked up my phone and texted Dr. Blanton. "Can I meet you for a cup of coffee? I want to ask you about the patient in quarantine."

"Becky, I'm so sorry about your sister," Blanton replied immediately. She had seen Riva's obituary online, and left me a voice message when I was in Long Beach.

Before I could respond to the first text, Dr. Blanton sent another message: "How did you know about the patient in quarantine? Let me guess. Lola knows all! Meet me in the cafeteria in 20 minutes?"

I replied: "Yes. It's Cinnamon-Roll Monday!" I often ran into Dr. Blanton while taking mid-morning coffee breaks on Mondays when the Holy Cross cafeteria served fresh-baked cinnamon rolls.

Blanton was one of the few scientists who didn't mind talking shop with me and answering my non-scientist questions. If Holy Cross had a TB patient in quarantine, Dr. Blanton would know all about it.

I opened my file cabinet and pulled out the paper file I had prepared regarding the previous TB-quarantine case. I had saved the relevant newspaper clippings. A *Colorado Tribune* headline from a couple of years earlier blared: "TB Menace in Lockdown at Holy Cross." At the time, news pundits painted TB as a newfangled bio-weapon for terrorists, as if the disease was previously unimaginable. Holy Cross doctors emphasized repeatedly that TB was as old as human history and had been known by many names—white plague, consumption, wasting disease—and had been found even in ancient Egyptian mummies. Tuberculosis had always been and continued to be a mass killer.

When TB ravaged densely-populated cities such as New York in the late 1800s, Denver's dry climate supposedly offered a miracle cure. Trainloads of desperately ill people started to arrive in the Rocky Mountain region. Holy Cross Home for Consumptives became the only sanitarium in Denver to serve poor people. Anna Prescott, the hospital's founder, was regarded by many as an angel of charity.

TB cases in the U.S. declined over the years, especially after World War II and the advent of antibiotics. Holy Cross repositioned itself as a research institution and an outpatient-care facility.

Rarely did a patient require an overnight stay on campus. Patients in quarantine were even more rare. Ghosts, however, were said to be common. Considering such a long history of disease and death on campus, employees at Holy Cross believed that the hospital was haunted. To me, it *felt* haunted. Even before I knew the history, and before I'd heard stories about spooky happenings at Holy Cross, I sensed disquiet in the air, especially after dark.

Lola gave me permission to come into the office late on most workdays—say, around 10 a.m., which Lola called *Becky's Whenever O'clock*—as long as I agreed to work later in the evenings. During the evenings, I heard strange noises. Perhaps these noises were audible during the day, too, but were masked by the sounds of a building full of administrative employees. For example, tapping and knocking inside the walls—these noises had something to do with the plumbing, I assumed. The sounds of people walking and whispering in the empty hallway outside my office were probably echoes of people on the floor directly upstairs.

The sound that I couldn't dismiss easily was the coughing—distant, persistent coughing. I had yet to imagine a likely, non-supernatural source for this sound.

I felt sure that I had encountered one actual ghost at Holy Cross. It wasn't like talking to Riva. No, it was something else, and not particularly dramatic. One day, I was walking in the maze of old tunnels beneath the medical campus. I heard someone behind me breathing hard. I assumed it was a jogger. Employees often jogged through the tunnels for exercise during cold Colorado winters.

I felt the person's presence. I heard someone wheeze and gasp. I turned to see if all was well, but there was no one there to be seen. Ever since this incident, I felt a *frisson* down my spine when I walked in the tunnels.

The tunnels were unavoidable. Long ago, Old Infirmary was built on hospital-owned farmland where dairy cows once grazed. Over the years, Old Infirmary became an island separated from the heart of campus by a major traffic intersection. The safest way for me to cross from Old Infirmary to the cafeteria to meet Dr. Blanton was to walk underground. I grabbed my notepad and headed for the tunnels. I waved my electronic identification badge in front of the tunnel door.

The first thing I noticed was the chill down my spine. The second thing I noticed was the smell. It always smelled strange in the tunnels, like a combination of mothballs, mold, and disinfectant coated with fresh paint. The lighting was strange, too; harsh and fluorescent but not bright enough to banish shadows. The underground ventilation system hummed. I walked briskly.

Suddenly, I smelled roses. I remembered the nun from St. Mary the Tower—she had smelled of roses. I turned around to see if, by chance, the ghostly nun was walking behind me. She wasn't. I kept walking. The fragrance of roses intensified. My footfalls echoed. The tunnel branched in three directions.

I heard a woman say: "Becky."

I turned in the direction of the voice. I saw an emaciated woman in a hospital gown. She had dark hair and dark, hollowed eyes. "You must help me," she said in a quiet but stern voice. "All three of us are needed to open the portal."

"Open the portal?" I repeated, puzzled. I blinked. The vision was gone. A fluorescent light flickered and dimmed.

"Hello?" I said. "Do you need help?" I walked to the spot where she had stood. "Hello?" I saw no one. Had I imagined her? I walked slowly toward the cafeteria, turning around every few moments. As I walked, the scent of roses gradually dissipated.

At the stairwell, I stopped and looked back for a full minute. In the distance, a fluorescent light flickered and brightened. I jogged up the stairs to the cafeteria.

The aroma of coffee and baked goods steadied me. I heard the comforting buzz of conversation. Plus, it was Cinnamon-Roll Monday. I filled a cup and picked up a roll. I joined Dr. Blanton at her table.

"Oh, Becky, my heart aches for you and your sister," Dr. Blanton said.

Blanton was ten years older than me. She wore her iron-gray hair in a military flat-top style. She waxed her hair to make the ends stand up straight. Her horn-rimmed glasses and lab coat made her look like a geek, but her haircut conveyed edgy cool.

"You look pale," Blanton said, troubled by what she saw in my face.

"I'm fine," I said, obviously still shaken by what had happened in the tunnel. I didn't mention my encounter with the woman, or ghost, or whatever it was. Doctors at Holy Cross greeted campus ghost stories with withering scorn. They had no patience for supernatural nonsense. I didn't want Dr. Blanton to think I was losing my grip on reality.

"I'm curious about your sister's cause of death. Was there an autopsy?" Blanton asked in a low voice, as if hoping to learn confidential details that she could analyze.

"Blunt-force head trauma," I said. "At least, that's my guess. The coroner's ruling has been deferred."

"That means they're still investigating," Blanton said, nodding, as if it made good sense from a medical perspective.

"I hope so. Believe me, when the coroner issues a report, I will want you to go over it with me line by line and explain it all. The woman at the mortuary told me that I might have to wait months to see the autopsy." I drank a sip of coffee. "Tell me about the patient in quarantine," I said brightly.

Blanton understood that I wanted to get back to work, and back to normality if possible. "The patient is a woman of Mediterranean descent in her late twenties or early thirties," Blanton said. "She says that she is a foreign national—an Italian—but she does not know how long she has been in the United States, or when she came to Colorado," she said, adjusting her glasses. "The woman speaks both Italian and English fluently."

Blanton tended to touch the frames of her eyeglasses when settling into her role as one of the world's foremost respiratory research scientists, as if adjusting her glasses somehow sharpened her focus on medical subjects. "The woman was found two days ago in Holy Cross Wilderness—in the mountains. Because of her emaciated state, she was presumed to be a lost hiker. Tests showed us that she is suffering from tuberculosis. It's a bacterial strain of unknown provenance, Becky. We haven't been able to connect the genotype to another case."

Blanton had explained this sort of thing to me previously. Medical researchers used rapid genome sequencing to identify individual kinds of bacteria. Doctors could trace various strains of bacteria and corresponding chains of infection all over the globe.

"Did she catch TB in the mountains somehow?" I asked, dubious. "That sounds odd to me."

"The bacteria itself is odd. It's an odd case," Blanton said, unable to disguise her wonder and excitement. She looked around to make sure no one could overhear our conversation, which skirted the boundaries of patient-privacy laws, we both knew. No one in the cafeteria paid any attention to us. People were busy chatting over cinnamon rolls or tapping on their laptops or phones. I glanced up at the security camera, which looked like an upside-down snow globe attached to the ceiling. I knew that it didn't record audio, just video, and was among at least two dozen identical cameras around campus, all monitored by one of three sleepy security guards in an office near the front entrance of the hospital. I felt confident that no one was eavesdropping on Dr. Blanton and me.

"There's something peculiar going on with her," Blanton confided. "I'm seeing something like a bacteriophage in her blood. A bacteriophage is a kind of virus that's attacking the TB bacteria."

Blanton sounded thrilled to be confronted with such a marvelous situation. She went on to explain that a bacteriophage is a special type of virus that can "eat" bacteria. Scientists had experimented with bacteriophages as alternatives to antibiotics to fight bacterial infections. "Trouble is, the eater-virus and the bacteria-to-be-eaten have to be compatible. You have to find the perfect match. In this woman's blood, there appears to be a perfect match," Dr. Blanton marveled. "This mysterious Italian woman has a rare strain of infection coupled with an even rarer infection-fighter. What's the likelihood of that?"

"Who is she?" I asked, drawn in by Dr. Blanton's excitement. "Where did she come from?"

"She gave us a name: Gemma Galgani." Blanton spelled the name aloud for me. "Our mystery patient claims that she was born in 1872. But, Becky, the mystery only deepens with this information."

"What do you mean?" I smiled, amused at Blanton's uncharacteristic flourishes of drama.

"We looked it up," Blanton said. "Gemma Galgani is the name of a Catholic saint who died of tuberculosis in Italy in 1903."

I tore off small pieces of my cinnamon roll and ate them rapidly, absorbed in the story Blanton was telling.

"If the woman in my lab is Gemma Galgani—*Saint* Gemma Galgani—well, that's not possible, is it?" Dr. Blanton looked at me with a skeptical expression as if wanting me to exclaim that, no, it was not possible.

"Is it possible? Could it be possible? I mean, other than the part about her dying of tuberculosis in 1903?"

"No, Becky, no. It's *not* possible Besides, Saint Gemma Galgani was born in 1878, not 1872."

"Why would she lie about her name? Why would she lie about the year she was born? I mean, it's so obviously false."

Dr. Blanton touched her glasses. "Our mystery patient is not necessarily lying. Her infection is very severe. Often, infection can make a patient delirious. A patient in her condition might hallucinate. According to what I've read, the real-life Saint Gemma suffered intense hallucinations because of her tuberculosis. Becky, she even thought she was being attacked by demons. Reports from the time attest that she had real, physical wounds from these struggles. Many people believed that she was literally fighting with the devil. But the Catholic Church dismissed her as a crazy woman. Only later, after her death, did they change their opinion and confirm her as a saint. It's entirely possible that our mystery patient knows

the story of Saint Gemma and, in her delirium, has confused
Gemma's story with her own. Sounds plausible, doesn't it?"

I nodded, unsure.

Blanton paused. "But it gets even weirder, Becky."

"How so?"

"Our mystery patient keeps asking us to contact Anna
Prescott. She says that Anna has a cure for her illness." Blanton
looked at me, waiting for me to see the strangeness of this
assertion.

"Anna Prescott?" I repeated. "You mean Anna Prescott
who founded this hospital more than a hundred years ago?" I
thought to myself but didn't say aloud: *You mean Anna Prescott
who, along with two other mysterious women named Anna, is suddenly on
my radar in a big way?* I felt a flush of urgency, as if pieces of a
puzzle might be coming together. "What does she say about
Anna Prescott?"

"She says that Anna works on the farm here at the hospital.
She keeps asking us to go get Anna and bring her immediately
because Anna knows how to cure the disease." Blanton offered
it as indisputable evidence of the patient's delirium. "The *farm*,
Becky. What farm?"

I drew my hands to my face and rubbed my forehead. Was
Blanton hoaxing me? A hundred years ago, Old Infirmary was
surrounded by acres and acres of farmland. I knew this from
Lola's institutional history project. "This whole place was a
farm," I said at last, keeping my voice steady. "You know that,
right?"

Blanton looked closely at me. "No," she said, "I had no
idea."

I explained calmly: "A hundred years ago, this was the only
place where the city fathers of Denver would allow Anna
Prescott to build a hospital for impoverished sick people—far

away from everyone else—in the middle of nowhere. Holy Cross was a farm."

Blanton looked baffled. "I didn't know that, and I've worked here for nine years, Becky."

"That's why Lola has made such a big deal about reviving all the archival stuff," I said. "No one remembers the history."

"That's my point," Blanton said, looking truly perplexed. "If I didn't know the history, and since it's not common knowledge—how did our mystery patient know it?"

I tried to think of the most obvious, boring answer. "Maybe she's a local history buff," I said unconvincingly. "Did you ask the police to help you identify her?"

Blanton sighed. "We've run every kind of background check we can think of. No one has been able to identify her. The FBI, CDC, and U.S. Immigration can find no record of a missing woman matching her description. She claims that she was born in Italy, but the Italian consulate can't confirm her identity. We have no fingerprint match. Nothing. It's as if she didn't exist before now."

My interest was fully engaged. "Can I talk to her?"

"She's under quarantine," Dr. Blanton said.

"If we both wear respiratory masks, it should be fine, right?"

"She has been interviewed by everyone, Becky. Police, social workers, Italian translators. I doubt you'll be able to make any progress." Blanton was trying to temper my expectations.

"It will take my mind off of other things," I said. "It will be good for me to sink my teeth into an unsolvable mystery." In truth, I knew that my teeth were already deep into a mystery that kept getting harder to chew.

Blanton studied me. "Okay," she said, as if dispelling mild doubts. "Okay. It can't hurt."

7

MYSTERY PATIENT

As Dr. Blanton led me through her lab, I noticed refrigerators and centrifuges crammed into small spaces. Glass tubes, vials, and presumably ghastly medical specimens occupied lab benches. All the labs on the Holy Cross campus looked chaotic and crowded, in my opinion, and Blanton's was no exception.

Dr. Blanton said hello to her assistant, a young woman who looked the way that Blanton might have looked thirty years earlier, with short blonde hair and thick glasses. I nodded to acknowledge the assistant, whose name I couldn't remember and whose security badge I couldn't see. On her lab bench was a thermal lunch bag imprinted with the Holy Cross logo. All employees had received one of these special pieces of promotional swag as an employee-appreciation gift during the previous year. I wondered whether the bag contained the assistant's lunch, or a medical experiment. I suddenly felt lightheaded and nauseated at the thought of baloney sandwiches intermingling with bacteria cultures.

"This way," Blanton said. She led me down a passage. We took a turn down a different passage.

"Keeping her in a janitorial closet?" I asked, half-joking.

Dr. Blanton stopped. She peered through a window in a wide door. "She's awake." Dr. Blanton raised her hand in greeting.

The woman in the room coughed. It was a long, rattling, phlegm-filled series of coughs, not quite severe enough to break blood vessels in her lungs. To me, it sounded far worse than the dry, persistent hack of TB's early stages. This woman was very sick. I secured my mask over my mouth and nose.

Dr. Blanton opened the door. The scent of roses enveloped us.

The patient sat propped up on pillows. She wore a white hospital gown. An intravenous drip line was taped to her bare, slender arm. I immediately recognized her. She was the patient I had seen in the tunnel. The woman had the same gaunt cheeks and dark, sunken eyes. She looked very weak. I doubted that she was able to walk across the room, let alone across the hospital campus. I felt as if my knees might buckle. I steadied myself against a wall. I glanced around the room, looking for a massive bouquet of roses. I saw no flowers anywhere.

Dr. Blanton adjusted the patient's respirator mask to make sure it was secure.

I looked closely at the intravenous line. If the patient had disconnected it, an alarm would have sounded. *How could she have wandered down to the tunnels without someone stopping her?* I felt a sudden, uncomfortable tightness in my throat, as if I was choking on important questions that I didn't know how to ask.

"This is Becky Pine from our fundraising research department," Dr. Blanton said. "Is it okay if she asks you a few questions?"

The woman turned her eyes to me. I saw in them a glimmer of recognition. She had seen me in the tunnel, certainly. The woman slowly raised and lowered her chin. Blanton interpreted this as a nod of consent. I saw it as a nod of familiarity.

Blanton pulled up a chair for me next to the patient's bed. I remembered the chair next to Riva's bed. I remembered the tubes and machinery surrounding Riva. I sat down. I opened my notebook. I fumbled with my pen.

The woman's large, dark eyes rested on me in a strange way as if she was looking into my face but also looking past me. I thought of the nun in the hallway in the Long Beach hospital. She, too, looked at me in a similarly intense yet distant way.

My voice cracked as I spoke. "We saw each other in the tunnel just now, right?"

"We don't let our quarantine patients wander the halls," Blanton said, sounding puzzled about why I would suggest such a thing.

"No, of course not," I tapped the point of my pen on a blank page of my notebook. I didn't want Blanton to think I was hallucinating along with her patient. "*In bocca a lupo*," I said in an attempt to be blandly conversational. "That's the only Italian I know. I think it means good luck."

The woman smiled. "*In the wolf's mouth*," she said in raspy, accented English. Louder, and in a clearer voice, she said: "Do you know Lucina? She is the wolf." The woman said it as if it was a joke that would make me smile.

"I don't know Lucina," I said, kindly, smiling anyway. I shifted in the chair. "Dr. Blanton told me that you know Anna Prescott," I ventured.

"Tell us more about Lucina," Dr. Blanton interrupted, trying to steer the conversation. "This is the first time I've heard you mention Lucina."

I picked up on Dr. Blanton's signal. "Is Lucina a friend or relative of yours?"

The patient said emphatically: "You must deliver a message to Anna."

I glanced over at Dr. Blanton, who offered me a subtle shrug. I looked into the patient's deep, espresso eyes. "I will give Anna your message," I said confidently, with every intention of following through, even though I knew it was an impossible task. "What should I tell her?"

The patient reached out her hand toward my face in a way that made wonder whether she was blind. She seemed to want to touch my face, to feel my features. I glanced at Dr. Blanton for permission to move close enough for the woman to touch me. Blanton nodded.

I put my pen in the wire spiral of my notepad. I scooted my chair closer to the patient. The woman reached out and tapped my forehead, just between my eyebrows. She tapped three times. A burst of purple filled my field of vision. That's the last thing I could I remember.

I must have fainted. The next thing I knew, I was sitting on the floor in the elevator lobby.

"Becky," Dr. Blanton said, her voice loud and authoritative. "Becky."

I was aware that I had blacked out. Dr. Blanton's hand was around my jaw as if she had been trying to wake me up. Her assistant held my wrist to monitor my pulse.

"What happened?" I asked. "Where did she go?" I knew that I had been talking to the patient in quarantine.

Dr. Blanton held up my eyelid with her thumb. She shined a light in my eye. "From the look of it, you fainted."

"I'm okay," I said. I tried to stand. "She wanted to give me a message for Anna."

"Sit for a minute," Dr. Blanton's assistant said, slightly annoyed.

"What was the message for Anna?" I asked Dr. Blanton. "What did she say?"

"She didn't say anything," Dr. Blanton said, perplexed. "She tapped your forehead and you turned to jelly."

I suddenly remembered. "The nun!" I said, excited, struggling to my feet. "Just like the nun in Long Beach. Everything went purple."

"Nun?" Dr. Blanton asked, half-laughing, as if I was talking nonsense. "Just sit back down for a few minutes and tell me about this nun."

"No, really." I tried to wave away her concern. "I'm fine. Everything's fine."

"Steady," Blanton said.

"Wait—*what* happened?" I asked.

"The patient touched your forehead, Becky. A moment later you were on the floor. No nuns were involved."

I became aware of a dull pain in my hand and arm. "Did I hurt my shoulder?"

Blanton's assistant asked me to rotate my shoulder. She asked me to make a fist. "Squeeze my fingers as hard as you can." She touched various points around my elbow. "You seem fine," she said, sounding a bit doubtful.

I paced up and down the hallway. "Except for this ache in my arm, I feel okay. Really, I do." I felt embarrassed that I had fainted and couldn't remember anything clearly. I saw my notepad and pen on the floor. I bent down and picked them up.

"Look, Becky, I'm going to call Lola and tell her that I want you to go home and rest," Blanton said, sounding motherly. "It was foolish of me to let you into a patient's room so soon after—I mean, it's my fault. I didn't even think." She sounded contrite, as if she had been responsible for my fainting.

"You mean, so soon after Riva," I said, pausing, remembering my sister's death. For the past half hour I had forgotten all about Riva. Now, remembering, I felt the return of weighty sadness.

"Becky, please give yourself time to adjust to everything that has happened. Don't rush back into your job routine too quickly."

I didn't like being the focus of Blanton's concern. I felt shy and awkward seeing furrowed brows and worried expressions directed at me. "Let's meet in the cafeteria for breakfast tomorrow," I said to Dr. Blanton as I pressed the button for the elevator.

"Tomorrow," Blanton repeated in a tone that conveyed doctor's orders. "Go home now, Becky. We'll talk in the morning."

Slowly and somewhat unsteadily, I walked back to Old Infirmary. In the tunnel, I paused at the spot where I had seen the patient in her hospital gown. It was impossible for her to have made it to that spot from Dr. Blanton's lab and back, I thought. She looked too weak to walk such a distance. Besides, she would have needed an electronic ID badge to gain access to the tunnels. I half-hoped that I would detect the scent of roses, but I didn't. The tunnels smelled of their typical weird odor, like a damp basement mopped with industrial cleaning solution.

The pain in my arm turned into a constant tingling sensation, as if an electrical current was running from my hand to my shoulder. By the time I made it to my office, I could feel the tingling in my neck and scalp. I felt overwhelmingly tired, as if I hadn't slept in days. The thought crossed my mind that I was experiencing symptoms of a heart attack. On second thought, and perhaps in denial of such a grave, life-threatening possibility, I diagnosed myself as suffering from heartbreak. My heart was broken, and it hurt. *Riva, Riva,* I thought. *My heart is broken and can't be fixed.*

Blanton had told me to go home, but I wanted to check a few things while they were still fresh in my mind. I looked at my notepad, hoping that I might've jotted down something useful about the patient in quarantine. I had written only two words: "Lucina" and "Anna."

The mystery patient had called Lucina "the wolf." I typed "Lucina" into a search engine. I discovered that it was the name of a river in Eastern Europe, as well as the name of the ancient Roman goddess of childbirth. Her name meant "she who brings children into the light." There was nothing about a wolf named Lucina, though. I clicked a few related links and ended up on a website about the city of Rome, Italy. I learned that the ancient mascot of Rome is a she-wolf who raised two infant boys. Still, I couldn't imagine what any of this might have to do with the patient in quarantine, or with Anna Prescott.

I typed the name "Gemma Galgani" into a search engine. She was indeed a saint in the Roman Catholic Church. Several black-and-white photographs of her were available online. Other than having dark eyes and dark hair, the woman known as Saint Gemma looked nothing like the mystery patient. I noted from her online biography that Saint Gemma died in 1903, the same year that Anna Prescott had died in a freak blizzard on a mountain hike. Gemma had died in April of that year from tuberculosis. Anna had died in late September on Mount of the Holy Cross. How and why were these two seemingly unrelated women—Saint Gemma and Anna Prescott—inhabiting the hallucinations of our mystery patient? Why did our mystery patient believe that I could somehow communicate a message to Anna Prescott? And what was the message she wanted me to convey?

My computer chimed softly, notifying me that I had received a new message. I clicked on my mailbox. There, at the top of my list of messages was a new notification from Riva Pine entitled "Great news!"

It was mortifyingly insensitive of Mack to use my dead sister's e-mail address to send messages to me at my job. Obviously, Mack now had total access to Riva's e-mail account. He could read all the e-mail messages that Riva had ever sent or received. This was a stunning violation of privacy, I thought—Riva's privacy and mine. Just because Mack was legally next of kin, did that give him the right to commandeer all of Riva's past correspondence, and to use her personal e-mail address however he wished? I assumed that the answer to this was probably yes. Yes, he could do whatever he wanted. Yes, it was all perfectly legal, and yes, it was all perfectly, tastelessly typical of Mack.

I opened the message. A photograph materialized on my screen. It was a picture of a used Toyota motorhome—essentially, a motel room on wheels. More pictures materialized. The recreational vehicle was painted in a camouflage pattern. I recognized the paint job as Mack's handiwork; he had painted the interior of Riva's garage the same way. I could see that the vehicle was parked in front of Mack and Riva's house. Mack had included close-up photographs of the surfing-related bumper stickers that he had plastered on the back of the vehicle.

Mack wrote: "Hey, Sis. I have cried so much that my tears burn my face, as they are like acid. I decided to seize the day and buy the RV that Riva and I had always dreamed of. It is a fixer-upper. I will trick it out with solar panels and cool shit. Riva had enough cash in her personal account for it. She liked to save for a rainy day. We know not when we shall die so we must live fully in the now. Much love, Mack."

My stomach churned. Riva would be absolutely sick to know that Mack had bought the RV with her hard-earned money. The

RV was something that they had argued about. She told me all about it when I saw her at Christmas. Mack had been pestering her to buy a motorhome that he could park at Huntington Beach, or wherever the "cool" surfer scene was happening. The vehicle would allow him to surf all day and hang out with his midlife-adolescent buddies like Roy Dumond and Samadhi Masterson.

I had joked that Riva should buy Mack the RV with the sole stipulation that he never return to their house.

Riva replied wryly: "I hate to think what he would do in the absence of adult supervision."

At the time, I laughed. But in retrospect, her words struck me as ominous. I saw it all so clearly: Mack had killed Riva so he could enjoy the absence of adult supervision.

I typed the name "Samadhi Masterson" into an identity database. The search returned no hits. A search on the name "Roy Dumond" returned several results, including a software engineer at the Catholic Health Authority Headquarters in Maryland. None of the "Roy Dumond" results fit the description of a Southern California surfer.

Had Mack invented these guys?

My computer chimed again. I received a new message—a message from Lola. The subject line was a succession of question marks. I opened it:

"Becky, your friend Dr. Blanton called me and said that you fainted in her lab. Please know that I support you during this difficult time. I gave you a sensitive assignment on your first day back at the office. I should have given you more time to settle in. Please take it easy and get some rest. Your job will be here for you when you are ready."

Lola! What a wonderful boss! I responded immediately. "Thanks, Lola," I wrote. "I am going home right now. I will be back in the morning, completely refreshed. I am fine, really. Thank you again."

The message from Lola had come at just the right time to remind me that dwelling on Mack would only make me miserable. Instead, I needed to focus on the supportive people in my life. I needed to focus on the fact that I was valued, and that I had a job to do.

Suddenly, I felt a sharp pain in my ribs. It hurt to inhale. I typed my symptoms into the search engine. I read a few articles and decided that my symptoms indicated something called *costochondritis*, an inflammation of the cartilage that connects the ribs to the breastbone. In typical cases, this inflammation had no apparent cause. It was not life-threatening and usually cleared up by itself. I read online that sufferers of costochondritis often mistake their symptoms as signs of a heart attack. *Yes,* I told myself, *I have given myself a case of costochondritis. No reason to worry.*

When I got home, I looked into my living room and nodded at the red-velvet bag containing Riva's ashes. "Hello," I said, as if politely greeting a guest. "Mack bought the awful RV. You probably knew that already. It's too disheartening to even contemplate. I'm going to sleep."

I put on pajamas and got into bed. I want to say that I slept and dreamed an unusually vivid dream. But the episode felt *too real*—too tangible to be a mere invention of my subconscious. I dreamed that I entered the archival photograph on the wall near Lola's office. I was with the Denver Ladies Mountaineering Society and Anna Prescott in 1903 on their fateful ascent of Mount of the Holy Cross.

I was there—*actually* there. The mystery patient was there, too, and I learned her real name.

8

BLIZZARD ON THE MOUNT

Mother Frances Xavier Cabrini, born in Italy, was the first naturalized American citizen to be declared a saint by the Roman Catholic Church. She traveled across the United States establishing schools and orphanages. Her ministry took her to Colorado mountain towns where Italian immigrants labored in hard-rock mines. In Denver, she founded Queen of Heaven Orphanage. In the spring of 1903, Mother Cabrini traveled farther west, leaving her Denver orphanage in the care of her nuns, the Missionary Sisters.

Sister Paul of the Cross was among the Missionary Sisters serving at Queen of Heaven. She was an orphan herself, born in the village of San Sebastiano al Vesuvio in Campania near Naples, Italy, in 1872. Her parents named her Graziana Contini. Soon after her birth, a volcanic eruption claimed the lives of her whole family.

Nuns from an order known as the Passionists rescued the infant girl. They raised her and gave her what little affection they could spare. She grew tall and thin. Her large chestnut-colored eyes gazed at the world with such softness and detachment that the nuns often debated whether the girl might be blind. When she was old enough, Graziana joined the religious order, taking the name Paul of the Cross.

Not long after joining the order, Sister Paul heard Mother Cabrini's call for nuns who were willing to accept difficult work in America. When she met Mother Cabrini, Sister Paul immediately felt a powerful sense of loyalty to the woman. She vowed to devote her life to supporting Cabrini's mission. She worked briefly in Cabrini's school in New York City. Later, she followed Cabrini to Denver to work at Queen of Heaven Orphanage. By that time, Sister Paul was in her mid-twenties.

Sister Paul spoke very little English. Instead of teaching school, she was assigned to manage the orphanage's farm. Cabrini's Missionary Sisters raised chickens, goats, and vegetables on their plot of land in northwest Denver. Sister Paul showed children how to milk goats, make cheese, and gather eggs. The children watched her with tiny, flashing eyes, admiring her, and wanting to be like her. They saw kindness and strength in her, but she was oblivious to other people's perceptions of her. She believed herself to be invisible to most people, most of the time. She believed that Anna Prescott was the only person who could truly see her.

Anna Prescott ran Holy Cross Home for Consumptives across town from the orphanage. People said that she was ageless; Anna didn't look a day over 30. The society pages in the newspaper often commented about Anna's striking beauty, her violet-colored eyes, and the silky sheen of her brunette hair. She had married a much older man of wealth and notoriety.

Her husband's money paired with her philanthropic ambitions kept Anna busy. Holy Cross Home for Consumptives was her life's work. Anna planned for it to be a self-sustaining hospital community. She insisted that the hospital be built on farmland so that the institution could raise crops to feed patients. In truth, wide-open farmland was the only place that the city fathers of Denver agreed to allow Anna to build her "warehouse of poor, diseased invalids with questionable moral character," which was how local politicians referred to the sanitarium. Anna was determined to use this exile-on-farmland to the advantage of her patients. As patients gradually regained their health, they worked on the farm, benefiting from fresh air and exercise while doing chores. The farm produced large quantities of eggs and milk, which patients needed for their doctor-prescribed diet. By every measure, the farming operation was a success.

Anna kept a herd of dairy cattle that produced more milk than the hospital could use. In early summer 1903, Anna sent word to Queen of Heaven Orphanage to say that she had extra milk to give to the children if someone would come to pick it up.

Sister Paul was sent with the wagon to collect the milk. This is how she and Anna met. It was mid-morning. The sun had just broken through the clouds, rapidly warming the air. Sister Paul slowed her horse and drew up to the barn.

Anna called out a greeting. She was dressed in a man's style of work clothes, which intrigued Sister Paul. Anna climbed up on the bench and sat next to the nun. "Over there," Anna pointed to several milk cans farther up the path.

With one glance at Sister Paul, Anna saw the Eternal potential. Lucina had always said that there would be special ones whom Anna would recognize immediately. She hadn't believed it until that moment. As they rode the short distance, Anna studied the nun's Mediterranean features: her long, narrow, aquiline nose, and the tanned, olive skin of her rough hands.

"What is your name?" Anna asked.

"Paul of the Cross," the sister whispered. She looked at Anna out of the corner of her eye, unnerved by the woman's scrutiny. When she reached the milk cans, she pulled the horse to a stop.

Anna jumped down. "All of my workers are in the fields today," Anna said. "It will take both of us to lift these cans." She wrestled with one.

Sister Paul rushed to help.

"Grazie," Anna said.

It occurred to Anna that the nun probably spoke little English. With effort and cooperation, they loaded the wagon.

"*Un abisso chiama l'abisso,*" Anna said when they had finished. It was a phrase in Italian that Lucina used to say. It meant, "*Deep calls to deep.*"

The sister looked quizzically at Anna. She recognized the line from the Bible, from Psalm 42.

Anna realized that her own heart was racing, and her face was flushed. She felt anxious. She didn't want Sister Paul to leave, but she couldn't think of a reason to ask her to stay. Anna said in Italian and repeated in English: "See you Wednesday." She added, "Next Wednesday. For more milk."

The sister nodded. "Grazie." She boarded the wagon and set off for the orphanage.

Anna knew that she couldn't wait until Wednesday to see the nun again. Her eyes—those gentle, dark eyes, like a horse's eyes, deep and calm, with a seeming blind spot in front. Sister Paul needed to be approached from the side, sincerely and with open hands, Anna thought.

That evening, Anna hunted for a Bible so she could read Psalm 42: *Deep calls to deep in the roar of the waves your vastness washes over me....*

It was a song about desire and despair. In the psalm, Anna recognized the line that she had muttered over and over when William, her first husband, had died of tuberculosis: *Like a lethal wound in my bones, my enemies taunt me: They ask, "Where is your God?"*

If not for William and his tuberculosis, and his ultimate death in quarantine in Livorno, Anna never would have met Lucina. Anna reminded herself of this fact: the "white plague" had led her to Lucina, and to her Eternal sisterhood. Lucina had shown Anna that their shared mission was to eradicate fundamental darkness, which was the source of all suffering.

Anna believed that tuberculosis in particular presented a personal challenge; curing this horrible disease was her specific task. If she succeeded, Anna was confident that a solution could be found for all other human maladies. Sister Paul had been drawn into her orbit, Anna believed, for their shared purpose of radical healing.

Sister Paul read her Bible that night, too. She wondered what Anna had meant by quoting Psalm 42: *I thirst for you but drink only my tears…Deep calls to deep….*

Such terrible longing, the nun thought. *Such pained words for such a beautiful woman.*

Two days later, Anna hauled a load of winter wheat to Queen of Heaven Orphanage by herself. The prioress at the orphanage made a fuss over Anna's unexpected arrival. Anna was well-known as a wealthy patroness of local charities. The prioress called the children to the courtyard to sing a song for the woman. Several Missionary Sisters introduced themselves. Anna looked around anxiously for the one she wished to see.

"Where is Sister Paul of the Cross?" Anna asked.

The prioress told one of the girls to fetch Sister Paul. The girl ran toward the barn. Anna ran after the child, leaving the sisters perplexed. The girl shrieked with laughter when she saw the woman chasing her. Anna laughed, too.

Sister Paul looked up from her work and saw them running toward her. She wiped grime from her hands and face.

Anna spoke in Italian: "Sister Paul, I will teach you English."

That was their beginning. They met for language lessons all summer. The other sisters didn't understand why the renowned Anna Prescott had taken such an interest in a nondescript Italian nun. Sister Paul didn't understand it either, but she was certain of Anna's authentic affection. Sister Paul returned Anna's warmth, but she sensed that Anna was keeping something in abeyance. She sensed that Anna had a confession to make, and perhaps would reveal a secret in her own time.

At the end of their summer together, in September 1903, Anna cajoled Sister Paul to join the Denver Ladies Mountaineering Society on their most ambitious trek. They would be the first women to reach the summit of Mount of the Holy Cross.

Sister Paul hesitated to accept Anna's invitation. She doubted that she had the physical stamina for the climb. However, the prioress at Queen of Heaven Orphanage insisted that Sister Paul go on the trek. She saw it as a chance for the sister to curry favor with wealthy donors on behalf of the orphans.

After days of strenuous hiking led by their guide Mr. Hodge, the ladies and Sister Paul did indeed summit the mountain. Mr. Hodge was a competent wilderness guide as well as a condescending former military man in need of the pay the ladies offered him. He seemed genuinely surprised by the women's toughness and determination. He confirmed that they were the first group of ladies to have made the perilous climb.

Rain started to fall as they began their descent from the peak. Soon, gray clouds turned to ominous thunderheads. Raindrops turned to snow, falling fast and thick.

When the brunt of the storm hit, they were above tree line. They had nowhere to shelter. Wind swept through trees in the distance. Branches snapped. Gusts surged toward them. Wind howled, whipping them blind.

Mr. Hodge shouted orders. The women in front of Sister Paul began to run. Sister Paul stumbled. When she looked up, she could see no one. Anna had been behind her but she, too, had disappeared. Sister Paul cried out. She could not hear her own voice above the gale. She didn't know where she was in relation to the steep edge of the path. Unable to see anything but a furious wall of white, she panicked. She started to run.

Anna grabbed her and pulled her to the ground. The nun clung to her. Anna covered them with her cloak. They huddled together, trembling. Sister Paul was certain they would die on the mountain. No one could come to their aid. No one would even miss them for several days, not until they failed to return to the town of Minturn.

Snow accumulated around them. Sister Paul prayed for the safety of the other women. She thought of the mules tied at camp. She prayed for mercy. She prayed for Anna. She always prayed for Anna. Sister Paul marveled at the inscrutable circumstances that led her to die on the mountain in Anna's arms.

Numb with fear, they hadn't moved in hours. Perhaps they were already half dead, suffocating under snow. Between their two bodies, huddled together, they generated warmth—more warmth than Sister Paul would have thought possible. Their situation was terrifying, but Anna's warmth and the intoxicating scent of Anna's damp hair thrilled Sister Paul in a way that felt more like elation than terror.

"The storm has passed." Anna's voice jarred Sister Paul. "Help me," she said. She pushed through the weighty snow that encased them.

Sister Paul pushed herself to her feet. She breathed and felt the chill in her lungs. Night had fallen. A full moon had risen. A sparkling, iridescent sea of snow covered the land. Sister Paul almost dropped to her knees in awe of the breathtaking scene.

"Hello," Anna cried. She waited for a response.

"Hello," they shouted in unison. There was no answer.

A large boulder had partially shielded the spot where they had huddled. Deep snow drifts surrounded them.

"We have to climb down to the trees and make a fire," Anna said. "Otherwise we will not survive the night."

"The snow is too deep," Sister Paul said. "Even if we can find the path, we will not be able to pass."

Anna thought for a moment. "If we stay here we will die. Follow me."

Instead of searching for the path, she threw herself down the slope. Sister Paul tried to stop her. Anna was already gone. She tumbled, slid, and swam. A boulder interrupted her progress and bruised her badly, as Sister Paul would later see. Anna adjusted her course and continued to fling herself toward the trees.

Sister Paul followed. The bumps were painful, but it was the most expedient route. Both women made it to tree line. Snow was not as deep under the trees. Still, the women had little hope of finding dry tinder. Anna pointed to a pine tree and told Sister Paul to tear away as many dead branches as possible. The sister worked until her hands were scratched and bleeding. She hunted for scraps of loose bark. Eventually, they had a pile of kindling.

Tree limbs were bent close to the ground under loads of snow. Anna threw her weight on them to snap them loose. She covered a patch of ground with pine boughs. With more branches she made a lean-to shelter under the slope of a fallen tree trunk.

The nun kicked through snow to find more dead wood. With Anna's flint, she made sparks and, eventually, a flame. She cupped her hands around it until it grew. They settled on a bed of pine boughs under their shelter. Between them, they had one metal spoon. They took turns melting snow over the fire and drinking water by the spoonful.

That night Sister Paul huddled close to Anna as they watched the flickering flames that might keep them alive. They prayed that the other women and Mr. Hodge would see their makeshift camp. They talked, trying to keep each other awake to feed bits of fuel to the fire.

Pain throbbed in Anna's hips and legs, but she didn't mention it to Sister Paul. The pain would fade if she rested, she thought.

Sister Paul woke with the first light of morning, surprised that she had slept at all. The sky was clear. The fire had burned out. The nun wrapped her arm around Anna. The woman felt cold and stiff. She pressed her hand to Anna's neck to feel for her pulse. She saw a faint cloud of Anna's breath in the icy air.

The sister touched her hand to Anna's cheek. "I will build the fire," she said. "You need warmth."

Anna's eyelids fluttered groggily. She tried to roll over. Searing pain electrified her body. She gasped.

"What is it?" Sister Paul asked.

"I am cold," Anna said, hesitant to admit that something much more serious was wrong with her.

Sister Paul rose to find more wood. She saw a dead tree several yards away. She tore at it. She scavenged for dead branches that had fallen. She was frightened by the uncertainty of the situation, but she could not deny her joy in being close to Anna. The chance to be of service to Anna gave her strength. She piled more branches around their camp to shield them from the elements. If snow were to fall again, they would be protected, and they would have adequate fuel for their campfire. Sister Paul revived the fire with broken twigs, which snapped and popped in the heat, filling the air with the smell of smoky pine. Anna watched as the nun stoked the flames.

"I have seen no sign of the others," Sister Paul said. "I fear the worst."

"They could not have gone far," Anna said.

Sister Paul remembered that her own instinct had been to run. What if the others had run or fallen, or gotten lost? What if they had survived and made a camp on the other side of the mountain?

"You're bleeding," Anna said.

Sister Paul's hands were cut. A drop of her blood fell into the fire.

"Come here." Anna tried to shift her body. She winced with pain. "Give me your hand."

The sister held out her hand. Anna took it. Her expression was apologetic. "I'm sorry that I could not show this to you until now, Sister Paul." Anna's velvety tongue caressed the sister's palm. Her mouth was tender and warm. The nun could not move. She watched, stunned. Anna licked her wounds. Sister Paul felt a tingling sensation spread through her hand and up her arm and into her chest.

Anna took the nun's other hand and licked it, too. She looked like a cat, licking with long, luxuriant strokes. Her saliva didn't cool in the chilly air. Rather, it burned. The nun began to perspire. She felt as if her whole body was ablaze. She closed her eyes in a swoon.

"Sister Paul," Anna said sometime later.

The nun did not open her eyes.

"Please look at your hands."

The nun blinked. Her hands were healed. There was no sign of any wound. "Anna, it is a miracle."

Anna's violet eyes darkened. "I would not call it that," she said. "It is a natural chemical reaction. Your origin cells respond to the chemicals in my saliva. I must share this method of healing with you, Sister Paul. I need you to do the same for me."

"I don't understand."

"I am badly injured. If we are to survive, you must heal me."

Sister Paul didn't know what Anna meant. She took off her heavy cloak and spread it on the snow next to Anna and laid down beside her, facing Anna. She was willing to do whatever was necessary to help. "I will try, but I am not capable of such miracles."

"Yes, you are." Anna held the nun's face in her hands. She pressed her lips to Sister Paul's. The sister's throat and stomach burned as if she was drinking molten gold. She could not tell whether she burned from cold or from heat. She felt as if she might faint. Several minutes passed. Sister Paul became aware of a strange feeling in her stomach—full yet empty. Hunger pangs stabbed. She needed to eat or to vomit, she wasn't sure which.

Anna lifted her skirts to show Sister Paul her injuries. Her hip and leg were badly bruised. Sister Paul helped her to take her boots off. Anna's ankle was horribly swollen and bent.

Sister Paul gasped. "There is nothing I can do."

"Put your mouth on me. Once you taste my skin, instinct will guide you."

"I can't," Sister Paul objected, although she wanted to do as Anna instructed. "It does not seem Godly, Anna," she protested, meekly.

"It isn't Godly," Anna said, with a note of stinging irony in her voice. "In this moment, I am asking you to discard every fearful rule and regulation that you have ever learned about God, and allow love to lead you. Sister Paul, I am asking you to find the eternal life that dwells within you."

Sister Paul blinked, bewildered, "I have eternal life?"

Anna smiled. "You are limitless, timeless, and capable of infinite creation." Seeing confusion on the nun's face, she added softly: "And you love me, Sister Paul, as I love you. This is the most important thing. Our love is what heals our wounds." Anna saw a flicker of recognition in the nun's eyes.

In truth, the dictates of the Holy Bible had never made sense to the nun. The only thing that made sense to her was service—serving others with kindness in her heart. *This* is what the Passionist nuns had taught her. *This* was her holy creed, not the words and commandments of an abstract God. Now, she had an opportunity to be of service to Anna, whom she cared for more than any other person. "I do love you, Anna," the nun said.

Tentatively, she pressed her cheek to Anna's skin. She touched her lips to Anna's bruises. Her heart pounded. She licked Anna's skin and tasted salt. Her stomach rioted. It was as if Anna's flesh was melting in her mouth. She swallowed and reflexively regurgitated fiery, viscous fluid, soaking Anna's wounded flesh. The nun tasted something that inflamed her wildly. She tried to open her eyes but the light was too bright.

As if from the inside out, the women melted into each other. Their bodies had melted into one vast pool of blinding light. In that light, Sister Paul felt blood vessels and capillaries dissolve. She felt each tiny neuron and nerve implode into brilliance. Light penetrated everything. Each and every molecule of their bodies was pure illumination.

From a pool of hot, sparkling radiance, bones and organs began to differentiate themselves. Light shaped itself into vertebrae and ribs, into muscle and sinew, into lungs and hearts. Two individual women emerged, separate, whole, and completely rejuvenated.

Sister Paul lay down next to Anna, her face smeared with tingling fluid. She struggled to catch her breath. The sun had crossed the sky. It was afternoon. Anna's injuries had been healed. Despite their dire circumstances, both women felt indestructible.

"I should have told you," Anna said. "How could I have explained it to you?"

"How do you explain it to yourself?"

"Lucina calls us Eternals," Anna said. She stroked the nun's hair with her fingertips. "Sister Paul, one day you will meet Lucina. She will teach you more than I know."

"Anna, I can no longer call myself Sister Paul of the Cross. My name is Graziana Contini."

9

MARYDALE

I awoke. The room was dimly lit with twilight. Whether the sun was setting or rising, I wasn't sure. The fact that I was in bed was the only indication that I had slept. Had I actually slept? I felt as if I had been climbing a mountain and fighting to survive a freak blizzard. As I tried to remember what had happened, the details of my dream became confused.

I became aware that I was not alone. The mystery patient from Holy Cross—the woman named Graziana Contini—sat at my bedside. Her cheeks were gaunt. Her eyes were sunken and dark, as they had been when I saw her in Dr. Blanton's lab at the hospital. She was no longer wearing her respirator mask. I could see a faint smile on her lips. Her smile made her look kind and wistful. I heard the click and whoosh of a ventilator, just as I had heard in Riva's hospital room. I heard the beeping and humming of hospital equipment. I saw that I was paralyzed—lifeless—in the bed, just as Riva had been. I couldn't move. I couldn't speak. I realized that I was unable to open my eyes. I was seeing the whole scene from a perspective outside my own body. I was in my body yet somehow I was outside my body at the same time.

"Becky," I heard Graziana say. "All three of us are needed to open the portal."

Graziana reached out to me with her right hand. She reached into my ribcage. She grabbed my heart. I saw her pull it out of my body. My heart quivered and thrashed in her hand like a cutthroat trout pulled from an icy mountain lake. With her left hand, Graziana reached into her own chest and removed her own heart. It was a sickly thing. Thick with scars, it labored to beat. She pressed her sickly heart through my ribs. Graziana put my heart into her chest. Almost instantaneously, Graziana's appearance changed. Her eyes were no longer dark and sunken. They sparkled. Her cheeks glowed with health. "This will take me far," she said. "Come find me so I can return it to you."

Graziana stood and walked out of my bedroom. Suddenly, I saw that it wasn't my bedroom at all—rather, it was Graziana's hospital room at Holy Cross. The bed was empty. The room was empty. I was there, but I *wasn't* there.

I awoke with a gasp. My heart raced as I looked around at the familiar items in my bedroom. I sat up. I grabbed my phone off the nightstand. *Yes, I am awake,* I assured myself. *This is real.* I checked the news headlines on my phone. *Yes, politics as usual. All is well,* I told myself. *And all shall be well.*

I paused—*and all shall be well?* I repeated the phrase in my mind. Why did I say that? This didn't sound like something I would say. Rather, it felt like a call and response, as if I had said to myself, "All is well," and some other voice had replied, "And all shall be well."

"Riva, is that you?" I asked aloud. "Are you telling me that everything will be okay? Nothing seems okay. Okay?"

According to the time on my phone, I had awakened 20 minutes before my alarm had a chance to sound. For me, this was unusual. I tended to hit the snooze button at least twice before I felt ready to greet the day. For the first time in a long time, I was uncharacteristically wide awake before sunrise. I sat in bed, trying to catch my breath, trying to recall what had happened. I had gone to Blanton's lab. I had fainted. Blanton told me to go home and rest. Mack sent me photos of a motorhome he had bought with Riva's money. Oh—and I had told Blanton that I would meet her for breakfast in the cafeteria.

Graziana Contini. According to my intensely surreal dream, this was the name of the mystery patient in quarantine at Holy Cross. If this turned out to be true—if Dr. Blanton could confirm this information—I would be astonished.

In the bustle of breakfast rush at Holy Cross cafeteria, Dr. Blanton watched me with calm, quiet, vigilant concern. "You're feeling better?" she asked.

"I'm not sure," I said. I pushed food around on my plate with a fork. I wanted to tell her about the name *Graziana Contini*, but I would have to admit to her that the name had come to me in a dream. How could she possibly take me seriously? "Let me ask you a medical question," I ventured, trying to sound sober-minded.

Dr. Blanton leaned forward and adjusted her glasses.

"Have you ever seen, I mean, have you ever heard of people somehow being able to spontaneously heal serious wounds and broken bones, or regenerate their bodies?"

Dr. Blanton looked sympathetic. Perhaps she thought that my question pertained to the irreversible brain damage that Riva had suffered. "We don't always know why people heal, Becky, or why they don't."

"Put it this way," I searched for the words to phrase my question. "Is there any such thing as one person's saliva reacting with another person's blood to create a fireball of spontaneous tissue regeneration?"

Dr. Blanton leaned back and rolled her eyes. "Becky, is this about vampires? Zombies? Is this a novel you're reading?"

"No." I rubbed my forehead, straining to think of what to ask. In my dream, Anna had mentioned a chemical reaction involving what she had called *origin cells*. "Is there a way to create a chemical reaction in origin cells with saliva?" I asked. "Would this chemical reaction make a bright light?"

"You mean stem cells?"

I shrugged. "I don't have much of a medical vocabulary."

"That was a hoax, you know," Blanton said dryly. "A researcher in Japan claimed that stem cells could be activated by dipping them in a weak acid solution. No one was able to replicate or confirm the result."

I should have known better than to ask a scientist my half-baked questions. Dr. Blanton probably thought I was losing my grip on reality—and maybe I *was* losing my grip. I drank a slug of coffee.

"Lasers are another story," Blanton added. "Intense light, such as laser light, can *possibly* activate stem cells. But there's still a lot we don't know about the process."

My expression must've brightened because Dr. Blanton smiled. "Did I answer your question?" she asked.

"Have you ever heard of—I mean, is there any such thing as two liquids coming together to create a bright light?"

Dr. Blanton smiled as if I was joking. "Ever heard of a glow stick?"

"Glow stick?"

"How do you think a glow stick works?"

"I've never given it a moment's thought."

"You have a flexible tube filled with liquid," Blanton said. "Inside the flexible tube is a glass tube filled with a different kind of liquid. You bend the flexible tube to break the glass tube. The two liquids combine to create a luminous glow."

"So it's possible," I clarified.

"It's commonplace. But that's not *laser* light," she clarified. "It creates a diffuse glow, not the focused, amplified light of a laser."

"Still," I said. "What about body fluids? Could a body fluid from one person come into contact with a body fluid from another person to create a luminous reaction?"

Blanton laughed in a stifled, embarrassed way, as if I was asking how babies are made. "Is this really what you wanted to talk about, Becky?" I heard a note of uncertainty in her voice. "Is there something troubling you about yesterday? About seeing the patient? About fainting? Is there something you noticed about the patient, or found out about her?"

"Yes." I had just taken a mouthful of food. I chewed, creating an unintentionally dramatic pause.

Dr. Blanton watched me with cautious, appraising eyes.

"I'm going out on a limb here," I said.

Dr. Blanton took a deep breath. "Okay."

"I think your mystery patient is named Graziana Contini."

"Why do you say that?"

"Don't ask. Please write it down. Check it out. *Graziana Contini.* If it pans out, I'll tell you my source. But you won't believe it."

Dr. Blanton wrote the name on her napkin. "It doesn't hurt to run it through the databases," she said optimistically. "Even if it came to you in a dream, it's better than nothing."

"It did come to me in a dream," I said flatly, and Blanton seemed to think I was kidding. "It might be a false lead," I added.

"Becky, it's our only lead." Blanton returned her pen to the pocket of her lab coat. "Let's meet again for breakfast tomorrow. Look, I know that being the focus of anyone's concern makes you uncomfortable. I'm not in the role of *doctor* with you. I'm interested in your well-being as a co-worker and a friend."

"Thanks," I said. "Seriously. Thank you."

"See you tomorrow?"

"Same time, same place."

On my way to my office, I opted to avoid the tunnels. I didn't want to encounter another mystery patient or rose-scented nun. Instead, I walked along the garden pathways that crisscrossed campus. The hospital grounds were filled with budding shrubs and trees. I saw only one other fellow employee as I walked toward my office. All employees wore electronic identification badges so we were easy to spot. We smiled at each other as if thinking the same thing: *What a shame that everyone takes the tunnels instead of the garden paths on beautiful spring-like mornings such as this.*

I looked into Lola's office to see if she was free. As usual, she was on the phone. She saw me and gestured for me to wait. I stood outside her door and studied the photograph of the Denver Ladies Mountaineering Society.

Yes, Anna Prescott was definitely the woman who appeared in my dream as the woman named Anna. The other woman in my dream-blizzard, the one who called herself Graziana, was in the photo, too. She bore a strong resemblance to the mystery patient in Dr. Blanton's lab. In the photo, all of the mountaineering women gazed into the camera except for Graziana. She looked at Anna. Maybe that's why I had dreamed that the two of them shared some kind of special relationship.

The name Graziana Contini was not on the placard accompanying the photo, but the names of Anna Prescott and the other women were listed. The placard referred to Graziana as "an identified nun, possibly from Queen of Heaven Orphanage."

I reminded myself that I had *not* actually been to the summit of Mount of the Holy Cross, no matter how real my dream had seemed. My subconscious mind was playing out a story that I had fabricated. None of it was real. I had looked at this photo several times a day for months. It was no wonder that these faces had appeared in my dream.

In reality, the women had died in a freak blizzard in 1903. This was a matter of undisputed, historical fact. My mind was trying to rewrite the story, somehow.

"Come in, Becky," Lola said, her voice welcoming. "If you'd like to use some of your vacation time, you have my approval."

"Thanks, Lola. It's not that." I didn't sit down. I didn't want to get into a detailed conversation with Lola because I wasn't sure what crazy-sounding thing I might divulge about my dream. "I told Dr. Blanton that I had a possible lead on the mystery patient," I said. "But now I worry that I got it all wrong."

"What's the lead?" Lola asked.

"I think that the patient's name might be Graziana Contini. Dr. Blanton is checking on it, but I have my doubts."

"Spelling?" Lola turned her attention to the electronic screen on her desk. She pecked the letters as I spelled the name. "We'll see if it rings a bell in anyone's database," she said. "Any lead is a good lead at this point. Take it easy today, Becky. Do something dull and administrative. Catch up on your filing."

I nodded. "There's one other thing."

Lola looked up at me.

"What you said yesterday," I began, my voice uncertain. "You used the word *Eternal.* I have a hunch. This patient might be related to that word."

Lola studied me. "Yes, you may be right," she said. She sounded cautious. "Let me handle it."

"Lola," I ventured quietly. "What does *Eternal* mean?"

Lola looked at me wearily for a moment. "It could mean a revolution in our understanding of medicine." She added: "Revolution is terrifying for some people, so let's not upset them." She placed her index finger over her lips.

"Okay," I said, understanding that she wanted to say no more.

Back at my desk, I looked at a stack of papers that I needed to file. Instead of doing that, however, I turned on my computer. I typed "Graziana Contini" into an identity database. The name returned no results.

Doctors like Blanton and executives like Lola had access to much more powerful search tools than I had at my disposal. They were authorized to access patient files from Holy Cross and other allied institutions.

I saw the note I had written the day before: "Anna Bartlet." I ran a fundraising database search. I saw that Bartlet was listed as the contact for the Ashton Foundation in New York, but no contact details were listed, no street address, no phone number.

I looked at fundraiser message boards and social media to see if anyone had ever posted anything about meeting Bartlet. Two years earlier, a fundraising officer from a Catholic charity had posted a photograph and remarked: "Lunch at Café Toulouse with raven-haired beauty Anna Bartlet. See! Her eyes really are violet!" In response, other fundraisers chided him for making sexist remarks and objectifying women. The photograph itself had been completely deleted, but the remark remained cached in a database.

I searched public records trying to find an Anna Bartlet in New York who might match the description of "raven-haired and violet-eyed." I found no one.

I clicked on my Holy Cross message inbox. Dozens of unread messages appeared. The quantity of them paralyzed me.

Some of the messages were from acquaintances of Riva's. They had heard about her death and wondered what had happened. I closed my message program without replying to anyone.

I realized that I'd spent the morning thinking about Graziana and my dream. I hadn't spent much time mulling Riva's death.

I started typing phrases into a search engine: *Husband kills wife. Iron dumbbell used as murder weapon.* I waded through pages of results. I read dozens of articles involving men murdering women by bludgeoning their heads with metal dumbbells. It was a common mode of assault, turns out.

I typed additional searches: *Head injury autopsy, head trauma accident versus homicide, how long does an autopsy take, how long can police wait to make an arrest for murder.*

I read pages and pages of information about coroners, death certificates, homicide investigations, and more. This pursuit absorbed my attention for much of the day.

I learned that, for a woman who's in an abusive relationship, the most dangerous time is when she decides to leave. At this juncture, men commonly resort to violence. Experts offered varying explanations. Some said that abusive men think of their partners as their property. By physically attacking her, the abuser asserts property rights, trying to re-establish ownership. Other experts said that violence was a matter of ego, of wanting to have the last word. An abuser might kill his partner as if to say, "Our relationship is over when I say it's over."

Sometimes an abuser is afraid that if his partner discovers that she's happier without the relationship, his "spell" over her will be broken. He will lose the emotional control over her that he has worked so hard to cultivate. For some abusers, the thought that she can live without him is interpreted as a personal insult. It's a slap in his face, and she deserves to die for it.

Any and all of these end-game motives could be ascribed to Mack, I thought.

Despite everything I knew about the myriad, demeaning ways in which Mack treated Riva, I had never conceived of their relationship as clinically abusive. I knew that Mack could behave in abusive ways, certainly. But Riva didn't fit my idea of an abused woman. She was strong. She knew her own mind. She had autonomy, money, and friends. She wasn't a victim. Her attitude was never helpless or defeated.

I combed through lists of warning signs and symptoms of abuse. Mack and Riva's relationship fit the bill. I had seen these signs—belittling, cajoling, sabotaging. For years, I saw that he was abusing her. It had never occurred to me that Riva was trapped in an abusive relationship.

Why hadn't I educated myself sooner about the clear, repetitive, and universal indicators of abuse? I could have helped Riva see that Mack wasn't a special case in need of her special care. He wasn't a unique, tarnished jewel. No, he was a textbook example of an angry, entitled, controlling man. Why didn't I do something to save her?

"You didn't see me as a victim because I didn't see myself as a victim, Becky," I heard Riva say. "I had no inkling that he was capable of murdering me until he murdered me. There's nothing we could have done."

I put my elbows on my desk and covered my eyes with my hands. *Oh, Riva, I failed you. I should have been smarter. I should have been more critical, more vocal, more strident.*

"You were strident enough," she said in a teasing tone.

It's not funny, Reeve. The signs were there. I saw. I knew.

"You don't want me to feel guilty about my death," she said. "I don't want you to feel guilty, either, Little Boz."

I'm so sorry, Riva. I'm so sorry.

I heard a knock on my office door. I looked up. It was Dave, the college-aged intern from the Mail Solicitations Department. "Did you see the helicopter?" he asked in a humorous, breathlessly gossipy tone.

"What helicopter?" As I spoke, I became aware of the distinctive *chop-chop* sound of a helicopter above the hospital. "It is from a TV news station?"

"It's a *black* helicopter," he said, as if this meant something ominous. "Go check it out."

He continued down the hall, spreading the news to other co-workers. I went outside. I looked to the sky. Sure enough, a black helicopter was circling the Holy Cross Health campus. As far as I could tell, the helicopter was unmarked. The aircraft made one more pass over campus, looped west, and disappeared toward the mountains in the distance.

Other employees had come outside to look, too. No one had the faintest idea what was going on. "Probably just a training exercise," someone said. "Remember when the president visited?" said another co-worker. "Those copters were Secret Service." Others disagreed. Somehow, this sparked a discussion about private-sector paramilitary organizations and corporately-controlled security forces. I wasn't interested.

I went back to my office. I grabbed a stack of paperwork and took it to the file room. I spent the next hour putting papers into folders. In the distant future, I thought, when my dismay regarding Riva's death had mellowed, and when my ridiculous dreams about Mountaineering Ladies had exhausted themselves, I would be grateful for well-organized paperwork. *Just because my personal world is collapsing into confusion and despair doesn't mean I can shirk my obligation to maintain departmental files.* When I finished filing, it was almost five o'clock. Time to go home.

I hadn't heard from Dr. Blanton. I wondered whether she had news about Graziana Contini. I picked up the phone. I quickly put it back down. Why call her? It was a lovely afternoon. I decided to walk outdoors across campus, and drop in on Dr. Blanton in person. I gathered my things. I hoisted my pack onto my shoulder.

Rush hour traffic roared through the intersection that separated Old Infirmary from the rest of campus. I was the lone pedestrian. When traffic paused, I ran across the boulevard.

This is stupidly dangerous, I thought. *This is why we have tunnels.*

Ahead of me on the garden pathway, I saw a woman. I wondered where I had seen her before. I could tell that she wasn't an employee because she didn't have a badge. She stood near an exterior stairwell door of Blanton's building. She seemed to be waiting for someone to exit the building so she could enter it. Her attention was focused on the screen of a mobile device.

The woman had shoulder-length, light-brown hair. She was in her mid-to-late forties, I guessed. She was trim, probably five-foot-seven. *She's pretty,* I thought. Even from several yards away, I could see that she had lovely features, with high cheek bones, large eyes, and a pronounced jawline. She pushed her hair back, and it hit me: she resembled the blurred photo of the woman standing in front of the Vatican, the woman in the hex-code photo I had seen at the library in Long Beach.

"Hey," I said as I approached her.

She turned to face me. One of her eyebrows was arched as she regarded me. Her mouth was small and full. She seemed to pucker her lips slightly as if sizing me up.

"Hey," I said, again. As I moved closer to her, I could see that she wore no make-up. Her skin was sprinkled with faint freckles. "Do you know that you look like Lillian Gish?"

"Like *whom?*" she said, sounding both wary and amused—sounding, to my ear, a lot like Lillian Gish.

"She was a movie actress," I said. "From Hollywood's golden age."

"Would you mind letting me in this door?" she asked impatiently.

"I can't," I said. "Hospital rules prohibit it." I realized that she didn't really look like Lillian Gish after all. While Gish struck me as waifish and fragile, this woman looked athletic and outdoorsy. I recalled that the woman in the Long Beach photo had also initially reminded me of Lillian Gish, but on closer inspection, the resemblance disappeared. "Have you ever visited the Vatican?" I asked, pointlessly, confused about why I was hallucinating visions of a long-dead actress.

"Vatican?" I saw the woman's watery-blue eyes dart to my employee name-badge. "Becky Pine," she said. I watched her study my face.

"Yes, and who are you?" I asked, sounding more imperious than I had intended.

"I'm Marydale. I'm with the Ashton Foundation."

I considered for a moment whether this was a simple coincidence or an elaborate, ridiculous hoax. "Marydale of the Ashton Foundation," I repeated, almost as if it were a punchline.

"There's a patient I need to see," she said. "The person at the reception desk told me there aren't any overnight patients. But there *is* a patient in this building. Can you let me in to see her?"

How could Marydale possibly know about the mystery patient in Dr. Blanton's lab?

"Look," I said, suddenly panicky. "I could lose my job for even talking about patients, let alone opening doors for unauthorized people," I stammered. "Besides, what's with calling yourself *Marydale*? What does the Ashton Foundation want from Holy Cross?" I realized that my questions sounded disjointed and unnecessarily belligerent, and I regretted my tone.

"It's just a name." Marydale smiled broadly, showing even, white teeth. Disarming, dimpled lines appeared on her lightly tanned cheeks.

That smile must open a lot of doors for her, I thought.

"The Ashton Foundation is interested in supporting medical research," she said. She spoke as if reciting a memorized mission statement.

I wasn't listening. Rather, I was distracted by her necklace. It was a silver circle on a silver chain. Inside the circle were overlapping circles forming a flower-petal design. It was the same design that had been carved into the wooden fob attached to the rosary that the nun in Long Beach had given me. The same symbol had been cremated with Riva.

Marydale noticed that I was staring at her necklace. She touched her hand to it, covering it, protecting it. "Becky, I think maybe *you're* the person I'm here to see." She sounded as if pieces of a puzzle were falling into place for her. "Do you know Graziana Contini? I need to get a message to her from Anna."

I looked into Marydale's eyes. She wasn't joking. So many questions competed in my mind, I didn't know what to say. After a moment of awkward silence, I asked, "Are you a nun?"

"A nun?" Her tone held a note of caution.

"I saw that same flower-petal pattern on a rosary. A nun gave it to me." I was about to explain about the hospital nun and Riva. Instead, I paused and folded my arms, defensively. "Tell me something. Tell me something honestly. How do you know the name Graziana Contini?"

"Anna told me that Graziana was here," she said innocently. "Anna said that Graziana had found someone here to help her. I am here to communicate a message."

"What's the message?"

"Greenwell Portal with Lucina as planned," Marydale said. "Does this mean something to you? Are you alright? Do you need to sit down?" She pointed to a bench on the grass nearby. "Here, let's sit," she said.

We sat. I told Marydale everything. The name Graziana Contini had come to me in a dream—a weirdly detailed dream—the previous night. Now, suddenly, here was Marydale, confirming the mystery patient's name, and mentioning Anna and Lucina. I felt myself starting to sweat as I spoke. Suddenly, I felt a sharp pain in my chest. "Look, I'm sorry if all of this sounds crazy. I've been dealing with personal issues."

"You're not crazy," Marydale said, reassuring. "The situation is convoluted, but it's not crazy."

"No, I mean—maybe I'm experiencing some kind of grief-induced psychosis," I confessed. "Here I am, spilling my guts to you because I think you look like Lillian Gish, as if that makes you familiar and trustworthy, and you don't really even look like her. That's just crazy. My sister died, and everything has gone crazy," I said, not meaning to mention Riva, but I was unable to stop speaking, as if a floodgate had opened.

The pain in my chest stabbed and ached. "I'm not having a heart attack," I said, aware that I was flushed and perspiring. "I have a broken heart because of my sister, and because Graziana pulled my heart out of my chest this morning and replaced it with her own. My sister is dead, and I did nothing to save her. She was an organ donor. Someone else has her heart now. That's what my dream this morning was really about. It was a dream about death and heart transplants, somehow. But now you're here asking about Graziana, and it all seems too real, or surreal. And the Greenwell Portal? Graziana appeared to me in the tunnel as a ghost and said something about opening a portal. I don't know what to make of it."

"Becky, I'm so sorry to hear about your sister," Marydale soothed. "What was her name?"

"Riva," I said, my voice cracking. "Riva Pine."

"All of these things that are happening in your life are interrelated," Marydale assured me. "If I could explain it all to you right now, I would. But things are in the process of unfolding. It's too soon for tidy summaries." Marydale's phone buzzed. She glanced at the screen. "I'm sorry. I need to run. Please, let's have lunch tomorrow. There's so much I want to tell you. Please give the message to Graziana."

"You know what I'm talking about?" I asked, dubious.

"I know exactly what you're talking about," she said. "We need to open the Greenwell Portal, and we will need your help. Before I can explain it to you, I'll need to clarify a few things with my boss." Marydale stood.

I stood, too.

"Please trust me," she implored. "There are valid answers to your questions. You're not psychotic, Becky," she said.

I was about to reply that this was the nicest thing anyone had ever said to me, when Marydale threw her arms around my neck. She hugged me tightly. I patted her back, expecting her to break the hug. Her hold did not weaken. She held on until I hugged her, too. She did not let go for a long while. When she pulled away, I couldn't speak.

She handed me a business card. "Lunch tomorrow," she said. She walked rapidly toward the curb.

I looked at the card in my hand. It read: *D. Marydale, CNM.* Under her name was a phone number. I turned the card over. It offered no additional information. I knew that CNM stood for Certified Nurse Midwife. I looked up again, and Marydale was gone.

I couldn't remember the last time that someone had hugged me the way she had. I felt suddenly giddy. I used my badge to enter the building. I ran up the stairs. At Dr. Blanton's floor, I pressed my badge to an electronic pad to enter her lab.

Inside, I saw three men wearing yellow coveralls. They stared at me.

"I just ran up seven flights," I said goofily.

"This floor is closed for cleaning," one of the men said sternly.

"Is Dr. Blanton here?" I asked.

"Everyone's gone. Floor closed. Exit the way you came."

I paused. A question half-formed in my mind, but I didn't pursue it. I planned to see Dr. Blanton at breakfast the next morning. My questions could wait until then. I turned around, went through the door, and jogged down seven flights of stairs.

The exertion of running had calmed me. I walked to my car feeling happy. I felt a spark of hope, much like a nascent romantic crush. I had met and been hugged by a beautiful woman who was privy to the details of a strange mystery. She knew all about Graziana Contini! Everything was going to be explained! Everything would make sense! My head spun with questions for Marydale: How is the Ashton Foundation involved with nuns in Long Beach? What does this have to do with Eternals?

I felt happy because, at last, I had decided to trust my perceptions. I decided to believe that I wasn't hallucinating an imaginary world. Rather, Riva's death had catapulted me into a deeper reality—a reality in which I could converse with my dead sister—a reality in which mystical beings could heal others. Renegade nuns weren't just a fantasy or a conspiracy theory—they were *real*, and one of them had hugged me.

I was in my car, driving home, buzzing with curiosity and excitement, when I remembered that Marydale had asked me to give a message to Graziana: "Greenwell Portal with Lucina as planned." I thought about the man in the hallway of Blanton's lab. He had said: *Everyone's gone. Floor closed.*

No, this couldn't be right. The floor *couldn't* be closed. One of the doctors must have been there, whether it was Dr. Blanton or someone else. Blanton would never leave Graziana alone without medical staff, not for a moment.

Also, since when did cleaning crews at Holy Cross wear yellow, hazmat coveralls? This question, too, would have to wait until morning.

That night, I dreamed that I was in a scene from *Night of the Hunter*, the movie that I had watched in my hotel room after Riva was hospitalized. Lillian Gish sat in a rocking chair with a shotgun on her lap to protect me from a depraved reverend who was stalking me. In my dream, I understood that Lillian Gish was my well-armed defender. Hers was the face of my guardian angel.

10

LIBERATION

The next morning, I went directly to the cafeteria. I was eager to hear what Dr. Blanton had discovered about Graziana. My brief talk with Marydale had given me confidence that the patient's name was indeed Graziana Contini, and that she was a person of great significance. I wondered what Dr. Blanton had been able to discover about the woman.

I carried my food tray past the cashier station. I saw that Dr. Blanton was already sitting at her customary table. Her arms were folded over her chest. As I approached, I saw that she had no food. A thermal lunch bag printed with the hospital logo was on the table next to her coffee cup.

"Good morning," I said. I slid my tray onto the table and sat down. "Everything okay?"

"I've been here all night, Becky. We all have. My whole lab." She sounded angry and frustrated.

My memory flashed back to the men I had seen in yellow coveralls, the ones who had told me that Blanton's lab was closed. "What happened?"

Blanton removed her glasses and rested them on the table. "The Catholic Health Authority has invaded my lab. I don't know how else to characterize it. This is an unprecedented, unprovoked invasion." She rubbed her eyes. "They are confiscating every tissue sample, every culture, and every file related to Graziana Contini. You were right, Becky. That's who she is."

"I don't understand. Who *is* she?"

"I have no idea, except that the Authority seems to be afraid of her." Blanton rolled her eyes at the absurdity of being afraid of an emaciated Italian. "They're making it impossible for us to care for her. The Authority is taking all of our records, all of our work regarding Graziana and her case. Why? Why would they do this? They say she's not important, and her case is not important. But she is important! I've seen it! Her blood has unique infection-fighting properties. I want to study it."

Yes, I thought. *This makes all kinds of sense: Graziana is an Eternal with profound healing capabilities. A scientist like Dr. Blanton is the perfect person to translate Graziana's disease-fighting characteristics into treatments and cures for other people. Yes, this could revolutionize medicine, as Lola had suggested.*

"Do you feel that the Catholic Health Authority is trying to prevent you from making a breakthrough discovery?" I asked in a way that sounded more like a statement than a question.

"That's absurd," Dr. Blanton said. "But that's exactly how it feels! My whole team has been arguing, stalling, and resisting the Authority all night. We even got Dr. Salzman out of bed to speak on our behalf. You know what he said, finally? He said that it all boils down to the fact that we're governed by the rules of the Catholic Health Authority. We either comply with their requests or we look for other jobs." Dr. Blanton said this with betrayal in her voice.

Dr. Salzman was a kind, grandfatherly pulmonologist specializing in pediatric care. He was in charge of running Holy Cross.

"Salzman didn't go to bat for you?" I asked. "Medicine comes before politics. Isn't that what Salzman always says?"

"I'm disappointed with him." Dr. Blanton put her glasses back on. She took a sip of coffee. This seemed to strengthen her to say what she would tell me next. "It gets worse, Becky. The Authority wants to transport Graziana to an undisclosed location later today. As her doctor, I told them it's out of the question. Moving her would jeopardize my patient's safety as well as the safety of people who might be exposed to the bacteria she carries."

"Move her?" I repeated, thoroughly baffled. "Why?"

"Why?!" Blanton slapped the tabletop with her palm. Her voice remained subdued, but the sound of her hand striking the table prompted a few people in the cafeteria to cast glances in our direction. "What do they plan to do with her?"

I had a terrible feeling that, whatever the Catholic Health Authority was up to, it was not in the best interest of the patient, and not conducive to the advancement of medicine.

"It smells fishy," I said.

Dr. Blanton leaned forward. "That's exactly what I think, too. I did something I might later regret, Becky. I made the call. I picked up the phone and called Atlanta. I ratted out the Authority to the CDC." She clenched her jaw as if assuring herself that her actions were justified. "No one can march into my lab and walk out with my case and my patient without a damned good reason. Federal marshals are up there right now making sure no one takes Graziana without CDC approval. Government officials are coming from Atlanta to review the case."

"Wow," I said, admiringly. "You escalated it."

"They escalated it," she countered. "Becky, they have a hazmat crew in my lab. They're swabbing everything as if we've had an outbreak of contagion. They're disposing of all the bacteria cultures we've been studying. It's like they want to destroy every possible biological trace of Graziana—every stray hair that might've fallen from her head, every dead skin cell of hers that might be in microscopic dust on the floor. It's as if they're trying to erase every trace of her from Holy Cross. Becky, it makes no sense."

To me, it made plenty of sense. The Authority knew about Graziana's healing powers, and felt threatened. The Authority was working to eliminate the threat by any means necessary.

Dr. Blanton slid her thermal lunch bag across the table toward me. She nodded at it. "That's for you," she said.

I didn't understand. "I already have one. We all have one, remember? It was the employee-appreciation gift last year."

"This one's yours," she said, calmly. "Take it home with you. Do not bring it back here until I ask for it."

"Oh," I said, dimly comprehending. "What's in it?"

"Your lunch, if anyone should ask. Don't open it. Don't handle the contents. Just take it home and keep it for me."

Blanton's assistant appeared in the cafeteria doorway, and urgently beckoned to her.

"What fresh hell?" Blanton said as she stood. "If I still have my job tomorrow morning, let's meet again for breakfast." As she walked past me, she leaned toward me and whispered: "Do not bring that bag back to campus until I explicitly request it."

When Dr. Blanton was gone, I contemplated the many disgusting things that might be in the thermal lunch sack. Biopsied bits of lung tissue. Bacteria cultures. Sputum samples. Suddenly, the cafeteria breakfast special was no longer appetizing to me.

I picked up the lunch sack and put it in my backpack. I followed the outdoor path back to Old Infirmary. I planned to call Marydale the moment I arrived in my office. Marydale and the nuns needed to know that Graziana was in grave danger.

When I sat down at my desk, I pulled Marydale's card out of my pack. I noticed that my computer screen was emitting a low-frequency, irritating hum. I hadn't even had a chance to turn it on. I checked the cables. Nothing looked amiss. I switched it on. The hum intensified. I switched it off again. The hum grew even more intense. I debated whether to call tech support.

I picked up my office phone to call Marydale. The receiver hummed in my ear. "Hummed" wasn't the right word. The sound was more like a low-pitched drone that, strangely, had the crazy-making qualities of a high-pitched, oscillating whine. I dropped the receiver.

I reached into my backpack to get my mobile phone. I couldn't turn it on. It was as if the battery was dead. I had just charged it. How could it be dead?

One of my co-workers appeared in my doorway. "Are you having computer trouble?" she asked. Everyone in our department was experiencing whiny computers.

I went to Lola's office. I leaned through her doorway and saw her at her desk. I quickly summarized what I had learned: "The Catholic Health Authority has commandeered Dr. Blanton's lab. Federal marshals are on campus to prevent the Authority from moving the quarantined patient. Officials from the CDC will be arriving soon," I said.

"Sit down," Lola said. "Close the door." I noticed that her office, too, was permeated by the increasingly annoying whine.

"Who is Graziana Contini?" Lola asked, with a look of bemused yet comic surprise. "I put her name through our allied-institution database yesterday, and all hell broke loose. Turns out, she's *wanted* by the Catholic Health Authority. Wanted, like some kind of criminal."

"She's an Eternal with amazing healing abilities," I said.

"I *knew* it," Lola said, excited and cautious at the same time. She tried to access the electronic screen on her desk. "Can you hear that? It's like a droning noise."

"My computer is doing it, too. Everyone's is."

"Wait," Lola said, perplexed. "Graziana's file is gone. It was here yesterday. Now the database no longer recognizes her name." Suddenly, her screen went dark. Lola rubbed her ears. "It's like the sound when you're under an electrical power line. Is it getting louder?"

"It's getting more annoying."

"I'm going to step outside," Lola said.

I was eager to find out what Lola had learned from Graziana's now-deleted file, but I was more eager to find relief from the nerve-grating sound.

The sidewalks around Old Infirmary were crowded with people. It looked as if we were having a fire drill. Everyone had come outside to get away from the noise. No one's mobile devices were working. We could see across the street that people were voluntarily evacuating the other buildings on campus. One of our interns told us that Technology Services was trying to locate the source of the problem.

I wondered if Dr. Blanton's lab was evacuated, too. What would they do with Graziana? I looked toward the research tower where Blanton's lab was located.

We had been standing outside for a few minutes when we heard sirens. Ambulances and firetrucks wailed toward us. With their lights flashing, police cruisers drove over the curb and onto campus. More emergency vehicles sped down the boulevard toward the main entrance of Holy Cross.

The growing crowd of our fellow employees murmured in concerned voices. Someone asked loudly: "Are we safe out here?"

"Stay calm," Lola said in a commanding voice to those nearby.

I thought about the lunch sack that Dr. Blanton had asked me to safeguard. I had left it in my backpack in my office. I wanted to keep it with me, just in case we were asked to evacuate the whole campus. While everyone was focused on the commotion across the street, I went back into the building. I noticed that the low, droning noise had stopped as mysteriously as it had started. I grabbed my pack and slung it over my shoulder. I went outside and told Lola that the sound had stopped.

I followed Lola back her office. She picked up her phone and called Salzman. "What's going on over there?" she asked. She looked at me as she listened. Her eyes widened. "I'll be right over."

"What?" I asked.

"Dr. Blanton was found unconscious in her lab. The patient we've identified as Graziana Contini is gone. Poof. Vanished. No one knows what happened." Lola grabbed her bag. "Let's go."

My heart pounded in my chest. Because of what had happened to Riva, and because Blanton had seemed so upset when I talked to her, I instantly concluded that Dr. Blanton had been a victim of foul play. I believed that the Authority had hurt Blanton and had kidnapped Graziana before the CDC officials could arrive from Atlanta. The Authority was erasing Graziana's presence from Holy Cross, and taking her away to an undisclosed location. Perhaps, I thought, they were planning to kill her, all for the sake of preventing a medical revolution.

On campus, I saw dozens of police officers and men in suits who looked like detectives. I thought about the night when police cars lit up Riva's street. I wondered whether all of this showy police activity would ever amount to anything resembling justice.

A half-dozen departmental leaders were engaged in an apparently contentious discussion in Salzman's office. Salzman saw Lola and a look of relief animated his face, as if the cavalry had arrived to save the day. Salzman closed the door on the meeting.

I walked down the corridor and stood with a group of staffers.

"Is Dr. Blanton okay?" I asked.

"Too soon to know," a lab intern said. "My boss said it looked like she had a heart attack."

Other people in the group murmured with disbelief and worry. "The police are reviewing the security video recordings," one woman said.

"The security cameras are monitored full time," another woman said. "The guards saw nothing. No one can figure out how a quarantined patient could leave the building without being seen by at least a dozen people."

I thought of the security camera in the cafeteria. Anyone reviewing the videos from that morning would be able to see Dr. Blanton and me together at breakfast. They would see Blanton giving me the thermal lunch bag. Eventually, someone was going to ask me about that bag. What would I do when the police, the CDC, or the Catholic Health Authority knocked on my office door?

I rushed back to my office. I pulled the thermal lunch bag out of my pack. I opened it and saw three glass tubes. I reached in and pulled them out. They were vials labeled *Graziana Contini*. These glass tubes held the Eternal's blood, laden with a virulent strain of tuberculosis. The liquid sparkled. It truly glowed.

I wrapped all three vials in a sheet of note paper and tucked them into a padded pocket of my backpack. I scrounged in other pockets of my pack. I found a few stray almonds and a crumpled wrapper from a candy bar. In another pouch, I found a coffee-stained napkin. I put these things into the thermal bag and placed it on the front corner of my desk. *If anyone comes looking for it, here it is,* I thought. *They can take it.*

I pulled out my phone. I saw that it was working again. I sent a message to Marydale: *Lunch where? When? Becky.*

I turned on my computer and checked the headlines. Local news sources were reporting a potentially explosive natural-gas leak at Holy Cross Health. According to the report, hospital employees were evacuated temporarily. Gas lines were inspected. No leaks were found. There was never any danger to anyone.

Nothing was mentioned about a missing patient carrying a deadly, communicable disease—and nothing about a doctor having a heart attack. *No wonder people don't trust the news media,* I thought.

My phone buzzed. I saw a reply from Marydale: "Zorba's Greek. Now."

I grabbed my pack and my car keys. My phone buzzed again. I saw a message from Mack: "Hey, Sis, I have my RV all gassed up and ready for a road trip to Denver. I can park on the street in front of your house. No worries. See you soon! With hugs of love, Mack."

He was coming for me. I imagined Mack jimmying a window to break into my house. He had done this once before. At the time, years ago, he and Riva were visiting me at Christmastime. I had lost my house keys. Mack had said, "No problem, Beck. Piece of cake." With unnerving dexterity, and using only a pocketknife and his bare hands, he popped one of my windows out of its frame and climbed into my house to unlock the front door from the inside. He popped the window back into place as if nothing had happened. If I hadn't seen him do it, I would not have suspected that he had broken into my home.

Riva was proud of him for "rescuing" me in this way. "Isn't he wonderful?" she cooed.

If Mack wanted to get inside my house, there was no way for me to stop him. My vision blurred. I felt paralyzed, like a terrified deer in the crosshairs of a rifle scope. Mack was coming for me. I was marked to be his next victim.

Suddenly, a wave of adrenaline hit me, as if my fight-or-flight response kicked in. I bolted out the door of my office. I drove fast and recklessly down Colfax Avenue toward Zorba's, and toward Marydale.

The restaurant was crowded as usual. The place had a distinctive aroma of French fries and coffee mingled with charred meat. The man whom everyone called Zorba flipped burgers over grease-fed flames. I apologized as I jostled through a group of people who were waiting for tables. I saw Marydale. Her face looked familiar to me yet miraculous, like suddenly seeing the moon rise on the horizon. She waved.

I slid into the seat opposite her. She reached over the table and squeezed my hand in greeting. This simple gesture instantly established a feeling of reassurance and trust. I felt as if I could tell her everything.

"Dr. Blanton has been hurt," I blurted. "Graziana Contini has been kidnapped. My creepy former-brother-in-law is planning to park a camper-van in front of my house, and stay with me indefinitely. I'm pretty sure that he plans to murder me. What's your news?"

Marydale blinked, as if needing a moment to consider my words. "He's not going to bother you," she said. "We'll cloak you."

Before I had a chance to interrogate her about this, she changed the subject.

"We have a complicated situation. The plan was for Lucina to liberate Graziana from the Catholic Health Authority. She has succeeded. Meaning, Lucina kidnapped Graziana from Holy Cross. Problem is, instead of bringing Graziana to the rendezvous point, Lucina has taken her somewhere else."

I was relieved to hear that Graziana had not been taken by the Authority. "Why is this a problem?" I asked.

"Because we need Graziana to open the Greenwell Portal. She is the only one who can do it. But now, Lucina has taken Graziana and disappeared with her."

"Why would she do that?" I asked.

"To protect her. We believe that Lucina is taking her to Rome to hide her from the Authority."

"Because the Authority wants to exterminate her," I said. "Because she is an Eternal and her biology can revolutionize medicine."

Marydale studied me for a moment. "Exactly," she said. "The upshot is that Graziana and Lucina have left us to figure out how to open the Greenwell Portal on our own. Angeline says that there must be a way that we can do it, otherwise Graziana and Lucina would not have left it in our hands."

"Who are you talking about when you say *we*?" I asked.

"Sisters of the Tower."

"You *are* a nun," I said.

"We're sort of like nuns," Marydale clarified. "With significant strategic and tactical differences. We use sonic technology as a diversion in order to liberate fellow sisters from hospital quarantine units, for example." She studied my blank expression for a moment. "The sonic disruption in your electrical system at the hospital this morning," Marydale said, confidently. "*We* did that. Actually, Bancroft did that."

I recalled the annoying hum and whine of the computers and phones at Holy Cross earlier that morning. "You're saying that a bunch of nuns subverted the hospital's security system and sneaked a patient past federal marshals?" I asked, skeptical.

Marydale nodded. "Intense, unpleasant sound is an overwhelming distraction."

The woman whom everyone called Mrs. Zorba placed two bundles of silverware wrapped in napkins on our table. "What do you want?" she asked in her no-nonsense way.

"Vegetarian plate and water, please," Marydale said. She had ordered exactly what I usually ordered.

"The same, please," I said.

Mrs. Zorba nodded and moved on to another table.

"I don't want to overload you with details," Marydale said. "We, the Sisters of the Tower, have a specific job to do. We need to make sure that the Greenwell Portal is opened. We have a narrow window of opportunity to accomplish this."

"Okay," I said. I didn't understand specifically what she meant, but I understood that she and the nuns had a pressing task at hand.

"We're connected with Eternals, but we are not the same as Eternals," Marydale said.

I recalled my dream of Graziana and Anna in the blizzard on Mount of the Holy Cross. "Is Anna an Eternal, too? Is Anna Prescott, Anna Ashton, and Anna Bartlet—are they—is she—the same person?"

"Yes," Marydale said. "Graziana, Anna, and Lucina are Eternals. We, on the other hand, are just Sisters of the Tower. Our order of contemplative warrior women was founded by Lucina."

Contemplative warrior women? I liked the sound of it. I wanted to know more. "Who is Lucina?"

"I'll get to that," Marydale said with an air of impatience. "Right now, we need to focus on the basics."

"Okay," I said, resolving to hold my questions.

"We, the Sisters of the Tower, are typical, flesh-and-blood, mortal women. We have received advanced training, and we have technology at our disposal. However, we don't have the spontaneous-healing capabilities of Eternals like Lucina. Eternals have a long, fascinating history. One day you will hear the stories. We can't afford to be distracted by history right now, though. We have a portal to open."

Lines around Marydale's eyes and across her forehead spoke of a woman nearing the age of 50 who had spent her life dealing with serious matters. She was attractive in my opinion, and I liked her. I knew little about her motives and plans, though, and about the role she expected me to play. Still, I was aware that I wanted to kiss her. I knew that my judgment was impaired by this desire. I knew that I was likely to give her the benefit of any doubt, and knowing this, I felt that I needed to be extra cautious.

"Becky, you and your sister," Marydale ventured, delicately. "You and Riva are perhaps the ones who can open the portal."

I remembered how, just yesterday, Marydale had listened to me ramble incoherently about Riva's death. "Riva is dead," I said. "How can she help?"

Marydale nodded as if she, too, wondered the same thing. "I'm not sure. For the past century, we've been relying on Graziana to open portals. I have no idea how it works. Angeline thinks that Graziana has selected you as her proxy. She transplanted her heart into you."

"No, not literally," I clarified. "It was just a dream. I don't have Graziana's actual heart." I fidgeted impatiently with my silverware.

I was tempted to mention the vials of Graziana's blood that had been given to me by Dr. Blanton. I looked at my backpack. The vials needed to remain a secret, I told myself. I had a duty to Dr. Blanton to protect them.

"We are pretty sure that the portal is in Rome," Marydale said. "We need to find it and open it within 72 hours."

"Rome, Italy?" I asked.

"Yes. We have to go to Rome."

Mrs. Zorba served us platters heaping with hummus, olives, cucumber, tomatoes, and fries. I felt guilty for ordering it. My stomach was clenched. I didn't feel like eating.

Mrs. Zorba put a slip of paper face down on the table and tapped it once with her finger as if punctuating the conclusion of her service at our table.

"Portal," I said, absently. The idea of running around Rome and looking for a portal struck me as ridiculous. I remembered a bronze-clad doorway at St. Peter's Basilica in Rome. It was a special entrance called the Holy Door. It was opened only during designated years of pilgrimage. I wondered whether the Greenwell Portal was a similarly huge, ornate doorway to which Graziana's heart was the sole key.

I watched as Marydale ate rapidly, as if we were in a hurry. I still couldn't find my appetite.

"Marydale," I said, as if pleading for her to indulge me. "I truly have no idea what's happening. I've been bombarded with a series of inexplicable, uncanny coincidences. I recently experienced a traumatic event—the death of my sister. I know that I'm in shock. I question my own perceptions, especially since my perceptions are at odds with the perceptions of other people, such as the Long Beach Police. Just this morning, something suspicious happened to a doctor at the hospital, and I can imagine only the worst. I feel that two women in my life have been victimized. People in positions of authority either don't care or are colluding in the victimization. I want to help you, Marydale. Really, I do. I'm not saying that *you* are crazy, but you do sound sort of crazy. I mean, *portal?* Portal to what?"

She wiped her mouth. She looked at my plate. "Eat while I talk," she recommended. "The portal is a doorway between our dimension and another dimension. It's a spillway between our present consciousness and vastly expanded consciousness. Think of it as a doorway between life and death. Or maybe."

She took a drink of water as she tried to think of a more accessible analogy. "Imagine finding a hidden doorway in your house that leads to a garden that you didn't know existed. You wouldn't be able to walk into the garden unless you found and opened the door." She paused to make sure I was following her.

"Okay," I said. "I can visualize that." I chewed a bite of food.

"Imagine a garden filled with wonderful fragrances, and soothing sounds—and beautiful rays of light," she continued. "The only way to let this beauty into your house, and into your life, is to open the door. This is our job, Becky. This is what the Sisters of the Tower do. We facilitate the opening of doorways like this for the whole world. Our job is to open doors so that the life-sustaining vibrations of the garden can be absorbed and shared by all."

"So you're opening doorways to other dimensions," I said, skeptically but not unkindly. "What's so special about Graziana's heart? Why is her heart the key?"

"All I know is that when she gave you her heart, she gave you a very sophisticated communications device. You will get messages. You will know things intuitively that you didn't know before." Marydale thought for a moment. "Maybe her heart will act as a kind of homing device and lead you to the portal."

This sounded both dubious and plausible to me at the same time. I wasn't sure what to believe. "I seriously doubt that the heart beating in my chest right now belongs to Graziana. It was a dream, Marydale. Graziana didn't swap our hearts. It's a metaphor at best. Besides, I can't flit off to Rome right now."

"You have no good reason to trust me, Becky. Still, I want you to know that we're in this together. You're not alone." She glanced at the clock on her phone. "We need to leave right now to catch our flight. All the arrangements have been made." Her tone was calm and competent, like a midwife issuing bedside directives while managing a difficult birth.

I tried to laugh but I knew she wasn't kidding about going to Rome. "I don't have my passport with me," I said. It was a feeble objection, but it was true.

"We have time for you to pick it up." She had opened her wallet and was selecting a few bills to pay for our lunch. "Maybe throw a change of clothes in your pack and we're good to go."

"Hold on, Marydale," I protested. "You can't just kidnap me the way you nuns kidnapped Graziana." I managed to offer a derisive laugh to punctuate the absurdity of the whole situation.

"Becky," she said. She looked at me with a combination of sternness and sympathy. "Yesterday, when you told me that your sister had died, I asked Angeline to check on her. I asked Angeline to see if Riva had a message for you."

"Check on my dead sister?" I asked, wondering what this might entail, wondering whether I should be amused or insulted. I braced myself to hear something trite and useless, such as, "Riva is in a better place now." What a cruel hoax, I thought. How cruel of so-called psychics and faith healers to claim that they can speak with the dead.

"Riva is fine," Marydale said, as if confiding this information to me. "She's in the archives right now researching her past relationships with Mack."

"Archives?" My eyes darted rapidly, as if struggling to see clearly. I remembered leaving the Long Beach Police Headquarters and walking to the bluff at Alamitos Bay. At that time, Riva "spoke" to me. She said that she had been looking up information "in the archives" about her relationship with Mack. How was it possible for Marydale or Angeline to know this? I had told no one about it.

"What was Riva's exact message for me," I probed. "What else did she say?"

Marydale shook her head as if preparing me for disappointment. "All she said was: *Little Boz.*"

Very few people knew this nickname. Mack was among them.

"Wait. You said that Riva was doing research on Mack. How do you know the name *Mack*?" I demanded. "I never mentioned his name to you. Did he put you up to this?"

A troubled expression clouded Marydale's face. "Becky, I know little about him. We've been warned that we should not even attempt to read his energy field."

"What does *that* mean?" I said, sounding petulant.

"It means, as your sister discovered, Mack is a fractured entity. He's like an army of fragments." Marydale said this with genuine sadness in her voice. "We have a plane to catch."

I agreed with her assessment of Mack, even though I wasn't sure what she meant. Still, I hesitated. Marydale could not have known about "Little Boz." She could not have known about Riva "visiting the archives" unless she had some way of communicating with my dead sister. I wanted to know more.

I was about to say this aloud when my phone vibrated with what seemed like an unusually strong jolt. I glanced at the screen. It was a message from Mack: "On the road now. I will be in Denver by morning. Please talk to me, Sis."

I pictured Mack driving his hideous murder-wagon through the blazing-hot Mojave Desert, singing along to the Dead Kennedys' *Holiday in Cambodia* at the top of his voice, his eyes wildly manic in anticipation of seeing me.

"Mack is coming for me, Marydale." I held up the screen of my phone to show her. "He wants me dead."

Marydale nodded. "Our best demonologist is handling it. You will be cloaked. Don't worry."

"Demonologist?" I repeated. "He's a typical, controlling, entitled man, not a demon," I said.

"Many men are the willing tools of malignant masters, and they don't even realize it," Marydale sighed impatiently. "Let's go now. You can talk to Riva about it yourself. When the portal is opened, you will be able to talk to her as easily as talking on the phone." She hedged a bit, "Well, at least that's what Angeline told me."

Oddly, I sensed that what Marydale said was true—ludicrous, but true. Faintly, I could hear Riva cheering me on: *Yes, Becky, go to Rome!*

"Let's go," I said.

I left my car parked on a leafy residential street just west of Zorba's. I assumed that it would be safe there. I might be "cloaked" by the demonologist, but my house was out in the open. *If Mack sets fire to my house while I'm out of town,* I thought, *at least my car will survive the inferno.*

Marydale pulled up to the curb next to my house. She left the engine idling. "Five minutes," she said as I got out of the car. "Hurry."

Inside, I grabbed my passport and tucked it into my backpack. I removed the paper packet of Graziana's blood-vials from the padded pouch. Notepaper opened like the petals of a flower, revealing a ruby-like gems. I couldn't just leave these vials behind, could I?

I imagined Mack breaking into my house and finding Graziana's blood. What might he do with it? He operated according to values and priorities that Riva and I could not intuit. He understood how our minds worked, which gave him a significant advantage. But his mind was unknowable to us. I couldn't guess—and didn't want to find out—what he might do with deadly blood specimens.

I decided to take the blood with me. But how would I explain it to airport security? I didn't want the vials to be confiscated or trashed. I glanced up at the fireplace ledge, and at the silent, imposing, red-velvet bag that held Riva's ashes. "Any ideas, Reeve?" I asked.

Yes, of course, I thought. *Riva, you're coming with me.*

I carried Riva's ashes to the coffee table. I loosened the metal clamp on the plastic bag of cremains. I pressed the vials of blood deep into the gray, sand-like ashes. I re-tightened the metal clamp, and packed it all neatly into the box.

I heard Marydale tap impatiently on the car horn.

I put Riva's ashes in my pack and zipped it closed. I had no idea what to expect, but I felt ready for anything. With tires squealing, Marydale and I took off for the airport.

11

BANCROFT'S HEX-READER

As Marydale drove away from my house and toward the airport, I realized how reckless I was being. I had jumped into a car with a stranger who planned to fly me to Europe. Did I truly believe that a group of renegade nuns needed my help to open a portal to another dimension? Did I truly believe that these nuns could communicate with my recently-deceased sister? It was far-fetched, certainly, but I *wanted* to believe it. *Just because it's far-fetched doesn't make it untrue,* I told myself.

The Long Beach Police found it far-fetched that Mack had killed Riva. People found it easier to believe that she had died haplessly of yoga than to see him as a murderer. It was bitterly ironic. Riva had been in mortal danger while in her own home, in the presence of someone whom she trusted with her life. I, on the other hand, was traveling to Rome with someone I had just met. *When is it ever safe for women to trust others?* I wondered.

"It would be worrisome for you to just disappear and not tell people where you're going," Marydale said, as if thinking what I was thinking. She asked me to take her phone out of her bag. She suggested that I copy our travel details and her contact information onto my phone and distribute it.

"Send it to your boss," she said. "And to your significant other, or your spouse, or whomever," she added, lightly, with what I perceived as a note of curiosity regarding whether such a person existed in my life. I noticed that she did not say "boyfriend" or "husband." I interpreted this to mean that she had surmised correctly that men played no role in my romantic life.

"I'm single," I confessed immediately.

"I, too, am recently single," Marydale said, as if she had been through a difficult breakup.

"Divorced?" I asked.

"We were never married," she said. "It was a long-distance relationship. She's French. It didn't work out."

I gasped involuntarily, audibly, and embarrassingly, as if I'd just received a windfall of good luck. "Me too!" I blurted. "I mean, about women. I'm not French. Obviously." I felt my face flush with awkwardness at my inappropriate expression of glee. "Not that I'm happy about your relationship breaking up," I explained, mortified by how reflexively uncool I was. "It's just unusual to meet single lesbians."

"You're about to meet a few more," Marydale said. She kept her eyes on the road. "You should send the travel information to your boss. Don't make her worry needlessly about you."

"Right," I said. I turned my attention to Marydale's phone and mine. Several questions percolated in my mind but I didn't say them aloud. I wondered, for instance, why celibacy was not expected of renegade nuns, and why lesbian relationships were acceptable, apparently, among renegade nuns. I wondered whether I might be eligible to become such a nun.

I interpreted it as a sign of Marydale's trust in me that she disclosed a tidbit of her romantic biography, as well as the fact that she allowed me to peruse her phone. She let me add myself to her contacts list and rifle through her calendar files to find our itinerary. Apparently, she felt that she had nothing to hide from me.

I wrote a message to Lola: "I am out of the office on an investigation related to Graziana and the Ashton Foundation. I will keep you posted." I attached a copy of our itinerary. I sent it.

It didn't occur to me that the Catholic Health Authority monitored all communications on the Holy Cross campus. I knew that administrators *could* eavesdrop on messages, but I didn't think about it at that moment. Maybe if I had been less flustered by my exchange with Marydale about our mutual, woman-loving singleness, I might've exercised caution. But I didn't.

Later, I would learn that this lapse had consequences. By mentioning Graziana, I guaranteed that my message would be flagged automatically by "sniffer" monitoring software at the hospital. This was precisely how the Authority had been alerted to Graziana's presence at the hospital in the first place. Lola and Dr. Blanton had searched in restricted Authority databases for records related to the name "Grazina Contini," thus inadvertently triggering an electronic silent-alarm system.

Further, the itinerary I sent to Lola was a goldmine for the Authority. I had handed them the precise address of a nun safe-house in Rome, along with Marydale's contact information and our exact travel plans. They knew where to find us. For the next several hours, however, I remained unaware that we were being hunted.

After I sent the fateful, soon-to-be-intercepted message to Lola, I wrote to Dr. Blanton: "Please let me know that you're okay. I'm going out of town. Details attached. Thinking of you."

I held my phone in my hand for a couple of minutes after sending the message. I hoped that it would buzz with an immediate reply from Blanton, but it didn't.

Marydale exited the highway at the rental-car-return ramp. I put my phone into my pack. I slid it into the same pouch where I kept the blue cloth-bound book that the nun in the Long Beach hospital had given me. I made a mental note to show the book to Marydale on the plane.

At the airport security checkpoint, a guard asked me to open my backpack. She examined the paperwork that was taped to the box of Riva's ashes. I feared that she would lift the plastic bag out of the box. I worried that the vials would shift and become visible. The guard swabbed inside the box to check for explosive chemicals. After a long minute, she said: "Sorry for your loss, ma'am. Have a nice flight."

Marydale gathered her scanned-and-approved bag from the security-line conveyor belt. "Your sister's ashes," she said in a concerned tone as we walked together toward the train. "Becky, I don't know what to say."

"There's nothing to say," I shot, sounding brusque. I knew that Marydale felt bad for me. I felt bad that she felt bad. I didn't know how to say: *Thank you for feeling bad for me. Your feelings are noted and appreciated, even though I don't know what to do with them.*

"We're made of stardust, they say," Marydale said to me as we waited for the train. I assumed that she was referring to Riva's ashes. "Or maybe we're made of starlight—starlight from Sirius, because it's the brightest. I don't know." She seemed discouraged that she couldn't find words to encourage me.

I smiled wanly, trying to appear encouraged.

Riva's vital organs had been given away to people who had needed them. Bits and pieces of her had been put into the files of the Los Angeles County Coroner's office. The rest of her body, along with the mysterious rosary from the nun, had been incinerated at 1,500 degrees. Whatever remained of Riva after this intense inferno had been pulverized during the cremation process. It amazed me that there was anything left of her at all. I thought about the grayish, sand-like grains. Riva's cremains didn't look like ashes; they looked like dirt from the moon, or maybe from the stars. I thought of Riva's happy, smiling face. Yes, I wanted to believe that her body had been converted into stardust. It would suit her.

Marydale and I were the last passengers in line to board the plane. We would be flying to Frankfurt to catch a connecting flight to Rome. Marydale turned her attention to her phone, which prompted me to do the same.

I saw that I had a reply from Lola: "I'm glad you're taking the vacation that I suggested yesterday. Safe travels." Without a doubt, she was the best boss ever.

I had a new voice message, too. It was from Dr. Blanton. Her voice sounded surprisingly relaxed and chatty, considering that the last time I had seen her, she was knotted with stress and frustration. Apparently, she had *not* had a heart attack:

"Becky, it's Ruth Blanton. I'm fine. Dr. Salzman put me on administrative leave. I'm at home now. Listen, I want you to keep that stuff safe—that stuff we talked about. Keep it safe. Will you do that? Remember when you asked me about spontaneous healing and glow sticks? Now I understand. I saw it with my own eyes. I saw a woman pick up Graziana from her bed. She literally breathed new life into her. The two of them dissolved together into a ball of light. It was miraculous! Am I crazy? The Feds think I'm crazy, but I saw it all. Salzman says it's head trauma. He says I fainted and hit my head. I don't remember fainting."

I had always known Dr. Blanton to be a rational-minded scientist. "Miraculous" was not a word she would use lightly.

Her description of Graziana's disappearance seemed to corroborate what Marydale had told me. Lucina had abducted Graziana under cover of some kind of magical-mystical hocus-pocus that allowed them to leave the hospital without being seen by federal marshals. Blanton's description supported this otherwise unbelievable story.

I wrote a quick message to her in reply. "You are not crazy. More to come." I turned off my phone for the flight.

Once we were in our seats, I asked Marydale: "When you said that men like Mack are compromised by demon masters, what did you mean?"

"Demons are not really our department," Marydale said. "It's a job for the Brothers of the Well." She saw that I was not satisfied with this answer. "There are a lot of theories," she sighed, as if it was wearying to consider them all. "You've heard about the degenerating Y chromosome?"

I was vaguely familiar with the theory because a prominent geneticist had written a well-publicized book called *Adam's Curse.* "You mean, the Y chromosome can't combine with the X chromosome to repair defects, and this is a problem because men feel threatened," I said. Over millions of years, supposedly, this inherent weakness could lead to the total extinction of the Y chromosome, which some pundits portrayed as an existential threat to maleness.

Marydale nodded. "Another way to look at it is that the Y chromosome is extremely vulnerable to a kind of behavioral hacking." Her tone made it clear that she was offering conjecture. "Some of the Brothers theorize that this so-called hackable-Y chromosome was deliberately bred into the human genome beginning around 200,000 years ago. By *deliberately,* I mean by use of violence and forced pregnancy."

"Awful," I grimaced. "But I don't see how a chromosome can be hacked."

"Genetic vulnerabilities can be exploited." She looked away as if trying to think of an example. "I'm not an anthropologist or a historian," she said. "But just look around at the world we're living in. Think of pornography—brutality dressed up as harmless fantasy. It's an effective way to exploit tendencies that, at some level, are presumed to be natural. Think about it. Once you introduce coercion and violence into a male's sexual fantasies, he's compromised. He is easily persuaded that coercion and violence are *natural* and *pleasurable*. Millions of men and boys enthusiastically train themselves to enjoy images of escalating objectification and degradation. They don't even know they've been hacked. They think they're exercising their rights and freedoms when in fact they're choosing to enslave their sexuality to sadomasochistic programming. Throw in drugs, alcohol, and females who have literally no choice but to bear offspring, including more hackable-Y babies, and we have a global orgy of male-propelled destruction on our hands."

Marydale paused to study my face, which must've registered surprise. I had never thought about pornography or its effects. "Sounds credible," I said. "As a theory."

"This is partly what we're talking about when we refer to the Captivity," Marydale added. "Brothers of the Well are resistance fighters against the Captivity, and so are we. But our job is less about fighting the darkness, and more about bringing the light."

I shrugged. "What does any of this have to do with demons and Mack?"

"Since the beginning of the Captivity, men have spoken about being hijacked by malign entities who make them do bad things against their will. They call these entities *demons* or *devils*,"

Marydale explained. "Truly, there *are* malign entities who look for human puppets. But these entities are powerless without the person's consent. Meaning, to do the work of a demon, you have to *agree* to do the work of a demon. You have to say yes. These entities win consent, usually with lies, flattery, and pretty promises. They promise increased power, or wisdom, or serenity. Almost always, the more lofty-sounding the reward, the dirtier the deal."

I was fascinated. "Do you think that Mack made a dirty deal with a demonic entity?"

Marydale nodded. "At the very least, he has allowed himself to be influenced by bad brothers."

I thought of Samadhi Masterson and Roy Dumond, the seemingly imaginary men whom Mack told Riva he admired.

Our plane started to taxi for take-off, offering an opportunity for us to pause our conversation. Marydale and I both sat back in our seats. I closed my eyes and tried to formulate questions that might sound intelligent.

I began as soon as our plane was in the air: "So, the Ashton Foundation, and you as a certified nurse midwife—you care about women's reproductive health *because*," I struggled to frame my question. "Because forced pregnancy is wrong for so many reasons?"

Marydale looked at me for a long moment. "Our primary concern is the liberation of humanity, starting with women," she said.

"Liberation from what?" I asked, at the risk of sounding obtuse.

"Liberation from the power-paradigm of domination and submission," she said.

"Which means *what*?" I ventured.

"We focus on consciousness-raising. You know what I mean by consciousness-raising?"

"Sure," I answered automatically. "Before people can be free, first they have to see that they are *not* free. They have to understand exactly how and why they are not free, and what they can do about it. That's, like, basic feminism."

Marydale nodded. "Except we're not talking about *that* kind of consciousness-raising. We're not talking about theory and education. Rather, we focus on opening broader consciousness through contemplative practice. We raise consciousness by raising the vibration of the planet. Opening a portal is like striking a tuning fork. It creates a vibration. People can harmonize. It resonates."

I didn't know what she meant. "Okay," I said, gently. "And Graziana's role in all of this—she has amazing healing powers, right?"

"It has to do with her genetics," Marydale said. "All I know for certain is that some quality or characteristic of her physical being is able to open portals. Just one cell of her skin is said to be extraordinarily potent. But there's more: Anna believes that Graziana's biology somehow holds the key to repairing and stabilizing the hackable-Y chromosome. I think Anna is toying with the idea of world peace through some kind of massive, instantaneous gene therapy."

I thought for a moment. "I can see why that idea would terrify the Catholic Health Authority. It almost sounds like *eugenics*, which no one can think about without also thinking about Nazis and the Holocaust."

Marydale shook her head sadly. "People claim that Eternals hate men, and that Sisters of the Tower hate men. It's a lie and a patriarchal reversal, of course. We believe that even the worst men are redeemable. Anna in particular has spent the past 240 years trying to save men from themselves."

This suggests that Anna is slightly older than the United States of America, I noted skeptically. I thought, too, about Riva and her dogged insistence upon seeing only the best in Mack. I wondered whether Anna was the same way, breaking her heart again and again to affirm the fundamental goodness of men who despised her.

Marydale leaned over and grabbed her bag from under the seat in front of her. She produced a device that looked like a phone. She handed the device to me. "What do you think of this?"

I touched the screen and examined it. It looked like a smartphone. I found nothing on it except a series of travel photographs featuring international cities, famous buildings, and stock-photo nature scenes such as sunsets and beaches.

"I don't get it," I said. "It's just a photo album. It's a waste of a phone."

"It's not a phone," Marydale said. "Do you know what a hex-reader is?"

The librarian in Long Beach had asked me the same question. At the library, I had used ordinary hex-reader software to extract a text document that had been hidden in a digital photo. The text was a story about Mary the Tower fleeing the Holy Land and teaching in the south of France. I was fairly certain that the story was a work of fiction authored by the librarian. Still, it struck me as an odd coincidence that Marydale, now, was asking me about hex-readers.

"Yes, I know what a hex-reader is," I said.

"This is the most amazing hex-reader ever," Marydale said admiringly. "Bancroft designed it. She's a genius."

Seeing Marydale's eyes light up as she spoke made me feel inexplicably envious of Bancroft, whoever Bancroft was.

"Look." Marydale pointed at what appeared to be a small camera-lens just above the device's screen. "This measures fluctuations in your irises. It also detects blood flow in your retinas. The device reads you as you read the device. It senses how the information you're seeing is resonating with you. It serves up content that's specifically tailored to your capacity to relate to it."

"Meaning what?" I asked, uncomfortable with the idea that a phone might be able to read my mind. "What's the point?"

"It shows you what you're prepared to know."

"I don't want an electronic device to decide what I'm capable of knowing," I retorted.

"You don't have to be defensive about it," Marydale said, somewhat defensively. "There are levels of code that can be revealed only when certain keys are present. This is not about whether you're a good person, or a smart person, or whether you're emotionally astute. The hex-reader is not *judging* you, Becky. The code is not judging you. It's impersonal. The code searches for keys and cues in people who are searching for information. Corresponding levels of code are unlocked according to the keys you have."

"Is it like a video game?" I asked, tentatively. "How do you get more keys?"

"It's not a game," Marydale said reverently. "You don't really get more keys. You already have the keys. Most of them are dormant or have not yet been revealed. It's an interactive process. As keys emerge, you discern messages from the content. These messages can, in turn, reveal more keys, and on and on. The hex-reader helps you to see what's in front of your eyes. Learning to see—to *really* see—is harder than it sounds. This device facilitates the process of stripping away filters that impede vision. Bancroft didn't invent the process, she just created this little gadget to facilitate the process."

"You mean, the process of revealing multiple messages encoded in hexadecimal language?" I asked, wondering if such a thing was possible. Knowing nothing about mathematics or coding, I was willing to believe that almost anything was possible. "How does it work?"

Marydale thought for a moment as if trying to find a way to explain. "Have you ever looked at the same picture again and again?" she asked. "You've seen it a dozen times. Suddenly, you notice something new, something you hadn't noticed before."

I thought of the old photograph of the mountaineering ladies, the one hanging near Lola's office at Holy Cross.

"What changed?" Marydale asked. "The picture? Your ability to see the picture? When you're able to look at one thing in a new way, you can start to look at everything in a new way. Bancroft's hex-reader is a teaching-tool for learning how to see."

"How do I run the application?" I asked as I tapped the screen to no avail.

"You just look at it. It will show you what you need to see."

Marydale left the device in my hands. She settled into her seat and closed her eyes.

As we flew from Denver to Frankfurt, I had no inkling that explosions and fires were happening in New York and Rome, and that Eternals and renegade nuns appeared to be under attack. I tried to look at Bancroft's hex-reader, but I think I slept instead. I dreamed of Riva. She was telling me secrets.

12

RIVA EXPLAINS

Little Boz, please don't worry that you're imagining my voice. It's me. Frankly, I worry that *I'm* the one who's imagining our dialogues. Am I making it up? From my perspective, I'm still here. You and everyone else have gone somewhere else.

It's not as if I'm hovering above you like an angel or a surveillance drone. I don't know where I am in terms of spatial coordinates. I just know that I'm *here*. I can perceive waves of light and sound. I can sense the changing expressions on your face. Somehow, when you talk to me, I can hear your voice.

Am I crazy?

I always thought we would end up as two little old ladies sharing a house on the coast of Maine or Nova Scotia—somewhere with rugged beauty—a place vaguely foreign to us, and magical. We saw a movie like this once in which Bette Davis and Lillian Gish played elderly, widowed sisters living in a remote, coastal cottage. I've forgotten the story, but I remember the setting. We would have spent our last days together on seaside cliffs watching for whales.

I want you to know that I did not "get myself killed." Choosing to be married to Mack is not the same as choosing to be murdered by him. My death was not my idea, and not my wish. Please resist all condolences that imply that I consciously or unconsciously chose the manner of my death. People might say that I had agreed to a "soul contract" with Mack, and that my murder was a predestined part of this agreement. This is victim-blaming. Not all deaths are part of a divine plan. My murder was Mack's plan—not mine, not God's. My murder was Mack's will, not the will of "the Universe." True, I bore the brunt of Mack's violence, but I bear no responsibility for his choices.

Still, I was involved with Mack. Why was I involved? Why are *you* involved? These are important questions to ask, Becky. I know you're already asking yourself, "Why Riva? Why did this happen to her?" Please resist sympathetic-sounding advice that counsels you against asking why. You won't necessarily find the answers you seek, but wondering why is the least you can do.

It's not true that people kill and are killed for no reason. There are reasons. I'm not saying that these "reasons" are reasonable or justifiable. Often, killers kill because they can. It's worth asking *why*. Why can they kill? Why can they get away with it?

The answers to these questions involve forces and influences that extend far beyond individual people and personalities. The answers extend beyond societies and cultures, too. You're going to laugh when I say this: the answers you seek are cosmic answers, Becky. Cosmic! I'm not kidding.

I loved Mack. I truly loved him. Maybe this is the biggest mystery of my life and death. I wanted him to know that I believed in him, so I didn't question him. My actions were based on love, not on fear or distrust. Even now, I don't think my approach was naïve, although I can understand why you always thought I was naïve. I tried to lift Mack up. I tried to show him his light. Love works miracles, Becky. It's not a mistake to believe this. It's not a mistake to stake your life on it.

"Don't throw pearls before swine." This is a famous saying that I've always found difficult to grasp. It means: don't give something of great value to someone who cannot appreciate it. If I made a mistake in my fundamental approach to Mack, it involves this lesson. To my way of thinking, everyone deserves love, whether they appreciate it or not. Taking it a step farther, people who appreciate love *the least* deserve it the most. Maybe this sounds like nonsense, but think of it as triage: the sickest people require the most care, and the strongest medicine. Likewise, the least-loving and least-lovable require the strongest love.

My mistake was believing that my love would make Mack a better person. I was always sure that I was a better person than he is. I still believe it. We are better than he is, Becky, and it's okay to say this. The world we want is far preferable to the world Mack wants. Mack works on behalf of the seductive Master of Fundamental Darkness. Sorry if this sounds melodramatic, but once you see him for what he really is, it all makes sense.

"Darkness" isn't even the right word. I'm not talking about an interplay of conceptual opposites, such as light and dark, or life and death. I'm talking about something darker than darkness, and *deathier* than death. I'm talking about extreme nihilism. I'm talking about stark, unrestrained, existential terror without end, and the impenetrable, toxic armor it wears as it walks through the world. This is what Mack has chosen for himself.

You should know that there is goodness in Mack. I've seen it. No one else has seen it, but I have, a very long time ago. He could never forgive me for seeing a glimmer of his tender, sweet vulnerability. Afterward, he fled into his toxic armor, and punished me ever since. He made a conscious, deliberate choice, Becky. He is the way he is because this is how he wants to be.

I mistakenly believed that, through our marriage, Mack would eventually become more like me. Remember the argument we had at Christmas? I said, "Mack is sad that you dislike him. Why can't you try harder to see the good in him?" We argued about it.

You said: "You can't rescue him from himself, Riva. He's not becoming more like you. You're becoming more like him."

I was really insulted! I was furious with you. Even after we agreed to drop the subject, my ears were ringing with what you had said. To be like Mack is to sneer at sincerity, introspection, and honest effort. To be like him is to reject everything that truly matters to me.

Now, I understand why I chose to be with Mack, and with Brad before him, and with Christian before him, and with Jim before him. Remember them? My litany of problematic boyfriends? Love was everything to me, Becky. But for these men, my love wasn't enough. They always wanted more. They accused me of withholding love. I needed to try harder. I needed to do better because, in their estimation, I was failing.

You know how I hated to fail. I refused to fail. Most especially, I refused to fail at loving someone. With Mack, I was fighting for ultimate success—as if a successful marriage with Mack would retroactively redeem all of my disappointments, wounds, and failures concerning men. I would prove once and for all the power and inevitable triumph of my ability to love.

My marriage to Mack was like an unusually long night in a casino. As years went by, I would win a little, and I would lose a little. The stakes seemed low. I had enough capital, enough love, to stay in the game indefinitely. I believed that, eventually, I would win everything. I didn't see that I was gambling with my life. All of a sudden, I realized that I had turned 50 years old. More than half of my life was gone. I had frittered it away on trivialities. I had never given birth to a child—although, ultimately, I felt a great sense of relief that I had not brought a defenseless child into Mack's world. I had a rewarding career and a strong business, true. But I had spent my adult life gambling away my heart, hoping for a "big win" that was never, ever going to be in the cards.

I wasn't giving up on love. I wasn't giving up on Mack. Rather, I was ready at last to find a new way to love. So much of love—or what I believed love to be—involved sacrifice and sublimating my own desires and concerns to something larger, something more important than myself. Love meant giving, waiting, enduring insult, hoping for better, and considering myself blessed with good fortune all the while, in spite of everything.

You would call it codependency or martyrdom, but it wasn't pointless martyrdom. The point, I believed, was to strip away everything false or provisional about myself—the qualities of my personality, my preferences and peeves, my whole identity—to reveal the *real* me, to reveal the deathless, immense joy that I knew to be my true self. I believed that this "center," this unconditional bliss, was everyone's true self.

After a decade with Mack, however, I began to wonder. I began to notice that, as I became less attached to my opinions and feelings, Mack became more attached to his. As I became more forgiving and less demanding, Mack became *less* forgiving and *more* demanding. I wondered whether I was doing this to him, making him worse, enmeshing him more deeply in his petty sense of self.

It occurred to me that, although my intentions were good, perhaps I was *using* Mack in some way. I was taking whatever he gave me, and using it to become more true to myself. I wondered whether I had inadvertently locked us into a zero-sum game in which my liberation entailed his deepening enslavement. It occurred to me that, perhaps, this wasn't an ideal arrangement for either of us.

It occurred to me that maybe I was doing love all wrong. I wanted to find a new way to love. I wanted to find a way to be in a relationship that was not contingent upon ideas of gain and loss, victory and defeat, domination and submission.

You'll be glad to know that I was planning to end my marriage. I had made the final decision soon after Christmas. I didn't want to tell you about it until the paperwork was signed. You would've insisted that I hire a lawyer before making any offers. Obviously, I would have handled everything differently if I had dreamed he might harm me.

He had been mulling what he called his "big project" for years, even before the time we went to Hawaii with you. Remember when I slipped and fell on my butt at Pahoa Hot Pond? Mack was thinking about his big project way back then.

He fantasized about it. He and Carleen Biggars talked about it, brainstorming ways to gain what they called "total freedom" by implementing Mack's big project. Mack had invested incalculable time and effort. Divorce would've ruined everything he had planned.

Carleen was leaving Mack, too. She told him that she didn't understand why he was stalling and delaying the project. She was unable to find a good nursing job in Southern California, she told him. She needed money. She was going to list her house for sale. She was going to sell everything and move back to Oklahoma where the cost of living was lower and more manageable for her than in Long Beach.

In Mack's mind, everyone was abandoning him—victimizing him—therefore, all of his actions were justified.

A few days after my death, Carleen put her house on the market. She suggested that Mack follow her to Oklahoma and live with her. "You'll need someone to take care of you now that Riva is gone," she'd said. Carleen knew exactly what Mack had done to me, but she wasn't afraid of him. She was confident that she was "the brains" and he was just "the brawn." Therefore, if an "accident" were to befall Mack in Oklahoma, it would ultimately be profitable for her.

Mack knew what Carleen was thinking. He's devastatingly perceptive when he wants to be. After Christmas, for instance, he saw that I had changed. I hadn't said anything yet about my decision to divorce him. But I had changed. Mack saw that I was ready to forgive him.

Forgiveness doesn't mean what you think it means. Forgiveness doesn't mean releasing him from guilt and obligation. It means releasing *myself* from guilt and obligation toward him. I owed him nothing. I wished nothing for him. I had no hopes or expectations toward him. I had neither charity nor ill-will to extend to him. This is what forgiveness really means, Becky. It means releasing yourself from every mental, emotional, physical, and spiritual cord that binds you to a person. It means severing every tentacle of a person's grip on you. It means to be free in every sense. This is what I did with Mack.

I thought that I had crafted a divorce offer that Mack wouldn't refuse. I was going to give him the house and everything in it. I assured him that nothing in his life needed to change. He could continue to do whatever he wished. All I wanted in exchange was to continue my life away from him. I hadn't decided where I would go. I thought about Denver, but I had my clients and colleagues in Long Beach to consider.

I presented this offer to Mack in the days before he implemented his big project. I thought he accepted my proposal graciously. I honestly believed that we would part amicably and relatively effortlessly. I couldn't have known that

Mack had spent the past several years remodeling our house, installing video cameras, and mentally rehearsing scenarios for his project.

I could not have known that many times, over many years, he'd had opportunities to "facilitate" my accidental death. He had always chickened out, or fate had always intervened. Remember the *other* times when I went to Hawaii with him— the two times when you weren't there with us? Mack would try to find the most secluded beaches to take me swimming. I don't know why, but I instinctively refused to get in the water with him. Instead, I joked that I would stay on shore so I could summon help in the event that he was swept out to sea. The surf was very rough at these beaches. He probably wanted to drown me, but I unwittingly failed to cooperate.

He would insist on going hiking in Hawaii, too, saying that he wanted to find a cliff that overlooked the ocean. Fortunately, we never found a panoramic, cliff-side view that wasn't crowded with tourists. Always, Becky, he was looking for an opportunity to kill me in a way that he believed would be ruled accidental.

As it turns out, his big project evolved over the years. After much consideration, he decided that my accidental death would not provide him with the "total freedom" he wanted. He would go back and forth in his thinking, unable to commit to one plan. He would have good times, which distracted him from his planning. For instance, remember when he started making heavy-metal jewelry in the garage? More recently, he had become interested in martial arts, loving to dress up in his karate uniform, pretending to be Bruce Lee or some-such. During these highs, Mack thought that maybe he could be "free" without completing his big project. But these highs didn't last for long.

The idea of manipulating a video-surveillance system had come to him while he was watching one of those forensic-investigation TV shows. He spent thousands of dollars testing different cameras and surveillance systems in our house, and remodeling the yoga room to install an exterior door. I always thought it was weird that he wanted to put cameras in certain locations, but not in others. Mack claimed that the video cameras would allow him to remotely check on Caldo when the dog was home alone.

I asked no further questions. I thought it was just another expensive, fruitless hobby that Mack would eventually discard, as was his way. The whole time, right in front of me, and with my money, he was working on his big project.

Why do people find murderers so interesting? Why do countless books and movies portray murderers as celebrities? As if murderers are fascinating, unfathomable anomalies of the human species! They're not. In reality, their self-absorption is boring. Their self-justifications are ultimately petty and circular. Their cruelties may shock the conscience, but there is nothing novel or creative about harming people.

Remember when I told you that Mack was obsessed with killer Joran van der Sloot, the man who notoriously got away with "disappearing" a Dutch woman who was on vacation in Aruba, only to be convicted years later for a sloppy, savage murder of another woman in Peru?

"Mack *admires* him?" you asked, incredulous.

I explained: "No, he hates him! He thinks Joran is a dumbass, and deserves to be in prison for being stupid."

Mack believed that he would be a much better killer than Joran. You and I laughed at this. We laughed because this kind of thinking is absurd to us. We laughed because we do not understand that many, many people fantasize about committing murder and getting away with it. People like us, people who are incapable of empathizing with what it means to have no empathy, mistakenly romanticize murderers as damaged heroes. We think that even the worst-of-the-worst can be redeemed if given enough love and understanding. Please count my death as compelling evidence to the contrary. I *want* to say that there's still hope for Mack, but I'm no longer certain.

Mack is what I call a light-devourer. He's like an insatiable parasite. He saps your light and leaves you in darkness while he moves on to another host. From the parasite's perspective, he's not *trying* to kill you. He's just trying to thrive. It's nothing personal. Your pain makes you more nourishing to him. He enjoys your pain, but he enjoys *everyone's* pain. It's not about you.

At the risk of sounding unjustly pejorative, I'm tempted to say that Mack and his master are like a disease. Like tuberculosis, maybe. With tuberculosis, the human immune system reacts to infection by trying to surround and neutralize the bacteria, forming little capsule-like lumps called *tubercules*.

This is sort of what I tried to do with Mack. I tried to coat him with good intentions and positive vibes to make him less harmful to me and to others. Mack outsmarted my immune defenses, I suppose. He's an infectious agent that can lay dormant for years, or he can sweep through a host-body and kill it in a matter of days.

This is an inexact analogy, of course, but maybe it gives you a better idea of what you're dealing with when you're dealing with Mack. There's no reasoning with an infection. There's no appeasement. It mutates in response to your attempts to contain it. It hides for years before roaring to life with infectious fury. It learns from your defenses and hides again, changing to become harder and harder for you to neutralize.

The disease has been with us always, since ancient times. We will never be rid of it. It cannot be killed once and for all. Rather, we must find new ways of living in spite of it.

Also—don't forget that Mack is good at camouflage. It's the dominant motif of Mack's personal aesthetic. He wears camouflage-patterned clothes. He buys camouflage-patterned accessories. He painted the inside of our garage with camo paint. Camouflage makes it hard for you to see contrast and depth, confusing your perceptions. Mack does this, too.

Mack doesn't fool everyone, though. The police know that something isn't right about his story. My surgeon in the emergency room told the police that, judging from the severity of my wound, a lot of blood would have been spilled wherever the injury had happened. And yet, paramedics saw very little blood at the scene. They described the amount of blood in terms of mere drops. Why wasn't the laceration in my scalp gushing blood all over the floor when the paramedics arrived? Why was there no blood on my clothes? The police wonder about this.

The police know that Mack could not have returned to the house from walking Caldo, bludgeoned me, and cleaned up all the blood before calling the paramedics. He had only a few minutes to do all of this, and it would have been impossible.

Plus, my tablet device was used to log on to a yoga website while Mack was away from the house walking Caldo. Police assume that I was the person who used the device. This would mean that I was alive and well in the house while Mack was out walking the dog. But I wasn't. I distinctly recall leaving my tablet device on the hutch near the kitchen. I didn't move it from that spot. And, actually, the police found it there when they searched the house.

It doesn't surprise me that the police are having a hard time piecing together what happened. I haven't figured it out, either.

Mack liquefied my brain with a devastating blow to my head, so that's my excuse for being an unreliable witness to my own death.

I was there at the time, but I don't know exactly *where* I was. I don't know exactly *what* happened to me. I did not understand that I had been hit. Does this make sense? My reaction was, "What?!" I don't recall feeling physical pain. I have a sense that two men were there with me. I don't know these men. This puzzles me. Who are these men? Mack did this to me, Becky. Have no doubt. So, again, who are these men?

At the risk of sounding self-contradictory—and to confuse matters even more—I know with total certainty that Mack did not mean to kill me. He did everything intentionally, yes. He killed me, yes. But killing me was not his intention. In fact, my death ruined his big project! This fact, too, puzzles me.

I saw my blood in pools and rivulets—so much blood you wouldn't believe that a person could contain so much blood. Caldo had tried to protect me. He was barking. The smell of blood frightened him. There was blood on his snout and on his paws. He ran in circles, spattering blood. Mack grabbed him. I heard Caldo shriek. My most urgent priority at that moment was to summon the police.

Somehow—I don't know how—I went to the police headquarters building in downtown Long Beach. I wandered among desks and cubicles where detectives worked. I was wearing a hospital gown. My hair was wet, as if I had showered. All the blood had been washed away. Because there was no blood, I worried that the police would doubt me. They walked past me as if I wasn't there.

"Excuse me, I beg your pardon," I said. "I would like to report an assault, and an incident of cruelty to my dog." They ignored me.

At last, a woman saw me. She was slender and willowy with long iron-gray hair that fell almost to her waist. Her skin was brown. The corners of her eyes were creased as if she'd spent years in the desert sun. She introduced herself to me by the name Bancroft.

She asked if I needed help. I told her that I didn't know what kind of help to request. She suggested that I do some research regarding my situation. She told me how to read the archives of light. So I went to the library. When I say library, I mean something more like a psychedelic waterfall of intensely-colored light that hums like a beehive. Everything you might want to know is there, encoded in frequencies.

I want to know exactly what happened to me to cause my death, but I don't want to face it alone. I want you to be with me, Little Boz. I want us to be together when we find out the grisly facts.

Bancroft said that there is a way for you to come visit me, and safely return to where you are. Opening the Greenwell Portal will allow you to do this. The portal is a passage from your dimension to mine and back. Think of it as a doorway from one room in your house to another. You could go through a wall to get to another room, but why bother when there's a door? This "doorway" analogy isn't exactly right. It's not as if you and I occupy separate rooms, or separate layers of reality, or different realms. I'm right here with you. We're all right *here*. Open the portal and you will see for yourself.

13

DETOUR

I awoke to a flight attendant offering me a hot, damp towel. I groggily swabbed my face and hands. The cabin was bright. The plane would be landing in Frankfurt soon. Marydale was wide awake. A map was open in front of her on her tablet screen. She noticed that I was awake, too.

"We'll be looking for a tunnel or passageway in Rome," Marydale said. "I've identified two areas where I think we might find our portal." Marydale turned the screen toward me. "This is where we should look first." She pointed at what appeared to be a church building located in the heart of Rome near the Pantheon.

I leaned toward her. "Santa Maria Sopra Minerva," I said, reading the map. "What's so special about it?"

"It's built on the site of an ancient temple complex," she said. "Thousands of years ago it was devoted to the great goddess."

"Oh," I sighed. I was annoyed by nouns that were diminished by the suffix -ess to make them sound somehow ladylike. Why did people insist on *gendering* deities and spirits? Unless there were a bunch of spirits or "energies" running around with sexually-dimorphic genitalia, how could the concepts "male" and "female" be applicable? If a spirit doesn't have a body, how can it have a sex? To me, it made no sense to describe the formlessness of spirit with form-specific terms.

"Great goddess," I said, mildly sarcastic. "Please tell me that the renegade nuns aren't into goddess worship."

"We aren't into any kind of worship," Marydale said, as if I had missed the point. "Ancient temple complex," she repeated. "Honoring the great womb, the great mystery of life and death. This *must* be a portal—or a portal cluster—with hidden tunnels surrounding it."

I didn't know what she meant. "Maybe," I said. "But according to the map, it's also a Minor Basilica of the Roman Catholic Church." I read aloud the descriptive text on the map: "It houses the relics of Saint Catherine of Siena." I looked quizzically at Marydale.

Marydale turned the screen to face her. She plotted a route on the map. "Often, when the church becomes aware of a portal, they build a structure around it to seal it and control who can access it. That's exactly what they did here." She read a block of text next to the map. "It says that the site was Christianized in the Eighth Century. *Christianized.* That's a euphemism for the church misappropriating power that doesn't belong to it." She read aloud: "*The gothic structure that now stands on the site was built by Dominicans.*" She turned and looked at me. "*Dominicans*, Becky." She said this as if Dominicans bore a particularly heavy burden of responsibility. "It adds up. What if the Greenwell Portal—or a path to it—is under there somewhere?"

"I don't know," I said, meekly. I could see that Marydale was passionate about exploring her hunch. I didn't know anything about Dominicans or Christianizing. "Maybe, but," I said tentatively. I remembered visiting the Pantheon one summer when I was a teenager on a school trip. I remembered teeming crowds and unrelenting mid-July heat. "Do you honestly believe that a doorway to another dimension would be located right next to one of the most popular tourist attractions in the world?" I asked, doubtful.

"Yes, I do," Marydale sniffed. "If you get any brilliant flashes of intuitive guidance, please alert me."

I exhaled a soft laugh. She smiled a little.

"If Graziana actually replaced my heart with her own," I began in tone of mockery. "And if this heart is supposed to act like a homing device that will lead me to the portal...." I paused.

Marydale was looking directly into my eyes. Hers were clear and perceptive. I didn't feel right using a mocking tone with her.

I began again: "Look, all I know is that my heart is telling me nothing."

"Nothing?" she repeated, studying my face. "Your heart offers no actionable intelligence?"

I wondered for a moment if we were still talking about the portal. "My heart is speechless," I said.

"Maybe when we get to Rome it will start talking to you," Marydale said. Her gaze fell to the screen in front of her.

I sat back in my seat. I glanced at Bancroft's hex-reader on my tray table. I picked up the device and handed it to Marydale. "I'm sorry I didn't get a chance to use this," I said. "I dozed off." Marydale said nothing as she took the device from me.

"I did have a weird dream, though," I said. "I felt as if I was talking to Riva. She said that I need to help her find out what happened to her." I paused for a moment, trying to recall details. "If we open the portal, I'll be able to see her," I said, hesitating, knowing how strange this sounded. "Is this possible?"

"That's sweet," Marydale said, sincerely. "It's nice that you have someone who is trying so hard to reach you, and that you're trying to reach her, too. A lot of times with death, it's as if one of you has moved away to Paris. You still think about each other, but staying in close communication has become too impractical."

I didn't quibble with her analogy. I wondered whether she was thinking of her French former-girlfriend, though, rather than someone who was actually dead.

After the plane landed, we walked through a series of hallways to the passport-control checkpoint. Mobile devices were strictly prohibited as we went through this process, so we left them in our bags. Eventually, Marydale led us to a restaurant on a concourse. We sat down. We noticed that everyone was looking intently at a television screen on the wall behind the bar. Apparently, buildings were burning in Manhattan and Rome.

I heard Marydale say "oh" in a way that conveyed both recognition and alarm. She stood and walked toward the screen. I reached for my phone to check the headlines.

Something strange happened. The screen of my phone blasted me with a burst of intense, purple light. The device felt hot, as if it had burned out.

Marydale grabbed the phone from my hands. She rifled through her bag for her phone and computer.

"Is everything okay?" I asked, idiotically.

"Follow me," she said.

Marydale dropped our electronic devices into a trash bin. "Trust me, Becky," she said. "They're useless now anyway."

I wanted to object, but I really did trust her. It was possible for someone to ping our phones, access our data, and use our devices to snoop on us, I knew. But who would bother to do such a thing?

We walked rapidly down the concourse. I recalled the dreams that I'd had right after Riva's death—Riva and I would be surprised to run into each other in an airport. She would disappear as soon as we remembered that she was dead. I half-expected to see her in Frankfurt.

At the gate of a French airline, Marydale rushed toward the counter. "Give me your passport," she said. I fumbled for it. In what sounded to me like fluent French, Marydale asked the gate agent for two tickets. The agent tapped on a keyboard. Marydale handed him our passports and spoke urgently. She asked me to unzip my pack, showing the gate agent the red-velvet bag that held Riva's ashes. I got the impression that Marydale was saying something about a funeral. The agent accepted Marydale's credit card. He spoke into a phone. A few moments later, he handed Marydale two boarding passes.

We boarded an immediately-departing flight to Marseille, France. It was a flight that Marydale had taken several times in the past. Her former romantic partner, the Frenchwoman, lived in Marseille. Marydale explained all of this to me in a calm, quiet voice, as if everything would be fine because she knew what she was doing.

"Things have taken an unexpected turn," she admitted apologetically after we took our seats. "Just give me time to think."

A flight attendant handed a newspaper to Marydale. A photo of a burning building was featured on that morning's front page.

"There were two explosions," Marydale said aloud, softly, translating the news for me. "The blasts happened simultaneously. International authorities are blaming an obscure terror cell. They have named the terrorists as Anna Bartlet, an executive in charge of New York's Ashton Foundation, and Graziana Contini, a fugitive who escaped from police custody in Rome."

My eyes opened, wide and mystified. "What?" I whispered, leaning closer to Marydale, trying to read along.

"Authorities say that Bartlet and Contini were planning separate attacks on unidentified targets in New York and Rome. They were killed when the bombs they were preparing exploded. No one else was injured. Police agencies are calling it a stroke of good luck."

"That's ludicrous," I hissed.

Marydale placed her index finger over her own lips, as if imploring me to stay composed. "The building that's burning in Rome," she whispered. She pointed to the front-page photo. "That's where we were going, Becky. That's the address you sent to your boss. It's one of our safe-houses."

"What? *Who?*" I didn't know how to construct my question. I suspected that I already knew the answer. I recalled what Dr. Blanton had told me—the Catholic Health Authority had wanted to move Graziana to another facility. The Authority had wanted to erase all traces of her at Holy Cross. They had killed her, of course. Was this so-called bombing just a ruse to cover up her murder? Had they murdered Anna Bartlet, too?

I recalled how credulous and bumbling the Long Beach Police had seemed regarding Riva's murder. They seemed to believe everything that Mack told them. Perhaps this was a common characteristic of *all* police agencies across all time and space: they served the seemingly powerful, and those whose stories they wished to believe at the expense of the seemingly vulnerable, and those whose stories were nuanced and complicated. If a powerful organization like the Authority wanted to kill two relatively-inconsequential women, they could get away with it easily, I felt certain.

"The Authority did this," Marydale said, definitively. "They must be monitoring communications at Holy Cross. To involve international police and news agencies like this—only the Authority would be able to pull it off. This is their doing."

"But why?" I asked. "It's a bewildering story. These alleged bombs accidentally destroyed *whole buildings* in major cities? But miraculously only the bombers themselves died? And these bombers were immediately identified as female terrorists who were terrorizing for no particular reason? It makes no sense. Why would the Authority concoct this implausible scheme, and then actually detonate bombs? Just to cover up the fact that they murdered two Eternals? *Eternals*, about whom the general public knows nothing in the first place. Why call attention to these women in such a dramatic way?"

"To disgrace Anna's name. To disgrace the whole Ashton Foundation. To disgrace Graziana and the medical advancements that may come from the study of her biology," Marydale offered, unsure. "They did it to discredit everything that Anna and Graziana are, and to ruin everything that they've accomplished. Once you're branded as a terrorist in the eyes of the whole world, it's hard to come back from that."

I thought for a moment. "*Come back* from that?" I repeated. "They're dead. They're not coming back."

"No, they're not dead," Marydale said, sounding certain. "Obviously, the Authority *thinks* they're dead, which is interesting. Or, maybe they *hope* they're dead. Regardless, Anna and Graziana are still alive in the conventional sense. They still inhabit this dimension of existence in their physical bodies."

"How do you know?"

"Bancroft would know," Marydale said. "If they were dead, Bancroft would've sent a different signal." Marydale saw that I didn't understand. "Your phone," she said. "I saw how the screen flashed in your eyes. Bancroft did that."

I blinked. "How did Bancroft access my phone?"

"When you copied the itinerary from my phone to yours, you were linked to our network."

"You mean, I unwittingly imported a renegade-nun spy tool."

"It's a good thing," Marydale insisted. "Bancroft disabled our devices. That's a signal. It means that all further communications must take place face-to-face with no electronics. Our mission is still in progress. If Eternals had been killed, there's a completely different protocol that would've gone into effect. We still need to find the portal and open it."

I rubbed my eyes, feeling confused, tired, and hungry. "Are we still going to Rome?"

"I think so," she said with a strained smile. "We need to focus on the portal, Becky. Please try to tune into your heart. Be silent. Be still. Let it speak to you."

This was corny advice, but Marydale said it earnestly, as if she truly believed that my heart was like a radio receiver.

"Just one question," I said, "before I settle into silent stillness. Someone—the Authority, perhaps—is setting off explosions. Two Eternals have been named as terrorists in the press. You said that the Authority must've intercepted my message to Lola. Does this mean I'm under suspicion now? Can I expect that my name, too, will be associated somehow with this ludicrous, non-existent, terrorist-bomb plot? And if someone has been tracking us—" I paused. "Are we in danger?"

"Possibly," Marydale said. "That's why we're changing course. I'm hoping that we can open the portal before this all blows up."

"Great," I said.

When we landed in Marseille, I half expected that we would be met at the airport by sinister-looking Catholic clergymen. I had no idea what the agents of the Authority might look like. Would they be wearing aviator sunglasses and tailored suits, or tropical shirts and baseball caps? I scanned the people in the airport. No one seemed to be paying particular attention to us.

We queued up at a taxi stand outside the terminal. "It's usually windy or rainy at this time of year," Marydale said. "We're lucky with this warm weather." Moments later, we were in a cab.

Marydale said nothing to the cab driver about being in a hurry. Even so, he drove as if we were under pursuit. We roared up a hill, erratically changing lanes, nearly kissing the bumpers of other cars. I glanced at Marydale to see whether she shared my panic.

"This is normal," she said, nervously.

The cab shot through a tunnel. The blue Mediterranean Sea spread out in front of us. I could see cargo-ship terminals and rocky, mountainous coastline. We sped through a residential area that overlooked a densely populated basin. I saw ochre-colored stucco houses with barred windows, palm trees, and brightly-blooming bougainvillea. Marseille reminded me of Los Angeles, except that I had never seen any California driver so expertly and terrifyingly negotiate heavy traffic in Los Angeles. After several hairpin turns and near-scrapes with scooters and motorcycles, our cab came to a sudden halt at the curb of a sidewalk café.

I followed Marydale through the small, cozy café. I smelled hints of fresh greens, fennel, garlic, and the promise of something delicious browning in an oven, mingled with traces of coffee and ever-so-faint tobacco smoke. It felt as if we had walked into someone's home. We walked toward the back of the café, toward what I assumed was a back patio. A door slammed shut behind us. We were in a narrow alley behind the café, amid the acrid stink of garbage and rotting fish.

"Almost there," Marydale said.

We exited onto a residential street. We walked fast past houses hidden behind high walls and metal gates. Sun sweltered in the clear sky. I was confident that no one could have followed us from the airport, but Marydale was being extra cautious. I felt my patience fraying.

"Can we stop for coffee?" I asked.

Marydale reached over and pressed the palm of her hand against my hip, as if pushing me onward. It was a gesture that presupposed an intimate level of personal familiarity, which I welcomed. After a moment, she withdrew her hand. This small, supportive gesture made me want to toughen up. I resolved to keep up with her without complaint.

We turned down another street lined with parked cars and motorcycles. We stopped at a gate. Marydale entered numbers onto a keypad. "Wait," Marydale said as she slipped through the gate. In an instant, she re-emerged with two helmets. She handed one to me. She walked to the curb and sat astride a powder-blue motor scooter. I stood awkwardly, not sure what to do. Marydale secured her bag in front of her. She patted the seat behind her, motioning for me to get on the scooter.

"Put your feet on the foot-pegs," she said. She reached back and pulled my hand around her waist. "Hold on to me."

The motor sputtered and jolted as Marydale pulled away from the curb. I wrapped my arms around her. I closed my eyes as we lurched into traffic at a cross-street. I felt the scooter swoop, sway, and strain to accelerate. I heard the roar of other vehicles around us. From time to time I heard honking horns and shouts in French. I didn't know whether we were the targets of these warnings and protests. With my body pressed against Marydale's, I honestly felt that it would be okay if I died.

Eventually the traffic noise grew less angry. I felt as if we were cresting a hill. I opened my eyes. The dazzling sea glittered in front of us. We descended into a small harbor crowded with fishing boats. A bridge with three large arches stood at the mouth of the harbor. Beyond the arches, chalk-white islands dotted the bay.

Marydale pulled the scooter to a stop near a boat dock.

On the dock, two men sat at a table, absorbed in a game of chess. Curls of cigarette smoke rose around them. The men looked up at us when Marydale cut the motor. "*Bonjour*," she said. The men squinted at her, curious. Their tanned faces were weather-beaten. Marydale asked them a question in French. They acted as if they didn't understand her.

She spoke again. This time, she said the name "Lucina." The men's faces lit up with recognition. They smiled and spoke warmly, as if offering their compliments.

Marydale pointed in the direction of the sea. She was asking the men for a favor. They nodded and stood up from their game, apparently eager to oblige. Marydale handed the scooter key and helmets to one man. The other man climbed into a motorboat.

The boat was a mere fifteen feet in length, and open to the elements except for a small covered area at the bow. The man took his place at the wheel behind a cracked, plexiglass windscreen. He started the engine. It burped in the water.

I stepped into the boat. The deck lurched under my feet. I quickly sat down next to Marydale. "Where are we going?" I asked, raising my voice above the noise of the motor.

"To Rome," she said.

I tried to imagine the geography of the Mediterranean. Certainly, Rome was at least a thousand miles from Marseille. We chugged into the harbor and under the arches of the bridge. As we passed the breakwater, the boat accelerated.

We pitched and rolled as we sped into the bay. Marydale noticed that I looked queasy. "Turn around and look at the shore," she shouted. "Focus on a stationary point."

I turned to look behind us. A beautiful church towered above us on a hill. I focused on the golden statue atop the church. I later learned that this was the Catholic basilica of Notre Dame de la Garde, or "our lady the protector." The seaside mountain of limestone on which she stood had been a place where people offered prayers and tokens of gratitude since ancient times. Under the church, I later learned, was a major portal—although, not the Greenwell Portal.

Our boat slowed. I heard someone in the distance shout. I turned to face the bow. There, in front of us, I saw a massive, gray yacht, almost 200-feet long with a fast, streamlined look. This, I presumed, would be our ride to Rome.

14

LUCINA'S YACHT

As Marydale led me to our cabin below decks, she told me that the vessel was owned by Lucina. The name of the yacht was *La Bonne Mère*, registered in the principality of Monaco. For my job, I routinely conducted research regarding the assets of wealthy people. For a yacht to be registered under the Monegasque flag, I knew that the owner had to be a resident or citizen of Monaco, a country with fewer than 50,000 inhabitants. I knew, too, that a conservative rule of thumb for estimating the price of a yacht was one million dollars per meter of length. *La Bonne Mère* was 50 meters, I guessed—meaning an estimated cost of $50 million.

Marydale told me that the vessel was crewed and cared for by a full-time staff of twelve women, all of whom were Sisters of the Tower. "Twelve crewmembers in the winter," Marydale clarified. "In the summer, there might be as many as 30 sisters working here, depending on whether Eternals are traveling."

At the moment, including the winter crewmembers, Marydale, and me, there was one other woman aboard the yacht—a woman whom Marydale called X.

"When you say X, do you mean that you don't know her name?" I asked. "Or is *X* her actual name? Or are you saying that X is your Ex?"

"Her is name is Xavier," Marydale said. "She's French. We call her X for short."

Our cabin was small and spare, with two narrow bunks and a tiny, efficient bathroom. "We can freshen up before we meet with X," Marydale said. She went into the bathroom and closed the door.

How did Lucina acquire her wealth, I wondered—and what was the purpose of this yacht? I was familiar with the story of an infamous religious organization that operated a small fleet of private ships. True believers of the religion were conscripted into serving as crewmembers on these ships, and, supposedly, they all wore naval-looking paramilitary uniforms. I hoped that Lucina's yacht was not a similar sect-at-sea. I recalled that the women who had helped us onto the yacht were *not* wearing uniforms. I took this as a hopeful sign.

I looked out the window of our cabin. Not far from where we were at anchor, I saw Chateau d'If, a fortress and former prison built on an island in Marseille Bay. It had been made famous by the novel *The Count of Monte Cristo*. In the story, protagonist Edmond Dantès was able to escape from the island prison by trading places with a corpse. Presumed to be a dead man, he was thrown into the sea. He swam to freedom. He recovered a treasure that had been hidden by one of his fellow prisoners. As a newly-wealthy man, Dantès plotted elaborate revenge against the people who had wrongly imprisoned him.

I wondered whether Lucina's story was similar. I knew that Eternals had faked their own deaths. Anna and Graziana, for example, had allowed people to think that they had died in a freak blizzard on Mount of the Holy Cross. Most recently, both women were still alive, according to Marydale, despite questionable news reports saying that they had perished in separate explosions.

Perhaps Lucina, too, had faked her own death countless times. Judging from her yacht, she had succeeded in acquiring a fortune. I wondered whether Lucina, like Edmond Dantès, was motivated by revenge, or by something nobler.

Marydale had told me earnestly that the nuns were working for the "liberation of humanity, starting with women," which had a lofty, zealous ring to it. I could not imagine that a group of women like Marydale would organize themselves around a sinister plot of revenge, or would play along with the narcissistic fantasies of a charismatic guru.

Besides, Dr. Blanton told me in her voicemail message that she had seen Lucina "miraculously" breathe new life into Graziana. To me, this suggested that, whatever Lucina was capable of doing, it far surpassed fake-guru parlor tricks.

I suddenly felt overwhelmingly sleepy. I stretched out on a bunk with my backpack on my chest. I wrapped my arms around it. I must've closed my eyes and dozed for a moment. The next thing I knew, I heard Marydale say, "No napping, not yet, Becky. Freshen up."

I carried my pack into the bathroom. I wondered absently why I had brought my whole pack with me into the cramped space. I splashed water on my face. I looked haggard and jet-lagged. "Okay," I said. "I'm gorgeous."

"You can leave your stuff here," Marydale said, glancing at my pack. "This cabin will be our home, at least for tonight."

I didn't want to leave my pack, and I wasn't sure why. "I know it sounds weird," I said, trying to understand why I suddenly felt a strong need to keep my belongings within arm's reach. "I have an odd feeling that I should not leave Riva by herself—Riva's ashes, I mean. It's too-little-too-late, I suppose, but I feel that I need to protect her."

Marydale didn't argue. I followed her out the door.

We were aboard a luxury yacht, but I didn't see garish décor or conspicuous indulgences such as hot tubs. Rather, the yacht's interior was elegantly simple and tastefully unadorned, as if naval architect John Trumpy had designed a seagoing convent.

"What does Lucina do with this ship?" I asked.

"It's a training vessel, mostly," Marydale explained. "Sisters gain nautical experience, and they immerse themselves in culture and history of the Mediterranean region. Lucina and her friends sail on it sometimes, to visit islands like Malta or Mallorca."

We ascended a narrow stairway. We entered what appeared to be a library or meeting room. The center of the room was dominated by a long, varnished-wood table suitable for at least a dozen people to sit comfortably. On opposite sides of the room, floor-to-ceiling windows offered stunning views of Marseille Bay. Shelves of books occupied most of the walls. Several comfortable-looking chairs were scattered around the periphery of the room.

Before Marydale and I had a chance to sit down, a door opened near one of the bookcases. A dark-haired woman entered. She was carrying a large tray. "*Bonjour!*" she said. "Welcome." She put the tray on the table. "I hope you are hungry," she said with a distinct French accent. "I am starving, so I hope you will not mind if I eat."

"This is Xavier," Marydale said as she helped Xavier move dishes from the tray onto the table.

I was startled when the woman thrust her face into mine, kissing one cheek, and then the other. "Victorine, welcome," Xavier said to me.

I probably appeared flummoxed by this customary but awkward-for-me French greeting, and by the fact that she had called me Victorine.

Marydale seemed amused by my awkwardness. "This is Becky Pine from the hospital in Colorado."

"Yes!" Xavier said. "Becky." She motioned for me to sit down. She greeted Marydale with the same French gesture of kisses.

Xavier was in her mid-to-late-thirties, I guessed, and no taller than five-foot-four. She was trim and energetic, with olive skin and a bright, wide smile. Her dark hair looked soft and abundant. I tried to recall where I had first heard the name Victorine. I wondered why X had associated the name with me.

Xavier had brought us a lunch that did not look inviting. It featured brownish-beige soup. She ladled some into a bowl for me. I smiled politely but grimly.

"It is not every day that the sea gives us the ingredients for real *bouillabaisse*," she said as she ladled a serving for Marydale. "Our Marguerite has done her best with what was available. We shall see if she has captured the true taste of Marseille." X placed unappetizing-looking filets of fishflesh into our bowls.

"We eat it like this." X took a round of toasted bread from a basket. She slathered it with thick, yellowish paste. She placed it in her bowl of soup. Marydale and I did the same. Xavier lifted a spoonful to her mouth. She closed her eyes and nodded as if it was, in fact, the true taste of Marseille.

Tentatively, I sipped from my spoon. I expected an unpleasantly fishy mouthful. I was overwhelmed by rich, briny deliciousness. I felt as if I had been deprived of a crucial nutrient all my life, and had suddenly found it in this bowl. I dipped my spoon again and again. What was I tasting that was so profound? The yellow paste on the crouton added notes of saffron and garlic to the symphony of flavor. The fish—and I had never cared for fish—was meltingly succulent. I could not stop eating. None of us could. We slurped and feasted without saying a word.

After all of the food had been eaten, we were full and groggy. Riva and I used to call this state a "food buzz;" we had eaten our way into altered consciousness. I leaned back in my chair. Marydale looked ready for a nap. Xavier sighed, immobilized with satiety. Bleary-eyed, we surveyed the empty dishes.

The door by the bookcase opened. In stepped a tall, slim woman with a boyish haircut. She carried a tray with demitasse cups of coffee and a plate of small, boat-shaped cookies called *navettes*.

"Franca!" Marydale exclaimed happily.

Franca placed the tray on the table. She kissed Marydale's cheeks. She greeted X in the same way. To me, she offered a cordial nod. She sat down next to Marydale.

"Franca is the captain of this ship," Marydale said as she served us cups of coffee. She introduced me as "Becky from Colorado."

Franca wore a crisp, white shirt with rolled sleeves, which made her look both business-like and relaxed. Her skin was deeply tanned. Her hair was dark brown with a shock of silver-gray that swooped over her forehead. She had large, brown eyes with dark circles under them, which made her look as if she had seen everything there was to see. Her manner was quiet and authoritative.

Franca sipped her coffee. I did the same. It was velvety, strong, and sobering.

Marydale explained to Franca and Xavier what had happened at Holy Cross. "We succeeded in implementing a distraction," Marydale said, referring to the ultrasonic disruption of the hospital's electronic system. "But instead of going to the rendezvous point, Lucina disappeared with Graziana. Now we're left to find and open the Greenwell Portal on our own."

"They went on holiday," Franca interjected. Her accent was different than Xavier's. I assumed that she was Italian rather than French.

"Holiday?" Marydale said, as if Franca was kidding.

"Yes," Franca said, acknowledging that it was funny, but it certainly wasn't a joke. "When Lucina and Anna were at Valletta in August, they told me about their plan." From the way Franca spoke, I could not imagine that she had ever kidded about anything. "They went to see the Grand Canyon. Together with Graziana they are car-traveling in America."

"They're on a road trip?" Marydale asked, incredulous.

"I thought they were under attack," Xavier said, perplexed. "We are on alert, preparing for the worst. Bancroft sent the signal. Is it a false alarm?"

"On alert, yes. The alarm is real," Franca confirmed. "Still, they go on the road trip. They are always under attack, so they must enjoy life, you know?"

I imagined ageless, supernaturally-gifted beings looking for a restroom at a gritty truck-stop in Arizona.

Marydale and Xavier exchanged astonished and semi-annoyed looks.

"They set this up? They planned this?" Marydale asked.

"This is why *La Bonne Mère* is in Marseille now," Franca explained. "Lucina said to me that I must be here, so I am here. Now Xavier is here. Marydale is here, too. This is all happening according to the plan that was told to me. Eternals have their mission, and we have ours. This is a time when we go on our different roads. Now I want to go back to Corsica before the wind rises."

"We have to open the portal first," Marydale protested. She explained our sudden detour from Rome to Marseille. "We have to *find* the Greenwell Portal before we can open it. This will take time, and the clock is ticking. How fast can you get us to Rome?"

"We are not going to Rome," Franca said, definitively. "This is not a racing yacht. I will not burn all our gas for no reason."

"But there *is* a reason," Marydale said. "We have 48 hours before the window of opportunity closes."

"Drive a car," Franca said dryly. "Fly a plane. *La Bonne Mère* is the slowest way. She is the most expensive way. Lucina would not want it. And I warn you: we should not be this far north at this time of the year. When the wind comes, you will see what I mean."

Marydale sounded exasperated as she explained about Graziana and Holy Cross. She pointed at me and said that Graziana had given me her heart for the purpose of opening the portal. Franca seemed skeptical. Marydale described the explosions that had been reported in the news, and how everything and everyone related to the Ashton Foundation was under intense scrutiny. "We can't rent a car or buy a plane ticket without using our passports and credit cards. We have to assume that someone is monitoring our credit-card activity and can follow us," she said.

Franca stubbornly resisted while Marydale persuasively implored.

As they wrangled, Xavier offered me a *navette* cookie. "Would you like one, Victorine?" She corrected herself immediately: "Becky, pardon me. I do not know why I call you Victorine."

Marydale and Franca were too engaged in their debate to pay any attention to us.

Xavier explained to me that the cookies were called *navettes de Saint Victor*, and were a special treat from Marseille. The cookies, shaped like the hull of an open boat, were said to commemorate a mysterious event during the 13th Century, when an unmanned boat floated into the old port of Marseille near the Abbey of St. Victor. The boat carried only a colorful, ornate statue of a beautiful woman, presumed to be a depiction of the Virgin Mary. This event was considered to be a miraculous visitation.

Xavier said that, in her opinion, the *navette* cookies were originally made to commemorate a much older event, which happened during the First Century A.D. According to legend, a rudderless, open boat carrying three women named Mary crossed the Mediterranean Sea from Alexandria, Egypt, and made landfall on the coast of the Camargue. "It is not far from here," Xavier said, "in a place called Saintes-Maries-de-la-Mer. The women in the boat were Marie-Madeleine, Marie Salomé, and Marie Jacobé."

Suddenly, I remembered the book that the nun in the hospital had given me. I dug into my pack and pulled it out. I opened the front cover. Written in block letters on the first page was the word "VICTORINE." I showed it to Xavier. Intrigued, she reached for the book.

Xavier held it reverently and studied the pages. I took a bite of the cookie. It was lightly sweet with a delicate flavor of orange blossom.

"Where did you get this?" Xavier asked in a whisper, not wanting to disturb Franca and Marydale's discussion.

"A nun gave it to me in California."

"This describes the Treasure Tower," Xavier said as she perused the pages. "It is said that when a portal is opened, the Treasure Tower rises from the earth. It's an immense tower made of precious gems. It emits joyous waves of light and sound. I have seen the opening of portals, but I have never seen the Treasure Tower. I think it is a metaphor for cosmic consciousness." She flipped back to the beginning of the book.

"These *mudras*," she said. "These poses and hand gestures." She looked at me with wonder and seriousness. "Yes, this is a set of instructions for opening the portal."

Xavier reached underneath the tabletop and pulled up what appeared to be a wireless keyboard for a computer. She tapped on the keys. A bookcase opened, revealing an electronic screen.

Marydale and Franca halted their conversation. A satellite-image map of the Mediterranean region appeared on the screen. Xavier consulted the book. She typed latitude-and-longitude coordinates on the keyboard. The map zoomed into the Languedoc region of the south of France. "Ahh," Xavier said as the map zoomed in closer. Gradually, a specific point came into focus: the town of Puivert.

I felt my heart leap in my chest. "Yes," I said, "Puivert." I had looked it up on my phone after I left Riva at the mortuary.

"Puivert?" Xavier repeated, as if it must be a mistake. After a moment, she began to laugh. It was the light, appreciative laugh of someone who finally comprehends a joke. "We have found the Greenwell Portal," she said.

"Where?" Marydale asked, her eyes scouring the map. "How do we know it's the Greenwell Portal?"

"Because of the French language," Xavier said. "The French word *puit* means *well*."

Marydale caught on: "And *vert* means *green*." She, too, smiled as if, in retrospect, it had always been obvious.

"Puivert is Greenwell," Xavier said, handing the book to Marydale. "And these are instructions for opening the portal."

I told Marydale that a ghostly nun had given me the book when I was in the hospital with Riva. "I've been meaning to show it to you," I said. "But I kept forgetting."

Marydale, like Xavier, held the book reverently as she studied it.

"Franca, can you take us closer to Puivert?" Xavier asked.

Franca took the keyboard. She adjusted the map. "You will not like my answer," she said evenly. "You can drive to Puivert from Marseille in just five hours. You do not need *La Bonne Mère* to take you there."

Marydale exhaled. "Franca, Franca," she pleaded. "We don't have a car. Even if we could get a car, I am too exhausted to drive right now. Becky and I have been traveling." She held up the book. "Besides, we need time to study these instructions."

Franca silently adjusted the map. "I have a friend," she said at last. "She lives in Sète." Franca magnified a coastal town on the map. The port of Sète was a two-hour drive from Puivert. "She works for the harbormaster. I will radio her. You will borrow her car."

Marydale's face lit up. "Franca," she said, surprised.

"I will go slow," Franca warned. "I will economize with the fuel. We will be at anchor before sunrise."

"Thank you, Franca," Marydale said. She threw her arms around the woman's neck and kissed her face. Franca lowered her head, pleased and suddenly bashful to be the recipient of Marydale's affection.

From this gesture, I deduced that Marydale was naturally affectionate toward everyone. Therefore, I should not take her expressions of affection toward me too personally. She had hugged me when I met her, and she had wrapped my arms around her on the motor scooter in Marseille. These were lovely moments for me. Still, I knew that it would be unwise of me to presume that Marydale liked me in a romantic way. Realizing this made me feel slightly melancholy.

Marydale and Xavier stayed in the library to analyze the old book. Franca left to plot a course for Sète. I hoisted my backpack and found my way back to the cabin. I was dead tired. I was also nervously energized. *Puivert*, I repeated to myself.

What will the portal look like? How will we open it? Will a Treasure Tower rise out of the ground? Will I really be able to talk to Riva? My mind spun with questions. Dazzling sun on the sea made me resist sleep. I took a hot shower to settle myself. By the time I collapsed into bed, *La Bonne Mère* was underway. The humming of the engine and the motion of the waves lulled me into oblivion.

"Becky," Marydale said, nudging my shoulder. "I'm going to meditate with the others. Breakfast is in half an hour."

I heard her leave the cabin. Morning twilight softly illuminated the room. I felt fully rested and wide awake. I heard seagulls squawking. Looking out the window I saw only the open sea. I assumed that, on the other side of the ship, I would be able to see the port of Sète. I got dressed and picked up my backpack. I followed a narrow staircase up to the aft deck.

We were at anchor near a quaint-looking town that was wrapped around the base of a hill. A cargo port just east of town clattered with activity. Blazing sunshine illuminated a parking lot filled with hundreds of identical, white, delivery vans. Whether these vehicles were recent imports, or exports waiting to be shipped, I didn't know.

The scent in the air was thrilling. It didn't smell like the sea. It smelled of eucalyptus trees and vineyards bursting into leaf. It smelled both fresh and prehistoric at the same time, as if the land of the Languedoc exhaled a mystical, immortal perfume. I imagined underground rivers rushing through undiscovered caves where Paleolithic people had painted sacred stories on limestone walls. I watched the fiery sky soften into clear blue. I had a feeling that this would be a big day.

After breakfast, Marydale, Xavier, and I boarded a smaller boat that the women referred to as one of the ship's tenders. It was an elegant-looking, 27-foot open yacht propelled by water jets. It was piloted by a woman whom I had not met. Marydale greeted her by the name Agnes. Flanked by Marydale and Xavier, I settled into an upholstered, sofa-like bench. I hugged my pack to my chest. Agnes jetted us to shore, like skipping a flat rock across a placid pond.

At the seaside quay, a woman was waiting for us. She was petite and blonde. She looked as if she had just dropped her children off at school. She seemed both nervous and happy to see us. She spoke in French to Xavier, and handed her a set of car keys. She boarded the tender with an eager laugh. Agnes whisked her away to *La Bonne Mère*.

Marydale commented that the woman wasn't happy to see us so much as she was eager to see Franca. Marydale and Xavier exchanged a knowing, approving nod. I wondered but did not ask: *what, exactly, is the deal with romance and nuns—and might I be a candidate for either?*

In the back seat of the woman's car, I found a plastic dinosaur, which I assumed was a child's toy. Marydale rode shotgun, and Xavier was behind the wheel. We rocketed out of Sète and onto a broad, fast tollway heading in the general direction of Toulouse. As we drove, Marydale and Xavier told me what they had learned from the book about opening the portal.

"We'll need to do it correctly, of course," Marydale said, as if feeling the pressure of high expectations. "Fortunately, we have several hours at our disposal. It involves a series of physical poses that must be enacted in the right order."

"We practiced yesterday," Xavier said. "We will show you how to do it, Becky."

"If we're careful and deliberate, everything should go well," Marydale said. She and Xavier sounded as if they were each trying to reassure the other.

I wasn't concerned about opening the portal; I presumed that whatever I needed to do would become obvious to me at the right moment. I was concerned about keeping my expectations manageably low. I would not see a tower rise from the ground, I told myself. I would not see Riva. No matter what was to happen, I would be disappointed. My sister was dead and gone, and there was nothing that would ever make this fact okay.

I watched the scenery roll past. I was surprised at how rural it looked: acres and acres of farmland in the shadow of rock-faced mountains. France was beautiful, and *La Bonne Mère* was beautiful. Marydale and Xavier were beautiful, too. My ability to appreciate their beauty told me that I had not lost my ability to appreciate life. All of this beauty felt wonderfully relevant and meaningful in the larger scheme of things. It was relevant to me, yet I felt irrelevant to it. All of this beauty existed without Riva, and it would continue to exist without me. What difference did I make? I was completely irrelevant in the larger scheme of beautiful things.

You're wallowing, Becky, I heard Riva say. *You need to cheer up and stop being so tragic.*

I pretended not to hear my sister's voice. "What's the significance of Puivert?" I asked Marydale and X. "Have you ever been there?"

Marydale shook her head. Xavier answered that she had been to Puivert only once, and could tell me very little. During the Middle Ages, the great castle of Puivert was the home of a wealthy family named Congost. They practiced the old religion of Occitania.

"At the time, this whole area of France was called Occitania," Xavier said.

I recalled the story about Mary the Tower that I had found hidden in a digital photo at the Long Beach Public Library. That story, too, had referred to the south of France as "Occitania."

Xavier explained that the grand chateau of Puivert had been built on a hill overlooking a large lake. Each year in springtime, the Congost family invited troubadours to Puivert to perform their songs in a friendly competition.

Troubadours were influential philosophers, political commentators, and pop-music stars all rolled into one, Xavier said. Nobles from across the region, including Eleanor of Aquitaine and Richard the Lionheart, would travel to Puivert for the troubadour competition. Political leaders took the opportunity to exchange ideas, form alliances, and fall in love.

During the nights in Puivert, the lake would light up with lanterns on boats as troubadours performed their love songs on the water. People described the scene as transcendent. A kind of musical-literary culture blossomed in Puivert hundreds of years before the European Renaissance.

Around this time, the Catholic Church declared all-out war on the people and the old religion of Occitania, in a campaign known as the Albigensian Crusade. Crusaders believed that they were fighting a holy war against the evils exemplified by Puivert—such as the "evil" of using wealth and art to celebrate love rather than to glorify the Church and its authority.

Regardless of moral arguments made in favor of war, the crusaders were in fact an immoral, cruel army led by perverse, sadistic men. They tortured and slaughtered the people of Occitania with a degree of horror that was unheard-of in Europe prior to that time.

Crusaders demolished the chateau at Puivert. They built a different castle near the site of the old one, but it was never the same. Members of the Congost family were burned at the stake. Later, in a hard rain, the lake of Puivert all but disappeared when it broke through its banks and flooded the town of Mirepoix.

"Now, there is just a small lake where the big lake used to be," Xavier said. "Puivert was beautiful, and it was destroyed. You can still see ruins of the old castle. To me, it is a terribly sad place. It feels very somber."

We all agreed that the most sensible place to look for the portal was on the grounds of the castle. We drove through a mountainous region. We passed miles of forests and vineyards. Eventually, we reached the town of Puivert.

Xavier negotiated a couple of hairpin turns as we drove up the hill to the castle. Ours was the only car in the visitors' parking lot. As we approached the castle, I wondered whether it was closed. Xavier expressed surprise when she saw a man sitting in a booth to sell admission tickets. He seemed surprised to see us, too, and blinked at us through his thick eyeglasses. Marydale paid our fee.

My impression of the castle had been influenced by the grim story that X had told us. To me, the façade looked bleak and sad. The entrance archway was flanked by unadorned walls. A turret on the right was still standing. A turret on the left had crumbled. The place had an air of desolation. My pack felt unusually heavy on my shoulders. Everything felt heavy.

"How will we recognize the portal when we see it?" I asked.

"We'll walk slowly. You'll be able to feel changes in vibration," Marydale said. "It's not going to jump out at us. It's going to be almost imperceptibly subtle."

The three of us walked through the archway and into a vast, walled courtyard. I imagined that, hundreds of years ago, knights jousted with each other in this yard. There was plenty of room for horse stables, an open-air market, and a crowd of people. To our left, one of the castle walls had tumbled down, opening up a gorgeous view of farmland below and mountains in the distance. The three of us stood and admired the view. We imagined the long-gone lake that had once shimmered with love and light. A faded placard on the spot displayed a historical timeline with information written in French. Marydale and X studied it.

I turned and looked at the eerily-empty yard. At the farthest end was another open archway. Suddenly, a woman appeared in the archway. I wondered where she and her group had parked their car. The woman just stood there, looking at me. I squinted, expecting to see yet another iteration of Lillian Gish. The woman wore a white jacket with a jaunty blue scarf, which reminded me of Riva. Riva had worn a similar jacket and scarf in one of her most recent photos before her death. The woman in the archway had blonde hair like Riva's. The woman smiled at me, and I knew—it was Riva!

I ran toward her. She waved me on, gesturing for me to hurry. I sprinted, speechless. I was still about a hundred feet away when she walked through the archway and out of my sight.

"Becky!" I heard Marydale yell in the distance. I turned and saw them running after me. "Becky, wait!"

I sprinted through the archway. Piles of rocks and crumbling walls from the old castle loomed in front of me. I ran along a path that had been cordoned off by ropes.

"Riva!" I yelled. "Riva, wait for me!" I paused. The area was clearly marked as dangerous and off-limits for visitors.

I saw a flash of blue scarf disappear behind a wall. "Riva!" I cried. I ducked under a rope and ran after her. I turned a corner. I pulled up short when I saw that I had entered a small, circular room. The room might have been a turret or stairway at one time. I heard a rushing sound, like wind spinning around me.

I felt someone violently grab my backpack and nearly lift me off the ground. I turned to fight, but there was no one. Rather, something was struggling urgently to get out of my pack. Wind swirled, accelerating. I pulled the pack off my shoulders. I pressed it to the ground, kneeling on the straps to keep it from jumping. I unzipped the main compartment. With two hands, I grabbed the red-velvet pouch that held Riva's ashes. It shook and shuddered. Wind howled in my ears. Above the din, I could hear Marydale shouting my name.

I opened the pouch. I lifted the plastic bag of ashes from the box. The box was torn from my hands and sucked into the roaring wind. The bag of ashes felt alive somehow, as if something inside was fighting to get out, and fighting to breathe. I tore it open. A cloud of dust whirled around me.

It wasn't just dust. It was Graziana's blood, too. The vials had opened. Her blood had mixed with Riva's ashes, glistening like a blizzard of rubies and diamonds. I stood in a thunderous tornado of swirling gems. A funnel cloud seemed to dig into the ground and grow into the sky, changing colors—topaz, emerald, sapphire, amethyst. It was wondrous.

It was terrifying. Shards tore at my skin. My blood turned to crystals in the wind. I put my arm over my face to shield my eyes. I felt that I was being torn apart by a stinging cloud of gem-dust.

"Riva!" I cried. "Riva!"

Except for the steady, periodic beeping of her hospital monitors, and the *whoosh* of her ventilator, there was no sound. I felt only Riva's hand in mine. I felt her pulse animating her fingers, letting me know that she was here. I was here. We were here together.

I opened my eyes. I looked at my small hand. Riva held it firmly in her small hand. We were children. I was four and she was six. We each had the same clear, wide, gray-green eyes. She led me into a cave. She paused in front of a rushing, underground waterfall. Its sound echoed around us. Riva squeezed my hand and led us through the wall of water. On the other side, we were in her house where she lived with Mack. As small, silent witnesses, we watched. We never let go of each other's hand.

15

THROUGH THE WATERFALL

Riva was frustrated with Mack that Sunday night. She was trying to pull together all of their tax-related paperwork and receipts to give to her accountant. Mack wasn't helping. He sat in the TV room watching the Academy Awards. "Don't stress out about it," he said to Riva, unconcerned. He knew that handling their taxes would be *his* responsibility for the rest of their lives.

Riva walked from the TV room to her office. She looked forward to the busy week ahead of her. She had client meetings, and floor-plan drawings to deliver. She had prepared a round of billing-invoices, too, and was grateful for how well her business was doing. She would need the money when she and Mack split up and she had two households to support.

Riva felt safe at home. She felt safe with Mack. Everything seemed relatively normal to her. She wasn't aware that she was on stage, inhabiting a scene that Mack had designed. He had contrived the setting to look unremarkable and completely exposed. This was the genius of his deception. Mack had placed the cameras so that they concealed more than they revealed—and yet they seemed to reveal everything.

Mack got up from his green leather reclining chair to let Caldo out through the side-patio door. Mack followed the dog.

He stood in the yard while the dog sniffed the grass. Mack gazed out at the darkened golf course behind their house. Fog had settled over the green. "You out there, Bro?" Mack asked.

Mack was following Caldo back into the house when the response came: "I'm here, Bro." Mack pretended not to hear. He kept the door open just enough for Caldo to hear the voice outside, but not enough for the dog to get out of the house. Caldo barked wildly, sensing that a stranger was in the back yard.

Mack walked into the guest bathroom and hid there without turning on the light. Mack wanted Riva to come out to see what was happening with Caldo. He wanted to make sure that she appeared in front of his surveillance cameras.

Caldo barked. Mack remained hidden. Eventually, Riva stormed out of her office and into the TV room to see why Caldo was barking. She let the dog out. She followed him to the back fence. With his tail wagging, he barked into the darkness and fog.

Riva heard, faintly, the voice of Carleen Biggars, who lived two doors down. Riva assumed that Caldo had heard Carleen talking to someone, and wanted to investigate. "Good boy," Riva said. "Keeping us safe."

Caldo, having done his duty, padded back into the house. Riva followed, smiling.

"Mack?" she said, as she closed the door behind her. "Mack?" She could not imagine where he had gone.

He slinked out of the bathroom. He faced her. He was aware that he was on camera. He was standing in front of the hallway closet. He had positioned the camera so that the closet would be in view at all times. Inside the closet was the all-important video recorder for the surveillance system. He wanted to be able to prove to the police that, throughout everything, he never opened the closet door. Therefore, it would have been impossible for him to manipulate the video.

"I just want to get our taxes done so we can finalize everything," Riva said. She tried to keep a scolding tone out of her voice, but she didn't understand why Mack refused to give her the interest statement for his savings account.

Mack glared at Riva but said nothing. He turned and walked down the hallway toward the yoga room. Riva went back into her office and sat down at her drafting table. Caldo settled in the hallway outside her office door.

A few minutes later, Mack brought her the piece of paper she had requested.

In the hallway just outside Riva's office, Mack pulled down the folding ladder that led to the attic. The attic-access ladder could not be seen on any of the surveillance cameras. When closed, the access hatch was hardly noticeable, except for a pull-rope that hung from the ceiling. Most single-story houses in their neighborhood had a similar pull-down ladder. It wasn't the type of thing that would draw the curiosity of the police.

Riva glanced at Mack's interest statement. His savings account had earned $100 in interest over the past year, which seemed to her like a paltry sum. She looked at the record from the previous year, when his account had earned $227 in interest. The year before that, it had earned $395. These seemed like small amounts to her, but she was struck by how the amounts had fallen over three years. She thought about asking Mack how much money he had in his account. Mack had never had much money, Riva knew, and this was a sore subject for him. She didn't want him to feel that she was judgmentally scrutinizing his finances. Still, she was curious.

She went into the hallway. She saw that he was in the attic. She was going to shout her question up to Mack, but she decided against it. Instead, she went into the guest bathroom.

She looked forward to a time when she wouldn't have to worry or wonder about Mack's finances. She would support him, of course, but it would be a relief to be divorced, and no longer liable for his choices.

Riva exited the bathroom. She walked through the open-floor-plan living room toward the kitchen, appearing on cameras six and seven.

Camera seven was a dome-shaped camera located in the ceiling just outside the TV room. It covered part of the dining table, the hallway-closet door, and the kitchen area in the distance. Riva stopped at the wooden hutch just outside the kitchen area. She opened the cover of her tablet device.

Camera six was a dome-shaped camera located in the ceiling just above the hutch where Riva stood. The camera lens was positioned in such a way that it did not show the surface of the hutch. Rather, this camera showed the front door, a limited view of the kitchen, and part of the living room. In the distance, the door of the guest bathroom was in view.

Riva stood at the hutch for several minutes as she tapped on the screen of her tablet device. She customarily kept the device plugged into a power outlet on the wall next to the hutch. Often throughout the day, Riva stood at the hutch to check news headlines and her messages.

On this night, she looked up airline fares to Denver. She did not book a ticket. She debated whether to mention to Mack that she wanted to visit Becky. She looked forward to telling Becky the news of her impending divorce.

Riva was about to walk away from the hutch when she decided to look up a savings-account-interest calculator. *At the rate of one-half-percent per year, how much money would Mack need in his account to accrue $100 in interest?* Riva typed varying interest rates into the calculator. She started to feel guilty for indulging her curiosity. If she wanted to know about his account, she should just ask him.

Riva left her tablet device on the hutch. For the last time in her life, she walked out of view of Mack's surveillance cameras.

From the attic, Mack saw Riva return to her office. He reached over to the power-and-video cables for the surveillance system. By unplugging cables, he could control which cameras were "on" and recording. He could unplug the whole system if necessary, leaving no traces of manipulation on the recorder. He cut the cameras. He descended the ladder. He neatly folded the ladder and closed the ceiling hatch.

He had crafted a weapon that he'd hidden in the attic. It was a foot-long steel tube that he had filled with concrete. It felt comfortable in his grip. It was small enough for him to hide easily, but heavy enough to do the job with one blow. He could not hit her more than once if he wanted it to look like a slip-and-fall.

Construction crews had been repairing sidewalks in his neighborhood, and Mack saw this as a lucky opportunity. After completing his mission, Mack planned to take the weapon down the street and drop it into an open bed that was being prepared for a new sidewalk. He would bury the weapon in the subbase. In the morning, new concrete would be poured. He would always be able to keep a watchful eye on this hiding spot, and no one would ever suspect it.

Mack carried the weapon to the yoga room. He opened a drawer of the Japanese *tansu* chest. He took out the special, black-dyed, cotton-fabric *gi* that he had bought for the occasion. He took off his favorite surf-logo T-shirt and his shorts, and put them in the drawer. He donned his martial-arts uniform. Already, he could feel the power of Roy Dumond's wisdom pulsating in his veins.

Mack recalled fondly the night that Roy had counseled him about attaining enlightenment for Riva. Mack and his brothers sat around their bonfire on the beach, as they had done on many nights while getting stoned. Roy's broad chest and powerful arms shined like gold in the firelight. He looked like a god. He was a god.

Mack explained to Roy and his brothers that he had always thought of Riva as a resource. She provided him with money, legitimacy, labor, and love. But there were strings attached. He wasn't free to do whatever he wished with the resources she provided. He had to account to her for his choices, and even for his feelings. She claimed to offer everything unconditionally, but she expected things in return, Mack complained. Riva was a hypocrite. She wanted to give him freedom, but she imprisoned him with her expectations and conditions. He wanted to help her let go of her expectations. He wanted to help her experience unconditional love.

Roy admired Mack's ability to maximize his resources. Riva would be nothing without Mack. It was because of Mack that she worked so hard. But why should she have to work so hard? She could take a well-deserved rest, and still provide Mack with ample resources.

Mack was smart, he told his brothers. He knew better than to sign up for a bunch of life-insurance policies. He knew that Riva's bitch of a sister would tell the police to look into his finances. The only policy that really mattered was Riva's long-term disability coverage. Fortunately for everyone, Riva had established this policy years before he had perfected his plan.

The real prize, Mack told his brothers, was money from Riva's family trust. His big project would at last give him access to Riva's rich inheritance.

Mack told his brothers that he planned to put Riva benevolently into a coma. According to the terms of their marital trust, Riva's incapacitation would immediately give Mack control of all of Riva's assets. Her long-term disability insurance would pay for her basic care and give him some income. Plus, he would reap quick cash from her small accidental-death-and-disability policies—the ones he had convinced her to sign up for through her credit-card accounts.

Mack explained that Riva's sister Becky would spare no expense to make sure that Riva received the best of everything. "Becky will pay for nurses and therapists, and for vacations for me, whatever I want," he said. "Becky will have to go through me if she ever wants to see Riva. She will have to pay me whatever I ask because I will have power of attorney. I will be in charge."

Money from the Pine Family Trust would flow from Denver to Long Beach. At last, Mack would have financial control, and finally Riva would be able to relax.

This arrangement would be universally beneficial in many ways, Mack explained. People would think well of him for being such a kind, selfless husband. His example would inspire generosity in others. Riva would be proud of his strength and courage in the face of tragedy. She would get a chance to depend on him, the way a wife is supposed to depend on a husband, not the other way around. Everyone would win something, Mack believed. Even Becky would benefit because she would have to stop being such a bitch. Becky would learn how to be respectful.

When Riva woke up from her coma, she wouldn't remember what had happened. Even if she could remember, no one would believe her. Mack knew this from his experience with Whitey, his stepfather. No one believed Whitey when he claimed that Mack had hurt him.

Mack had successfully undermined Whitey's credibility. Mack had sneaked into Whitey's house in Menifee. He took

Whitey's walker, and hid it in Whitey's garage. Confused and upset that his walker was missing, Whitey accused his sister-in-law of taking it. Later, after days of family drama about the missing walker, Whitey's nephew found it in the garage. After this episode, everyone agreed that Whitey couldn't be believed. Mack was prepared to use the same medicine on Riva if necessary.

Mack's brothers concurred that Mack's plan was well-reasoned, thoughtful, and compassionate. With sufficient resources from Riva's family, they all could continue to deepen their brotherhood, and Riva would be at peace.

But Roy looked pointedly at Mack and said, "Think." He spoke in the hypnotic, compelling way that the brothers longed to hear. "If you want total freedom. If you want true liberation. *You* must become enlightened," Roy said. "*Riva* must become enlightened, too."

"But how?" Mack asked humbly.

The bonfire crackled and sparked. Roy told them the story of the little princess who loved the ocean.

The first time that the little princess visited the seashore, she fell in love with the waves. She loved the ocean so much that she insisted on bringing it to her castle in the mountains. At her command, men worked to build a system of pipes to bring the ocean several miles inland. They devised a series of pumps to bring the ocean up the mountain to the castle. Eventually, ocean water trickled into a bowl in the castle. When the little princess saw this, she was disappointed. What she had loved about the ocean was its immense, uncontrolled energy. She suddenly understood that she could not bring what she loved into her own home.

"This is a love story," Roy said. "Riva is the little princess. You are the ocean. It is your wild nature that she loves. Give her what she loves. Give her the raw power of nature in her own home."

"But how?" Mack asked again, more humbly.

Roy explained about sacred masks. An enlightened mask is carved by an enlightened master. It is not a prop in a performance. It gives the wearer a spiritual identity. It gives the wearer a sacred mission. When a man fulfills his mission while wearing the sacred mask of the divine masculine, the truth is illuminated for all to see.

"You will become the instrument of a force greater than yourself," Roy said. "No harm can come to you. No guilt or blame will trouble you. Both you and Riva will become enlightened through your deed. If you wear the mask of wrathful masculine nature, I will give you my blessing."

Mack heard Riva brushing her teeth in the master bathroom. Roy had told him that the master bath would be the ideal place for the sacrificial ceremony.

Clad in his black karate-uniform, Mack faced his brothers. They gazed admiringly at him from the wall. "We're with you, Bro," they whispered. "Roy is with you."

Bold and resolute, Mack lifted his own mask from where it hung among the others on the wall. It was the face of a leering, horned demon with red-and-black skin, and bulging, green eyes.

Mack placed the mask over his face. He tied two silken cords behind his head to secure the visage over his own. Just as Roy had promised, Mack felt himself transformed into an instrument of true freedom. He felt calm, focused, and indescribably powerful. He was a man-god! He had no fear, no hesitation. His physical vision was impaired by the obstructed eye-holes of the mask, but he felt that he could see everything clearly at last. He picked up his weapon. He went to prove his sacred devotion to Riva.

Riva had changed into her pajamas and was ready for bed. She was still thinking about the airfares to Denver that she had seen online. They were reasonable. She should go ahead and book a ticket, she decided. She didn't need Mack's approval to visit Becky. She walked down the hall, past the yoga room, and back to the hutch near the kitchen. Caldo followed her. Riva opened the cover of her tablet device. She tapped on the screen, unaware of Mack's approach.

Caldo barked and rushed at Mack.

Mack landed a crushing blow. The sound was loud and sickening. Mack caught Riva before she could fall. He gently placed her face-down on the floor. "Don't worry," he said. "I'll take care of you."

He returned to the yoga room to celebrate with his brothers. Mack removed his mask and replaced it on the wall. "Yes," his brothers whispered, hissing their approval. Mack added to their chorus: "Yes, yes." This was a moment to savor.

Caldo stood over Riva. The scent of her blood frightened him. It was on his snout and paws. In distress, he paced rapidly and circled the room. He nudged Riva's face.

When Mack saw that Caldo had spattered Riva's blood, he tried to grab the dog. Caldo evaded him and ran toward the dining-room table.

Caldo shrieked when Mack lifted him off the ground and carried him to the guest bathroom. Mack dropped him into the bathtub. Mack closed the door and left the dog in the dark. He would deal with Caldo later.

From the hutch near the hallway, Mack grabbed a newspaper. With it, he tried to wipe up some of the blood that Caldo had spattered. "Shit," he said, watching smears of blood melt into the stained-concrete floor.

Mack saw Riva's blood pooling. He went to the yoga room and got one of Riva's rubber-backed terry-cloth yoga mats. He wrapped it around her head to contain the flow. He picked her up and carried her into the master bathroom. He laid her on the floor of the shower stall.

Caldo whined in the guest bathroom. Mack fetched a sponge, a bucket, and cleaning solvents from the garage. He wiped up the blood. The concrete floor was already colored with a brownish decorative stain. As Mack cleaned, he saw that the solvents stripped away the floor's decorative color, which made his clean-up efforts look obvious. To adequately conceal everything, he would need to apply a fresh coat of floor stain.

Mack went to the garage. He selected a can of reddish-colored stain. He applied it everywhere that Caldo might've spattered blood. He did an excellent job of blending the colors together. No one would suspect that traces of Riva's blood had been mixed into the décor.

Mack failed to notice, however, that he had overlooked some blood spattered on a leg of one of the orange, molded-resin chairs at the dining table. In addition, Mack had missed a thin streak of blood running down the back of the same chair. Later, this spatter would be visible in police photographs.

Caldo wailed forlornly as Mack returned to the guest bathroom. Mack wished that he could strangle the dog, but he couldn't. He needed Caldo for his alibi. Mack ran the water in the tub. He cleaned Riva's blood off the dog. Again, he left the dog shut away in the guest bathroom. He walked to the master bath to work on cleaning up Riva.

Mack had left her in the shower, but she had crawled out somehow. The mat had unfurled from her head and spilled blood all over the floor. Trails of blood had soaked into the concrete. "Shit," he said.

Mack stripped off Riva's pajamas. He put her back in the shower, along with the bloody mat. He turned on the water. He rinsed her blood down the drain.

He wrung the water out of the mat and out of Riva's clothes. He put these items into a plastic trash bag. He placed the bag near the back door. He returned to the bathroom. He saw a fresh pool of blood spreading around Riva's head where she lay in the shower. "Shit," he said again. He would have to call Carleen.

Mack changed out of his karate uniform and back into his T-shirt and shorts. He put on his sandals. He stuffed his black *gi* into the bag of items near the back door. He put the weapon into his waistband and covered it with his shirt. He turned off the motion-activated lights behind his house. Carrying the bag, he exited his house through the golf course. He walked two or three blocks.

In Mack's neighborhood, many of his neighbors kept their trash bins out in the open. Noiselessly and randomly, Mack deposited items from his bag into several different trash bins. He returned to his own street. He buried his special weapon in the new sidewalk bed that had been prepared near Carleen's house.

He went home and called Carleen.

"Something bad happened," he said, calmly. "Come now," he commanded. "Come in through the back, through the bedroom. It's dark. No one will see you."

A few minutes later, Carleen left her house. She walked along the foggy golf-course path. She entered Mack's house through the back door of the master bedroom.

"I know how it looks, but I didn't do anything," Mack told her. He led Carleen to the bathroom. He showed her Riva's still-bleeding body.

"I was asleep," Mack explained. "I must've heard a noise, because I woke up. I could hear the shower running. Riva sometimes takes a shower before she comes to bed. I got up to check on her. I found her like this. She fell and hit her head."

Expressionless, Carleen turned her gaze from Riva to Mack. She knew that he had assaulted Riva somehow, but she didn't know how. "Mack," she said in a frank tone. "This looks bad for you."

"I know," he said. "But it was an accident, I swear. You have to help me make it look like an accident."

Carleen stepped into the shower. She turned Riva's head. She looked at the gaping scalp wound. It continued to bleed profusely. "She got her bell rung," Carleen said.

Riva was still alive, although her brain had already swollen perilously. Her life might have been saved if Carleen had called for help in those early hours. Instead, Carleen's priority was to protect Mack. She assumed that he was following the plan that they had discussed. According to the plan, Riva would be rendered comatose, and Carleen would be hired to serve as her full-time nurse throughout her recovery. Riva's family trust would pay top dollar to ensure around-the-clock care. Carleen would have good, steady income.

Carleen had experience dealing with medical emergencies and cops. She knew what first-responders looked for at the scene of an accident, and what would seem suspicious to them. "If paramedics see all this blood coming out of her head, they'll call the cops," she said coolly.

Mack explained that he wanted Carleen to clean up Riva and place her in the yoga room. He planned to tell everyone that Riva had hurt herself while doing morning yoga.

He told Carleen that he would scrub the bathroom floor. He would apply a coat of stain to camouflage any remaining traces of blood. But before he could apply the stain, they would need to move Riva out of the shower and into the yoga room.

Carleen hosed Riva down with the hand-held showerhead. "We'll have to stop the bleeding before we can dry her hair and dress her," she said. Using layers of shop towels from Mack's garage, Carleen applied pressure to Riva's wound for a full hour, slowing the bleeding to an ooze.

"What's your alibi?" Carleen asked.

Mack explained his motion-activated surveillance-video system. The police would look at the video and see that he and Riva were not arguing or fighting. Mack had disconnected the system's power around 10:30 at night, but the police wouldn't be able to know this. Rather, it would appear as if Mack and Riva had simply gone to bed, and the system stopped recording because there was no activity in the house. In the morning, Mack would reconnect all the cables, turning the system back on. He could access the cables from the attic without being seen on camera.

Mack planned to take Caldo out for their customary morning walk. The cameras would show them walking away from the house. While he was away, he would use Riva's tablet device to access his household wireless network. He would use Riva's credit card to buy something online. Next, he would log on to a website that Riva had subscribed to, a website that showed videos of yoga routines. After clicking "play" on a yoga video, he would have 22 minutes to walk home with the dog, and "find" Riva injured in the yoga room.

"I'll be able to prove that I wasn't anywhere near her when she fell," he said. "They'll see from the video that I called for help right away."

It was a clever plan, Carleen acknowledged. She was thrilled to share a conspiracy with Mack.

Riva's wound continued to ooze, and dawn was fast approaching. Mack and Carleen moved Riva into the yoga room. Carleen scrubbed blood off the floor. Mack painted reddish-colored stain onto the concrete in the bathroom.

Carleen selected clothes for Riva—a lavender tank-top and teal capris. Carleen wanted to dry Riva's hair before she clothed her. She didn't want to risk smearing blood onto Riva's fresh clothes.

To Carleen's annoyance, Riva's wound continued to ooze. Carleen knew of a product that she could apply to the wound to help seal it. She doubted that any paramedic or emergency-room nurse would suspect that this particular first-aid product had been applied. Rather, it would look no different than a bloody scab or a hematoma concealed by Riva's hair.

Before she could stage the scene, Carleen needed to run to a 24-hour pharmacy to buy the substance to seal Riva's wound.

Mack didn't want Carleen to leave the house. He explained that he needed to reactivate all of the cameras at the same time, especially the back-yard cameras. His routine was to stand in the yard with Caldo first thing in the morning. He could not wait around for Carleen to return from the store. It would look suspicious.

Carleen and Mack agreed that, when she returned from the store, she would park her car in front of his house. That way, he would be able to see her car through the kitchen window. This would be the signal for him to go up to the attic and disconnect just the back-yard cameras. Carleen would then be able to return to the house from the golf course without being recorded. When she returned from the store, she would finish staging Riva in the yoga room. Meanwhile, Mack would stay on camera in the kitchen area in order to prove that he had been nowhere near the yoga room during most of the morning.

Neither Mack nor Carleen could find fault with their plan. In fact, they were impressed with their ingenious problem-solving. They had the kind of clarity and energy that came from battlefield-levels of adrenaline. They were having fun.

Just before dawn, Carleen exited through the back of the house. Mack retrieved Caldo from the guest bathroom. At around 6:00 a.m., Mack went into the attic and re-activated the surveillance cameras. In the back yard with Caldo, Mack watched the day dawn on his brand-new life of perfect, enlightened freedom.

He had no intention of killing Riva. Riva's death was truly an accident. Her demise devastated him, and angered him. Mack saw it as a cruel joke that, after all his hard work and care, Riva had abandoned him.

16

LE CIMETIÈRE MARIN

Riva looked at me with a brave smile. She let go of my hand. The instant she let go, I spun to the ground. I landed on my butt with a painful thud. I heard her say: "Sorry. Still learning. Now *you* have an ass tattoo." Next to me, three stones hit the ground in rapid succession, as if punctuating Riva's joke with a comic rimshot. The stones looked like rubies fused with diamonds. I scooped them up. The elongated, oval shapes fit into the palm of my hand. I immediately recognized them as the three vials of Graziana's blood, transformed. How would I explain this to Dr. Blanton?

"Becky," I heard Marydale cry out. She and Xavier scrambled toward me as if I was a survivor of a natural disaster, emerging from rubble.

"You're bleeding," Xavier said. She knelt in front of me. She pulled a cloth from her pocket and touched it to my face.

I saw that the backs of my hands were scratched as if I had been pruning wild rosebushes without wearing gloves. Marydale knelt next to Xavier. She examined the cuts on my hands. She opened my right hand, revealing the three, mysterious stones. "Where did these come from?" she asked, awestruck by their beauty.

I was about to tell her about Graziana's blood when the bespectacled Frenchman from the admission booth appeared in front of us. He looked indignant. When he saw blood on my face, he looked apoplectic. I did not understand exactly what he said, but it was clear to me that we were being kicked out, and forever banned from the castle grounds at Puivert.

Xavier spoke apologetically to him in French. "We have broken the rules," she said to us. "We must go."

Marydale and X helped me up. I put the three stones in my pocket. I lifted my pack, which was now lighter because I no longer carried Riva's ashes. I looked around in vain for the plastic box and red-velvet bag that had contained them. I felt a massive bruise throbbing on my hip. I walked as fast as I could. The man from the ticket window followed behind us, shooing us out.

"Did either of you get caught in the tornado, too?" I asked.

"We can debrief in the car," Marydale said.

I tried to remember everything that I had seen, but it was a blur, like a movie on fast-fast-forward. I felt shaky and oddly giddy. I had been in a windstorm, I knew. Riva's ashes and Graziana's blood had been sucked into a funnel cloud. Riva had rescued me from the storm by pulling me into an underground cavern.

We reached the parking lot and the car. We climbed inside and closed the doors. Both Marydale and X wheeled around in their seats, wide-eyed. "Becky, what happened?"

"I saw Riva," I said. "I ran after her. I ran into that circular room in the ruins. You must've seen the tornado. That's how I got these cuts. From the shards of gems, or whatever. You guys, we did it. We opened the portal."

Xavier looked puzzled by what I had said, as if she wasn't certain that the portal had opened. She and Marydale exchanged a look.

"We didn't see a tornado," Marydale said.

I wondered whether they were kidding. "I'm pretty sure it was the Treasure Tower. I couldn't really get a good look at it, though, because of all of the sparkling jewel debris in the air."

"No, Becky," Xavier said. "We saw a woman. A woman in a hooded cloak."

"It was unsettling," Marydale added. "I was yelling at you, but you couldn't hear me. You just stood there, frozen, in front of the woman. She was twice as tall as you. Her face was hidden by her hood. We could see her long hair hanging down. It was the color of crow's wings. I remember thinking that she must be *Badhbh Catha*, the Battle Crow. She threw her cloak around you and hugged you like a child. Next thing we knew, she was gone, and you were on the ground with cuts all over you."

I thought for a moment, trying to remember what Marydale had described. I couldn't. "This woman who hugged me," I said. "Did she seem nice, or was there something malevolent about her?"

"A little bit of both," Xavier said. She turned the key in the ignition. "Let's go." The sunny day had suddenly given way to gathering, darkening clouds. "We have never opened a portal before by ourselves," Xavier admitted as we drove out of Puivert. "Maybe we succeeded, but I cannot say for certain."

We drove several miles before we connected with a major tollway. As we drove, I explained that Riva had pulled me through a waterfall and into her house in Long Beach. As I talked, I recalled more details about what I had seen. "Mack was having a dialogue with some people. I wasn't sure if he was talking to actual people, or whether it was all in his imagination. He spoke to someone named Roy. Roy sounded a lot like Mack. He twisted everything. He talked as if hurting Riva was an act of kindness. He said it was a pathway to enlightenment."

"Becky, he sounds like the Master of Fundamental Darkness," Xavier said tartly. "Reversals and inversions are his stock in trade."

Marydale added: "Roy could be *both* an entity attachment *and* an aspect of Mack's fragmented ego."

I shrugged, not sure what they meant. "I saw what he did to Riva—that's the important thing. The police need to examine the floors in that house. They'll find blood in places other than the yoga room."

I recounted more details, excited that the truth had been revealed to me. As I spoke, my excitement gave way to bafflement and outrage. "They were having fun," I said. "Riva was totally helpless, and they were congratulating themselves." I felt my outrage collapse into despair. I started to cry.

Xavier exited the tollway at a gas station. I wiped my eyes. Xavier glanced at me in the rearview mirror. "Maybe you can let yourself cry," she suggested, softly.

I sniffled and contained my tears. "I'm fine," I said.

Xavier pulled up to a gas pump and stopped.

"I want to clean those abrasions on your face," Marydale said.

Together, we went into the gas station. It was a glorified convenience store with several vending machines that served coffee. Marydale bought a bottle of antiseptic and other first-aid items.

In the bathroom mirror, I could see why Marydale and Xavier had been alarmed by my appearance. My face was marked by a half-dozen scratches like the ones on my hands. Blood had dried in streaks, making the cuts look worse than they actually were.

With the professionalism I would've expected from a nurse, Marydale cleaned my cuts. She applied ointment. She said nothing as she worked. At last, she looked into my eyes and said, "Okay."

We walked out of the bathroom and into the store. We passed a rack of postcards. "Wait," I said. I stopped to pick out a postcard for Riva. In that instant, it hit me that I had nowhere to send it. I had forgotten—and remembered—that I could never again share a simple postcard with my sister. The enormity of this fact drove me to my knees.

I sank to the floor and onto my bruised haunch. It smarted. I started to cry. I covered my face with my hands. My mouth was open but no sound came out except sharp exhalations that could have been mistaken for laughter. I just sat there, in the middle of a gas station in France, convulsing, as tears and snot ran through my fingers, stinging the cuts on my hands and face.

I didn't mean to make a scene. People were looking at me, I knew, wondering what was wrong with me. If Riva had seen me, she would have teased me about having a mortifying, public meltdown. The thought of Riva seeing me—and not seeing me—made me convulse even harder.

Marydale and X said nothing. They didn't try to comfort me or hurry me out of the store. Instead, they stood guard around me, quietly protecting the space, and politely deflecting the inquiries of others. They gave me room to fall apart.

After a long while, I lifted my head. Xavier gave me a handkerchief. I wiped my face and blew my nose. X handed me another handkerchief. At last, I reached up. X and Marydale helped me to stand.

On the ride back to Sète, Marydale sat in the back seat with me. She invited me to lay my head in her lap. It was comforting to feel Marydale's hands resting on my head and shoulder. I was in an almost fetal position. From this vantage point, I saw a yellow, plastic toy wedged in the back of the driver's seat. I reached out and pried it loose. It was a star with a smiley face. I thought of Riva, converted into smiling stardust. I smiled wanly at the toy and returned it to its hiding place.

Back aboard the yacht, we planned to meet for a formal debriefing in the library, provided that Marydale could connect us with Bancroft.

At some point during the day, Franca must have moved *La Bonne Mère* closer to shore. The ship was anchored near what appeared to be a cemetery on a hillside beneath a lighthouse. In the distance, dark clouds massed over the land. The air smelled like a damp forest. Rain must be falling inland, I thought, washing over the vineyards.

Xavier stood next to me on deck. "The weather is changing," she said. "Franca is eager to get underway."

We would be sailing for Corsica, Xavier told me. From there, Marydale and I could fly back to Denver, presuming that it was safe for us to travel.

I tried to imagine returning home. I thought of Mack sitting in his RV in front of my house waiting for me. I almost mentioned this to Xavier, but she spoke before I had a chance.

"That is a very famous cemetery, *le cimetière marin*," she said, looking at the shore. "Do you know the poet Paul Valéry? He wrote a poem about this place."

"I don't know anything about French poets," I said apologetically.

We gazed out at the rows of tombs on the shore. The cemetery looked like a neighborhood of small, stone houses, some with doors facing the sea.

"Maybe you will recognize a famous line: *Le vent se lève, il faut tenter de vivre*," she said. "The wind rises. We must try to live."

Xavier folded her arms. She raised her chin and closed her eyes against the gusting wind. There was a sadness about her that I hadn't noticed until that moment.

"*Courons à l'onde en rejaillir vivant*," she said. She opened her eyes and looked at me. "It means to be pulled under by the waves, and to spring up again, renewed." She smiled in a way that struck me as very French—ironic, melancholy, and optimistic at the same time. "Becky, it means to go running into the sea and be washed back to life."

Marydale called to us: "We have a link-up with Bancroft."

"At last," Xavier said. She went into the library.

I lingered for another moment at the rail. I had much to tell the sisters—about the portal stones made from Graziana's blood, for one thing. I had dozens of questions to ask, too. All along, with each answer I sought, a new puzzle or fresh mystery arose. I hoped it would always be this way. I hoped there would be no end to marvels and mysteries, not even in death.

Over the months to come, I would remember looking out at the maritime graveyard at Sète, picturing myself running into the Mediterranean waves, and being washed back to life. I found this imagery to be particularly helpful when the Los Angeles County Coroner officially ruled that Riva's death was accidental.

"The cause of death is listed as blunt-force head trauma, presumably from falling to the floor," Dr. Blanton explained to me as she studied the coroner's report. "They took the extra step of hiring a neuropathologist to examine Riva's brain. Because of this, they can say conclusively that she did not suffer a stroke or an aneurism. Her fatal injury was not caused by a pre-existing head injury." Dr. Blanton told me that this last point was particularly significant because there was a suggestion that Riva had fallen and hit her head previously.

Sure enough, the autopsy report noted: "The decedent experienced a falling episode one year ago while in Hawaii. She reportedly fell and struck the back of her head. She was evaluated and was reported to be fine. During the past three months, the decedent was reported to be moving in slow manner while having difficulty getting up in the morning."

This was a bunch of lies told by Mack to mislead investigators. I wanted to know why the coroner would include such statements in the report without fact-checking them first.

"Statements made by Riva's husband are regarded as evidence," Dr. Blanton explained.

"It doesn't offer any rationale for *why* the coroner called it an accident," I said, despondently flipping through the pages. "The coroner implies that Riva died *days* after being admitted to the hospital, as if she was fine when she was admitted, and somehow took a turn for the worse. This is false. She was brain-dead on arrival."

"Can you meet with the coroner and ask your questions directly?" Dr. Blanton suggested, sorry that she could not be more helpful.

I tried to get a meeting with the coroner. I requested a copy of Riva's entire coroner file, too, so that Dr. Blanton might have more information to analyze. I learned that the coroner's office was beleaguered by budgetary problems. Staffers complained of being overburdened. Later, the chief medical examiner resigned in protest, telling reporters that it was impossible for him to do his job properly. Maybe these were the reasons why the coroner's office ignored my inquiries.

After months of my phone calls to the Long Beach Police Department, two homicide detectives and their sergeant finally agreed to meet with me. At last, I met Detective Anderson face to face. He really did look like Martin Milner—clean-cut with wavy blond hair, blue eyes, and a care-furrowed forehead. I sat directly across from him.

"The last thing I want is for a murderer to walk free," he told me. "We've looked at everything. We see no proof of a crime."

I talked at length, telling them what I believed had happened to Riva. The police flatly dismissed it all.

The sergeant told me: "Your opinions have no probative value in a court of law."

Detective Anderson added: "The coroner took one look at your sister's head and knew right away that she had fallen."

"If that's true, *why* did you get another search warrant and search Mack's house again, right after the autopsy?" I knew that the police had conducted an additional search because the warrant was a public record.

Detective Anderson left the room. He returned with glossy photographs. He spread them on the table in front of me.

They were pictures of the back of Riva's head. I was aware that her scalp had been split with a laceration, but I had never actually seen the injury. The photos showed a wound that was larger, deeper, and more horrible than I could have imagined. It looked as if Mack had swung a nine-iron into her head while she was face-down on the floor.

"From a fall," Detective Anderson said.

"Off a roof?" I demanded, mocking, outraged. "Did she fall off a roof?"

The detective leaned forward and looked at me in an unsettling way. His gaze was piercing and almost menacing. Every muscle of his face was rigid with rage. I realized that I had never seen anyone look so profoundly angry, yet so composed.

I assumed that he was angry at me and my disrespectful taunts. Later, as I replayed the scene in my mind, I came to believe that he was angry at the situation. Perhaps he was as frustrated as I was. No reasonable person could look at those photographs of Riva's wound and conclude that she had fallen from a standing height onto a smooth, flat floor.

Yes, obviously, something brutal and ghastly had happened to Riva. But a wide chasm yawned between *knowing this* and *being able to prove this beyond a reasonable doubt in court*. Unless this chasm could be bridged with more evidence, Mack would remain un-incarcerated, and Detective Anderson would remain thwarted.

Mack had killed Riva. I had proven this to myself. I wanted to prove it to the world. At the same time, I had to wonder: what would be gained by accusing him in court?

I was well aware of murder trials in which the victim was denigrated, and the perpetrator was acquitted. Could I endure a months-long trial in which Mack disparaged my sister, finagled sympathy from a jury, and ultimately walked away feeling vindicated for what he had done?

No murder case can ever be thought of as open-and-shut, especially when a man kills his wife or girlfriend. In such cases, the crime is minimized as *domestic homicide*—as if it's an ordinary, understandable, somewhat cozy occurrence in most households, akin to *domestic bliss*, a private matter between consenting adults.

The Sisters of the Tower persuaded me that, although justice might never be won in court, Mack would engineer his own come-uppance. In the meantime, I needed to learn how to quarantine him.

Marydale explained that Mack and his army were like the Nightmarchers of Hawaiian legends. Supposedly, hordes of dead warriors marched across the islands at night, pounding drums, chanting, and wreaking havoc on people who found themselves in the marchers' path. The only way to survive was to energetically and emotionally disengage from the fearsome phenomenon. In other words, I needed to hide from these marauding forces. Unseen, I would be able to grow in strength.

"Mack's brotherhood is like a band of disruptive frequencies that you can't fight in any conventional way," Marydale explained. "Your time for battle will come, but it won't be in the way that you think. The only way you can be ready to fight is to fully inhabit your bodies of light."

In truth, I understood little of what Marydale and the sisters taught me, even when they praised me for making swift progress. I knew only that Mack and his murder wagon never came to my house. He stopped contacting me, too. It was as if he had forgotten abruptly that I existed.

Riva, on the other hand, visited me frequently. Marydale urged me to keep a notebook and write down our dialogues. On Lucina's yacht, as we skimmed across the mysterious Mediterranean on our way to the mythic coves of Corsica, I recorded our first, formal, post-death dialogue:

"We have work to do, Little Boz."

"Toward what end?"

"There is no end."

"I mean, for what purpose?"

"To cross the sea of suffering."

"Can you avoid metaphors, Reeve? I want to know what you're really trying to say, so please just say it."

"Don't let one person—no matter how much you love her, or feel obligated to her—do not let one person shrink your dreams. Don't think badly of yourself just because some people hate you, or because someone wants to harm you."

"Who do you mean, specifically? Who hates me?"

"This is what I want you to understand, Boz. You can't go around wondering who hates you. You can't waste time worrying about rejection."

"Okay, Riva, but do you have a specific person in mind? I can think of several possibilities."

"Just assume that you're hated by fools. You live in a foolish world that's ruled by fools who believe themselves to be geniuses. Fools have a death-grip on everything, and they want to squeeze the life out of you. Don't let them. Find the people who aren't fools. There are lots of them."

"I derailed you into a rant about fools."

"You did. You should daydream about happy things like success and love."

"I don't, though."

"You should try. It's like you're sabotaging yourself into a lifetime of isolation and misery. You need a partner."

"Says the woman who was murdered by her partner."

"Becky, I know you feel as if you've been in the doldrums for a long time, doing nothing. But you've been busy *becoming*. A lot happens when you sit still. Remember the days when we would take a long walk on the beachside path, and end up at The Library in Belmont Heights for lemon bars and coffee? Those were the days. Whole days when we talked and talked—treasure troves of sistering! But it sure felt as if we were doing nothing. Brad was such an ass. I can't believe how much time I wasted on him. I was in a process of *becoming*, then, too. Hooking up with Mack so soon after Brad was a low-self-esteem move, you were right. I was trying to prove that *love wins, no matter what!* Is this premise flawed? Or is this game of proving going to be an extraordinarily long one? Maybe unwittingly, you're helping me to prove my point—love wins!—because I love you, and I can still reach you, and we will not be defeated by people who sneer at love."

"Am I sneering at love?"

"A little. Relationships fail. You're right. But love wins, and love is about *you*—how *you* feel—how *you* conduct yourself. Love is not contingent on a relationship."

"Still, maybe it *would* be nice to have a partner."

"Do you have someone in mind?"

"I like Marydale, but I'm not sure if she likes me. Do you have any top-secret intelligence? Are there things you're allowed to know only after death? Like, can you give me omniscient advice about relationships? Can you tell me if Marydale and I are destined to live happily ever after?"

"What do you like about Marydale?"

"What's *not* to like?"

"I think she's actually very guarded, and you don't recognize it. She's self-protectively shielded to the point of being unable to see you."

"She can't see me?"

"You want someone who can see you."

"Can I see her?"

"If you two ever meet, it will be love at first sight."

"I can't tell whether you're being cryptic or just sarcastic."

"Becky, it's like you want reassurance that it's safe to love her. When is anything ever safe? I just wish you would shine like a giant, radiant sun of love and safety for your own sake rather than waiting for her to extend love and safety to you."

"I like her hands. She has competent hands."

Riva and I talk endlessly. In sisterhood, nothing is hopeless, nothing is final, and no one gets the last word.

ABOUT THE AUTHOR

Lisa Jones is a writer in Denver, Colorado. Under the pen name Beryl Barclay she wrote *Daily Scoldings: A Bracing Tonic of Criticism, Rebuke, and Punitive Inspiration for Better Living* (Running Press, 2010.) Her first novel *Up* (Sticky Press, 2002) was reissued as *Southland Auto Acres* (Verbal Construction, 2010.)

www.VerbalConstruction.com

CPSIA information can be obtained
at www.ICGtesting.com
Printed in the USA
FSOW01n2336060317
31468FS